NIGHT COMES FALLING

A DCI Bone Scottish Crime Thriller
(Book 6)

T G Reid

GLASS WORK PRESS

COPYRIGHT

NIGHT COMES FALLING

GLASS WORK PRESS

DEDICATION

To Jean and Sylvia

PROLOGUE

Martin Burns pedalled to the top of the hill and pulled into a lay-by to catch his breath. It had been a long shift at the factory, and the six-mile journey home was taking its toll on his forty-two-year-old legs and lungs.

He opened the belt bag strapped tightly around his expanding girth and plucked out a joint he'd rolled in the bogs before leaving work. He sparked up and took a deep drag, holding the smoke in for a few seconds to maximise the hit. He exhaled and slumped forward against the handlebars, the skunk gently massaging his muscles and brain, instantly making him feel a little better after his headache had forced him to cut his shift short. He took a couple more quick tokes and nibbed the remainder for later.

"Two more hills to go," he wheezed, and continued on.

Conquering the final brae, he spotted the lights of his local garage up ahead. His stomach rumbled at the welcoming sight, and he turned into the entrance for his nightly supplies. The garage's new extended hours were both a blessing and a curse. While he could now buy food and smokes at any hour of the day, including on his way home, his weight had almost doubled, and he was too afraid to calculate the unit count on his alcohol consumption.

He jumped off, parked the bike on a stand at the side of the forecourt, and snapped the D-lock around the rear wheel. He glanced through the window, the bright fluorescent lights dazzling him for a second.

"Oh God, no," he muttered.

An elderly woman in a purple company uniform and matching cap stood behind the till, going through some receipts. He considered a hasty retreat.

"Fuck it." He went in.

When he'd collected three bridies from the hot counter and family-size bag of Doritos, he reluctantly approached the till.

The elderly employee had already fixed her stare on him.

"Evening, Jean," Burns said.

"It's Mrs Black to you," the woman snapped back, her ferocious stare burrowing into his skull.

"You're on a late one tonight, aren't you?" Burns attempted some friendly banter.

"You think I should be locked up in a care home, is that it?"

"No, I just mean it's quarter to one in the morning, and quite remote out here, you know?"

"Is this a holdup?"

Burns laughed. "Don't be daft."

"I might be eighty-seven, but I can handle myself, so don't even think about it."

"I don't doubt it. Not one bit." Burns winced.

He dropped his haul on the counter in front of her.

"Dining alone again, I see," Mrs Black said sarcastically.

"Here we go," Burns mumbled. "Look, Mrs Black, I've had a long night shift and I just want to get home."

"So another round of comfort eating. Has your supply of vulnerable women run dry then?"

Burns shook his head, deciding not to engage. "A packet of Golden Virginia and large roll-up papers, please."

"It'll be the death of you, you know. All this rubbish you're squeezing into that ever-increasing gut of yours." She fished the smokes out of the unit behind her.

"Could you just till this up, please?"

"I'm telling you. You'll be lucky to make it to fifty, which will be a huge sigh of relief I'm sure to all the women in the future you'll be messing about with."

"Right, that's enough. If I wanted a lecture, I'd enrol in a class at the college."

Mrs Black ran the groceries through the scanner.

3

She held out her hand. "Seventeen pounds fifty-six."

He tapped his card on the machine and dropped the supplies in his rucksack.

"I don't know what it is I've done to you, Mrs Black," Burns complained, wrestling his bag onto his back.

"It's what you've done to all those unfortunate exes of yours who fell into your web. You need to get your arse into the twenty-first century, young man, and stop treating women like bloody doormats."

"Sermon over?" He threw up his hands.

"I've been married three times, and every one of my men treated me with the utmost respect and dignity, and they'd been through the war. No excuse."

Burns blew out his cheeks and escaped to the door.

"I know exactly who you are," Mrs Black said, pointing her bony finger at him.

He dashed outside, quickly unlocked his bike, and pedalled back onto the lane.

As he shifted down a gear, his foot slipped off the pedal and he scraped his shin on its edge.

"Witch!" he hollered into the dark of the night.

He continued along the lane, and the faint lights of Cullenbrae hamlet appeared in the distance. With another heavy sigh, he put his legs into the final push for home.

The lane ahead suddenly illuminated. A vehicle approached from behind. He steered the bike closer to the verge to allow it to pass, but it seemed to slow and follow him.

He waved it on, but it refused to overtake. He tried again and glanced around but almost wobbled off.

The vehicle screeched past him, its wing mirror catching his shoulder. The bike careered off the lane and up the bank. He tumbled sideways, landing on a clump of overgrown heather, his leg still wrapped around the bike frame.

Winded, he tried to clamber free, but the tangle of wires and metal was too tight.

"Fuck's sake!"

The car sped on, the red of its rear lights slowly shrinking into the distance.

Then it stopped.

"Aye, come on then. Let's do this!" Burns shouted and tried to free his ankle again.

The vehicle remained still.

"Let my bloody foot go!" He lifted the bike frame on top of him, but a searing pain shot up his leg. "Oh Christ, no!"

Something was wrong with his ankle. He glanced back at the vehicle. It reversed towards him.

"What are you doing?" he cried out at the oncoming lights.

The car continued to accelerate.

"No, stop!"

He raised his hand, but the rear bumper of the car hit him square in the face. His torso catapulted backwards, and the back of his head smacked against a rock sticking out of the verge.

The screaming engine stopped, and the car rolled forward a few feet. The buckled frame of the bike flipped up, and the front wheel hooked onto the exhaust pipe, dragging it along with Burns' bloody, battered body into the centre of the lane.

Despite the extreme impact, Burns was somehow still semi-conscious. Raising his head from the cold tarmac, he squinted through bloodied eyes at the rear of the car.

The driver's door opened. A trainer and a trouser leg appeared.

Burns moaned through a mess of broken teeth and shattered jaw bone. His head fell. He was losing consciousness. He tried to call out again, a cry for help, but the only sound that would come was the wail of pain. His head hit the tarmac.

The trainer moved closer to his face. A figure loomed over him. He lifted his hand to appeal again. The figure knelt. His throat gurgled, and he reached up to grab at his attacker.

But in one swift, lethal movement, the figure drove a thin metal spike into Burns' left eye socket, obliterating any hope he had of surviving the assault. As death throes twisted and contorted his mangled limbs, and the bike frame danced up and down on the road, clanging like a discordant funeral bell, the vehicle's red lights slowly diminished and finally disappeared into the impenetrable dark of the night.

ONE

"Duncan Bone?" the nurse called.

DCI Bone put the well-thumbed copy of *Good Homes* back down on the coffee table in the middle of the packed hospital waiting room and followed her down the corridor to the consultant's office.

"One moment, please," she said when they reached the door. She knocked, went in, and shut the door behind her. A few seconds later, she was back. "In you go then. He won't bite." She smiled and returned to the reception area.

"Duncan, hello," Dr Malcolm Sewell, Bone's consultant neurologist, said, sidling around his desk to shake hands.

"Morning, Doctor," Bone replied anxiously.

"I think we've known each other long enough now for you to call me Malcolm." The consultant smiled.

"I'll stick to 'doctor' if you don't mind. I find it reassuring."

"Good to hear." Sewell nodded. "Take a seat."

"Is that a 'take a seat' or 'you'd better sit down' take a seat?"

The doctor gestured, and Bone complied.

"I have to say, your appointment time took me a little by surprise. I thought we started early, but seven-thirty?"

"We're trying to clear a backlog. I don't mind it as I can hit the squash courts early."

Bone sighed. "Okay, procrastination over. What's the damage then?" He unconsciously ran his finger along the length of the scar, from his hairline down his temple to his cheek.

"Well, first of all, there's absolutely no need for you to be worried or concerned about anything, Duncan," Sewell began.

Bone sank into his chair with relief. "So what's going on with the dreams, the new hallucinations I told you about?"

"This is where it gets interesting," the consultant said. "Let me just put this up on the monitor." He tapped at the keyboard in front of him, and the screen on the wall behind him flashed to life. The profile of Bone's skull appeared.

"Okay, so this is your MRI from Tuesday, and if I zoom in…" He adjusted the image.

8

"...here you can see where the fragment of bone is lodged, deep within the upper temporal lobe."

Bone leaned forward. "And no sign of infection or tumour?"

"Clean as a whistle."

Bone sighed again.

"Are you okay?" the consultant asked.

"It's always disconcerting to see that murdering scumbag's DNA still locked in there."

"It's certainly an unusual injury, but as I've told you many times before, you are a very lucky man. If the fragment of femur had been any bigger or entered further up or down, it would have been curtains for you."

He turned back to his computer. "But interesting as that is..." He glanced up. "from a medical point of view..." He smiled. "There's something even more intriguing going on." The screen flickered, and a second image appeared. He repositioned both so that they sat side by side.

"Right, so on the left is your MRI from six months ago." He let Bone study the two profiles for a moment. "Notice anything?"

Bone shrugged.

"The foreign object, in this case the fragment of bone, is demonstrating what we call in the trade, Intracranial Spontaneous Migration."

"What's that?" Bone's worried expression returned.

"In layman's terms, the object is on the move."

"You've got to be kidding."

9

"It's rare, but not entirely uncommon."

"So, does that explain the recent hallucinations I've been experiencing?"

"Most probably, yes. The fragment has moved deeper and further into the temporal lobe, so this may cause alterations in how your PTSD manifests itself, but as always, this is your brain's way of developing resilience."

"Is it dangerous? I mean, should I be worried?"

"I can't see any immediate risks. Obviously, if it keeps moving, then we will have to reassess impacts and effects, but in the vast majority of such cases, this unusual phenomenon is usually short-lived and the object settles down again."

"To a quiet life of tormenting its host."

The consultant switched off the monitor. "So, are these manifestations on the increase again?"

"No, not really, but the wee lad is rather unsettling." Bone frowned.

"Remind me, sorry," Sewell prompted.

"Well, you know all about the creature as I've moaned to you for years about him."

"Indeed. Sometimes it feels like I know more about Peek-a-boo than I do about you, Duncan." Sewell raised his eyebrows.

"Sorry about that. My PTSD counsellor encourages me to overshare."

"So has your femur friend deserted you then?"

"I'm not sure. But instead of him, a small kid comes to visit."

"A child?"

"A flame-red-haired boy, around nine or ten years old."

"And what does he say or do?"

"Nothing. I wake up and he's at the bottom of my bed, staring at me. Or I'm at the cooker and he's over by the window, just there, watching me."

"So he comes to you when you are up and about?"

"Up and about, in bed, middle of the night, just like Peek-a-boo, but as he's not burnt to a crisp; it's less unsettling. Strangely, he makes me feel quite calm."

"I'd say this is progress."

"Really?" Bone questioned.

"I'm a neurologist, not a psychiatrist, but I would venture that if the perceived threat has diminished, then this is symptomatic of receding PTSD." He rubbed his chin. "And before the boy arrived, were your encounters with the creature also diminishing?"

"Absolutely, and I think that's partly down to my amazing counsellor and group sessions."

"You're still attending those?" the consultant asked.

"Twice a month, sometimes more if I feel the need," Bone replied. "That, and the lifestyle changes I initiated last year along with my home life, which is now more settled than before."

"Ah yes, the wild swimming and outdoor activities will most certainly have helped the healing process, not to mention your fitness levels."

"Not tempted to give it a try? It has literally saved my life."

"The psychological benefits are unquestionable, but then you have to balance that with the trauma of frozen genitals." He smiled. "So to conclude, you are physically and mentally healthier than most medical staff here, and there is no need to be concerned about your latest encounters with your PTSD." He stood. "But if these hallucinations change or worsen, or your headaches return, please book another appointment, okay?"

Bone nodded and got up.

"See you in six months. I'm not expecting you before that." Sewell opened the door.

Bone left.

Out in the car park, he slumped down in the driver's seat of his reassuringly ancient Saab 96 and took hold of the steering wheel as though to anchor himself back to the earth. His mobile rang, shaking him from his moment of meditative stillness.

He cleared his throat and answered. "Hi, love."

"Any news?" Alice, his worried wife, asked on the other end.

"All clear, no problems," he said, choosing not to mention Peek-a-boo's latest adventures round the inside of his cranium.

"Aww, love, that's such a relief. I've been sitting here chewing my coffee mug."

"Sorry it took so long. The waiting room was rammed."

"And no complications or changes?"

"No, just…"

"Are you coming home?" Alice interrupted. "There's a young lad here who wants to give you a big hug, not to mention his stressed-out mum."

"I'm going to go for a quick swim."

"At the cabin?" Alice said in surprise.

"God no, up at the reservoir. It's on my way back, and I could really do with clearing my head after all that."

"Okay, but don't be long."

"Hour tops, so hold those hugs."

Bone said his goodbyes, his young son shouting in the background.

"What's Michael saying?" Bone asked.

"He says bye-bye, heid the baw."

"Charming. I've no idea where he gets that from." Bone laughed and hung up.

He started up the Saab. It coughed, spluttered to life, and he reversed out of the car park. "Life in the old machine yet," Bone muttered and turned towards the exit.

TWO

At Auchenbarrie Reservoir, he'd just completed a lap of the man-made loch when he spotted a member of staff waving to him from the jetty. He swam across, dodging passing swimmers, and climbed up onto the deck.

"An urgent phone call for you, Duncan," the young lifeguard said.

"Who is it?" Bone asked, shivering.

"A Detective Inspector Walker from Kilwinnoch Police Station. Is that your colleague?"

"Aye, is she on the line now?"

"No, when I told her you were in the water, she said to ring her back. You'd better get warm and dry," he added.

"Thanks. Why is it so cold today?" Bone asked, and he rubbed at his goosebumped arms.

"No more than usual. Why, does it feel colder?"

"Absolutely freezing." Bone's teeth chattered, and he dashed back to the changing rooms for a quick shower.

Ten minutes later, he fished his phone out of his canvas rucksack and called his colleague.

"Rhona?"

"Sorry to disturb, sir, but there's been an accident up near Cullenbrae that needs our attention."

"Where?"

"You know, the hamlet up in the Campsies between Kilwinnoch and Drumbeck?"

"Aye right, I've got you. That's the back of beyond out there." Bone sat on the changing bench. "What sort of accident?"

"A hit-and-run. The victim was found dead this morning. SOCO are already at the scene."

"Bloody hell, the man in black is quick off the mark this morning."

"They've been very quiet of late, so the fangs will be out," Walker said.

"I'll pick you up shortly, okay?"

"My pool car is comfortable and reliable, sir. I'd be more than happy to drive."

"No, I'm up at the quarry. I'll swing by with Bertha, no worries." Bone smiled.

"When it comes to your banger of a car, there are always worries attached, sir."

"Ye of little faith." Bone hung up, then rang Alice back to let her know he was going to be a little longer than first expected.

When Bone reached Walker's house, he tooted the car, and moments later, the door opened. Walker emerged, followed by her partner, Maddie, clutching their two-year-old daughter, Erin, who wriggled around, trying to escape her grip. They all came down the path to greet him. Bone got out.

"Look at you, you beautiful girl!" Bone said.

Erin spun round.

"I'll take that, thanks," Maddie said. "Especially after only two hours' sleep last night, with this one giving it Beyoncé in her cot till the wee small hours."

She tickled her daughter, and the toddler screamed with delight.

"Say hello to Duncan, Erin," Walker said.

Erin buried her head in Maddie's chest.

"I have that effect on all the girls."

"We know," Walker replied.

"Have you had some yoghurt this morning then?" Bone asked.

Erin shook her head in denial.

"Well, I don't know what that is all over your face then, but whatever it is, I want it." He reached over and tickled her under the arms. She squealed again.

"Are we off then?" Walker asked.

"Do we have to?" Bone sighed. "Good to see you, Maddie and Erin. You should come round to the

17

holding. Alice has worked wonders. Erin would love the hens and the ducks."

"Quack-quack!" Erin shouted.

"Very good, and how does a hen sound?" Bone asked.

"Moo!" Erin mouthed.

"That's a cow, silly billy," Maddie cut in.

"Moo, moo!" Erin carried on.

"Let's go before the whole herd arrives." Walker chuckled. She kissed her daughter and Maddie.

"Say goodbye to Duncan, Erin," Maddie said.

Erin waved sheepishly and then buried her face in her mum's dressing gown again.

The detectives went back to the car and climbed in.

"She's grown so much since the last time I saw her," Bone said, fishing the keys out of his pocket.

"Literally by the hour. We spend most of our days constantly moving the entire contents of our house out of her reach. If she can grab it, she can eat it."

Bone turned the key, and his ancient Saab started the first time.

"Oh my God. I mean, how is that possible?" Walker threw up her hands in disbelief.

"She's just been for a service. She usually behaves for at least a couple of weeks."

"That's bollocks. A few days and it's back to cough-wheeze."

"Might have exaggerated slightly. Fair dos." He grinned at her.

"What?" she asked, sitting back.

18

"I was at the car boot at the weekend." He continued to smile.

"Oh God, no! What did you buy?"

He remained silent.

"This isn't fair. What the hell are you going to spring on me this time?"

"I managed to snag another box of sounds for our retro seventies cartridge player here." He tapped the 8-track music player slotted into the dashboard.

"That thing doesn't still work, does it?"

"Oh yes, and guess what I found in among the weeds?"

"Not free jazz? Please don't inflict that on me again. I've had more than enough of that sort of cacophony from last night's circus show with Erin."

Bone pushed the massive play button on the front of the panel.

The machine clicked and clacked as the cartridge inside attempted to engage with the mechanism.

The opening bars of *'Delilah'* suddenly kicked in.

"Not Tom Jones! Oh, bloody hell!" Walker groaned.

Bone fished the box out of the door pocket and handed it to her.

"Look at him? Bloody hell." She grimaced at the cover of Jones dressed head to foot in all his seventies leather and lace glory.

Bone sang along. He glanced over at her.

"Come on, you know you want to," he urged.

"Oh no, I bloody don't!" Walker folded her arms.

He drove the car onto the main road and accelerated out of Kilwinnoch.

When they reached the edge of the Campsies, he turned up the volume to full for the chorus. Walker held her head in her hands.

He roared out the lead-up. "Don't be shy." He nudged her elbow.

"It's a totally offensive song!" she hollered over the din.

"I know. It's brilliant, isn't it? Here it comes."

"Oh shit." Walker winced.

Bone crooned the chorus badly.

Walker mumbled along.

"I've got you now!" Bone laughed.

"Delilah!" they both yelled in unison and carried on through the song, Walker's voice soon soaring higher and louder than Bone's.

Out in the hills, a driver filling up his car at a petrol station gawped at the noisy pair as the Saab roared past.

When the song finally ended, they both laughed.

"That was actually quite liberating," Walker croaked, her voice almost completely shot away.

"I told you. Who can resist a bit of the Welsh Elvis?"

"Well, at least it wasn't that strangled cat music you usually listen to."

"I'll have you know, if it wasn't for the likes of…"

"Looks like we're here," Walker interrupted. She nodded to the collection of forensic vehicles and cordon tape straddling the lane.

He drove up to the roadblock. Slowing up, he wound down his window. A young officer in a Hi-Viz jacket approached the car.

"DCI Bone." He flashed his lanyard.

"Morning, sir. Could you park up over there?" He stepped back and gave the Saab a once-over. "Nice wheels, by the way." He smiled and then looked back at Bone. "Sorry, sir, I've overstepped."

"Why, are you being sarcastic?" Bone asked.

"No, no, not at all. I'm a massive fan. My granddad had loads of them."

"Gee, thanks." Bone smirked.

"No, no, I don't mean you're old or anything, well, I mean you're my senior, so you are older but not ancient but... er... anyhow."

"Did he own one in lovely lurid green, like ancient Bertha here?" Bone saved the lad from the hole he'd fallen into.

"No, it was red, I think. Yea, definitely red, as I remember thinking it was a spaceship." He glanced up. "I was five, by the way. It wasn't last week."

"What's your name, son?"

"Constable Green, sir."

Bone's eyes widened.

"No, it really is Green, Norman Green."

"Well, Officer Green. I am very impressed and I have to say you're probably the first in the force who hasn't taken the piss out of my choice of transport."

"Far from it, sir. I love it."

"I'll let you take her for a spin sometime if you like."

"That would be tremendous. Thank you, sir."

Bone parked up and, with a wave to the overenthusiastic recruit, he ducked under the cordon tape and headed towards the bank of bright lights on the brow of the hill.

Halfway, an officer in a white scene suit approached.

"I know what you're going to say," Bone said, and held out his arms.

"Morning, sir." DC Harper's face and glasses emerged from his hood.

"What the hell— Will?"

"I was just passing, and I thought this looked like the hottest ticket in town."

"We really need to work on your humour, Will," Walker said.

"No, I was over at Catriona's place in Stirling, and this is on my shortcut to work. They had me in this before I could say…" He leaned in. "What is it you call the SOC team again?" he whispered.

"Teletubbies."

"Chief Forensics Officer Cash instructed me to give you both these." He handed them scene suits and protective shoes.

"Have you been in, then?" Bone asked.

"No, not yet," Harper replied, pushing his glasses up his nose. "I have to say, I feel like a chicken in a roasting bag in this."

"It suits you, Tinky-Winky," Walker said.

After a few exhausting minutes wrestling the gear on, and after Bone ceased cursing, the detectives set off for the battery of lights set up on the lane ahead.

Bone approached an officer who was unloading boxes from one of the forensic vehicles. "Where's Cash?"

"There." The officer nodded to a group of SOC officers huddled together under the lights.

They went over.

Chief Forensic Officer Cash was on his knees by the body of a man lying flat out on the tarmac, the twisted, buckled bike frame and wheels still tangled around his legs. The man's face was almost completely pulverised, his features barely recognisable, and his left eye was missing from its socket.

Harper recoiled.

Alongside Cash, two officers straddled the victim, one taking photos with a long-lensed camera, while the other took samples from under the nails of his bloodied hand.

"Morning, Andrew" Bone alerted the CFO.

Cash turned in surprise.

"Ah, I was just thinking: I wonder what DCI Bone is doing this morning? I bet he'd love to hang out with me again in the arse end of nowhere."

"You've met DC Harper?" Bone asked.

"Ah, so that's who's hiding under there. Welcome to the house of fun, DC Harper. And good morning to you, too, DS Walker."

Walker nodded and pushed an errant lock of red hair back into her scene suit hood.

"So what's the story, then?" Bone asked, kneeling by the victim.

"This morning at approximately seven-thirty, a local jogger discovered the body of this male, late-thirties to early forties, with severe head injuries, possible multiple skull fractures."

"You say a local jogger?" Bone asked.

"Yes, Cullenbrae resident, a Mrs Annie Hepworth."

"Where is she now?"

"I believe officers have taken her back to her house in the hamlet. I would assume she's pretty shaken up."

"Not the best start to anyone's day," Bone said.

"Except ours, eh, Duncan?" Cash grinned.

"So was it a hit-and-run?" Walker continued.

"Well, that's what we thought at first. There are tread marks on the road up ahead there that look fresh. Traffic might be able to determine the speed of the car, and we could get lucky and pull sufficient markings to identify the brand, but they look pretty rough, so don't hold your breath."

Bone glanced along the lane. Two officers grappled with either end of a measuring tape, while a third crawled alongside.

"There are also additional scrapes and marks on the tarmac that suggest the victim was dragged from the verge to his final resting place here." Cash pointed to a trail of dried-in mud and grime leading across the road and disappearing into the bank. "So a veritable potpourri of evidence-gathering this morning. Isn't

24

life such a joyous cornucopia of mystery and wonderment?"

"At first?" Bone asked, steering Cash away from another of his oncoming existential cliff edges.

"Ah yes. And just to add to the fiesta of fun, there's this." Cash pointed his rubber-gloved finger at the hollow eye socket. "I'll need to take a closer look at the wound, but initial inspection suggests that the eyeball has been completely minced rather than blown out by the impact, as it were."

"Nice." Harper winced again.

"Are you okay, Will?" Bone asked.

"I might just step back for a sec, if that's okay?" Harper slowly reversed.

"The lad's muesli must be disagreeing with him this morning." Cash chuckled.

"Could it be a protruding part of the vehicle that struck him?" Bone continued.

"Possibly. There's some fragments of paint visible around the wound. We'll get that off to the lab and see if it throws up a vehicle make and model." Cash glanced over at Harper, convulsing on the other side of a van. "Sorry, wrong phrase." He smiled.

"What's that logo on his jacket?" Bone asked.

Cash removed a spatula and a small plastic evidence bag from the kit belt on his scene suit. He gently prised off a few specs of mud clinging to the fabric and dropped them in the bag. He looked up. "Love Candy."

Bone knelt and examined the red lip-shaped design embroidered onto the chest pocket.

"You don't know?" Cash said.

"No?"

"Well, you must be the only person in Kilwinnoch who doesn't."

"It's the sex toy company," Walker said. "Their factory is out at the Bantone Mill."

"Sex toys in Kilwinnoch? Now there's an oxymoron I never thought I'd hear."

"A growing industry apparently, so to speak," Cash said.

"I can't believe you haven't heard of them," Walker said. "They've been operating for three or four years now. The owner started the business from his bedroom, and it's now one of the biggest and most successful start-ups in the region."

"I live a sheltered life. So, he was on his way home from this factory?"

"A reasonable deduction," Cash said. "It's very late to be out for a leisurely ride in an accident black spot."

A cry from further up the lane interrupted the CFO.

They got up and went over to a SOC officer, who was down in a ditch adjacent to the tyre marks in the road.

"Harry?" Cash asked.

"I've found this, sir," the officer said, pointing to an object protruding from the mud.

Cash carefully negotiated the bank and knelt by his colleague. After a moment, he looked back at the detectives. "It's a corkscrew. And a perfect fit for an eye socket." He scrambled back up onto the road.

"Excuse me a sec." He returned to the officers by the body.

"And here was me thinking we'd have a quick sign-off on this and traffic would deal with it." Bone sighed.

"All roads lead to murder," Walker said.

"We'll have to wait and see what SOC and traffic come back with, but this is clearly not a straightforward accident gone wrong."

Cash returned, accompanied by the photographer.

"The bike has a security tag on it, with a number," Cash said.

The officer clicked buttons on his camera and turned the screen.

Walker removed an iPad from her bag and jotted down the serial number the officer had snapped.

"Hopefully that'll give us a trace on the poor sod," Bone said.

"Unless the bike was nicked, of course."

"Aye, there is always that." Bone glanced up the road. "So how far is Cullenbrae?"

"It's literally at the bottom of the hill, about a mile," Cash said.

"So, foul play then?" Bone asked.

"Off the record?" Cash paused. "I've always wanted to say that." He smiled. "Murder most foul, but again, don't quote me." He sighed. "Sorry, I've been binge-watching *CSI*."

"Isn't that a bit of a bus driver's holiday for you?" Walker asked.

"I know. Blame my wife. She's completely obsessed. She says she wished she'd married the star instead of me. I only started watching it to pick holes in it, but God, it's addictive." He blew out his cheeks. "What the hell is happening to me? I used to be a reflective, philosophical kind of guy, and now I'm saying things like 'don't quote me' and 'off the bloody record.' Our journey through the world can be very tiring sometimes."

"We'll leave you to it, Andrew," Bone interrupted.

"Yes, you're right. I'm ranting again. I'll let you go as we seem to be literally up to our necks here in crime scene flotsam."

"That's a line from *CSI*, isn't it?" Walker said.

"Jesus, you're right, it is. I need help." Cash shook his head. "I'll keep you updated."

"Thanks," Bone said. "Let's get the show on the road." He smiled.

"Just don't." Cash frowned and returned to the victim.

Bone and Walker deposited their protective clothes with the PC at the cordon.

Harper emerged from the other side of a vehicle. "Sorry, sir."

"You don't have to apologise, Will. We've all been there, and some things really get to me, too."

"Yes, remember that case where the victim's skin had been completely shredded after he fell into that combine harvester?" Walker asked.

Harper grabbed his mouth and dashed behind one of the forensic Land Rovers.

"You are so bad," Bone said.

When Harper returned, Bone held up his hand before he could apologise again.

"Will, can you trace the owner of the bike? Rhona got the security number etched on the frame. Rhona, you'd better interview the witness while it's still fresh in her mind and get a couple of uniforms up here to start door-to-door."

"I'll give you a lift. My car's on the other side of the cordon," Harper said.

"Okay, just give me a minute to write up a set of questions for the uniforms. Where are you going?" Walker asked Bone.

"I'll head back to the incident room and alert the Super. I'll call into the garage we passed on the way in and check if they saw anything last night."

"Good thinking." She looked over his shoulder. "Careful, though, the mighty paps have landed." She nodded to a huddle of journalists gathered by the cordon tape. "That was quick."

"Tapping into police radios again, the weasels."

"But no sign of Weasel One."

"Always a worry when McKinnon's not in the slurry pit. Where the hell is he, then?"

"I'm sure we'll find out sooner rather than later, sir."

"Indeed. Okay, let's reconvene at the station for a catch-up." Bone checked his watch. "At ten? The man in black should have sent through the images by then, and hopefully we'll have a bit more to work on."

He approached the tape and ducked under. The journalists surrounded him, firing questions, cameras and mics raised. He pushed through, jumped in the Saab and turned the ignition key. Nothing.

"Come on, Bertha, don't let me down." He tried again. The engine spluttered, wheezed, and coughed to life. A plume of black smoke billowed from the exhaust, smothering the incoming journos in a cloud of fumes.

"That's my girl." He crunched the gearbox into first, and the car juddered back up the hill.

THREE

The hamlet of Cullenbrae was situated at the bottom of a dank gully, tucked between two steep hills that towered high above and blocked out the sun for most of the day.

A cluster of buildings huddled around a pub whose glory days had long since gone. Harper parked his Yaris up alongside the pub's mouldy sign, hanging at a precarious angle on a half-rotted hardwood post. Ahead, a modest war monument sat in the centre of the hamlet, with a few faded wreaths still clinging to the stone façade.

A squad car approached and parked behind. Two PCs climbed out.

"Okay, I'll sort them out," Walker said. "Here's the security tag number." She handed Harper her iPad.

"On it. Then I'll come and find you."

Walker got out and went over to the PCs. She flashed her lanyard.

"Morning. Can you start knocking on doors at the far end of the hamlet and work your way back to the square? She produced her hastily written script. "Here are the questions you need to ask." She handed the note page to the first PC. "Please make sure you stick to them, okay?"

"Ma'am," the officer said.

"Do either of you know where Cullenbrae View is located?"

The two officers shrugged.

"I presume it's up higher than here if the street's called View," the second PC said.

"Very helpful, Constable, thanks for that." She rolled her eyes. "Right, let's get on with it then."

The PCs set off across the square.

"And don't forget to complete descriptive forms. We don't want to miss anything here," she called to them.

The first officer waved and they carried on.

Walker scanned the buildings around the square and spotted a steel-and-stone new build perched close to the clifftop edge of the gorge teetering over the hamlet. She set off up the steep incline. At the top, she stopped for a moment to catch her breath.

The house was straight ahead and appeared to be in the middle of a major renovation, with building materials piled up in the driveway and two skips out front. She approached the front door, sandwiched between two ground-to-roof tinted glass windows that seemed out of place stuck on the front of the old Edwardian building. She was about to knock, but the door was open.

"Good morning?" she called, but there was no reply. She nudged the door further and stepped into an open-plan modern living room. "Hello?" she called again. She scanned the room. An enormous six-seater corner sofa dominated the space, along with a massive flat-screen TV that stretched the width of the side wall. She turned. The hamlet and surrounding hills filled the spectacular view from the windows.

A thirty-something man in a navy suit appeared in the open archway at the rear of the room.

"Who are you?" he asked briskly.

"Detective Inspector Walker from Kilwinnoch station. Sorry, the front door was open."

"Oh right, yes. I presume you want to speak to Annie," the man said, his West London accent laced with a hint of Central Scottish brogue.

"Mrs Hepworth, yes, that's right."

"She's in here. She's pretty shaken up," he said.

"And you are?"

"I'm her husband, Simon Hepworth." He ushered Walker through the archway and into an expansive kitchen with more wall-to-ceiling windows.

Annie Hepworth was in her dressing gown, slumped at the kitchen table. Her wet hair clung to the side of her face, obscuring her features.

"Annie, this is Detective Inspector Walker."

Mrs Hepworth glanced up and pushed the hair from her red, swollen eyes.

"Sorry to disturb you, Mrs Hepworth. I have to ask you a few questions."

"Do you know when the road will be open?" Mr Hepworth interrupted. "It's just that I have to get to my office."

"We're working as fast as we can. When there's a fatality, there are certain procedures and protocols we have to go through," Walker said.

"It's just that I have an important meeting this morning and I'm already late. It's bloody inconvenient. When the lane's shut, we are literally trapped here." Hepworth exhaled.

"This is a major incident, sir."

"Surely, you could just let me squeeze through."

"You could drive out using the lane on the other side of the hamlet. That's still open."

"Are you kidding? It's either flooded, or blocked by sheep or by farm machinery, and I'd have to drive practically all the way to Stirling before I could get off it."

"As I said, sir." Walker shrugged.

"And in the meantime, our business goes down the pan," he said.

"Simon, please, just leave it," Annie said.

Mr Hepworth shook his head, then marched back to the living room.

"Sorry, Detective Inspector. My husband is an arsehole sometimes."

Walker sat next to her at the table. "I know you've probably already been through this with a uniformed officer, but could you tell me what happened this morning?"

"It was just so horrible. I don't know if..." Annie brushed the moisture from her cheek.

Walker produced a packet of hankies from her pocket. "I'm sorry. Just take your time."

Annie dabbed at her face. "I go out for a 5K run every other morning."

"What time was that?"

"At six-thirty. It helps set me up for the day."

"What is it you do?"

"I'm in marketing, but work from home mostly."

"So you set off at six-thirty?"

"Yes, my usual route; through the square, round the back of the old mill, and then down the farm track onto the lane." Annie stopped and took a couple of deep breaths.

"Did you see anyone?"

"When I ran past the Dow's farm. The farmer was out in the yard, but he didn't see me."

"And then?"

"I dropped down off the track onto the lane. I usually carry on to the petrol station, and then about-turn and retrace my route back to the house. But I was only a few hundred yards further on when I spotted him on the road. At first, I thought it was someone who'd just come off their bike, or maybe had been struck by a car, but I didn't expect..." Annie puffed. "He was in a horrible, horrific state. My brain sort of froze for a minute. I checked his wrist for a pulse but couldn't feel anything."

"And then you called 999?"

"I presume so. To be honest, I can't remember. I was in shock. I knew he was probably dead, but my brain just wouldn't believe it, you know?"

"And then what did you do?"

"I stayed on the line, and the woman told me to wait for the police and ambulance. Then you all came."

"And did you recognise the man you found?"

"His face was so battered, and his eye... God, I'll never forget it. I hope to God it's not, but I think it might be Martin Burns."

"Is he a Cullenbrae resident?"

"Yes. He lives at number twenty-eight Brae Hill. I've seen him out and about on his bike a few times. I think he cycles to work as well. I just can't believe it."

"Do you know Mr Burns, then?"

"He made and installed our kitchen."

Walker glanced around the solid oak, bespoke units and doors, some inlaid with intricate designs. "Wow, that's impressive work."

"Yes, he's very... Sorry." Annie blew her nose. "He's a carpenter."

"Does he also work at the Love Candy factory?"

"Yes. As a cleaner, I believe. He doesn't earn enough money on his cabinet-making, so he supplements with jobs like that."

"When did he do the work for you?"

36

"It was probably a year ago now. We bought the bungalow back in 2019, but it took us ages to get it up to a point where we were ready to install. And he was very slow, too. But it was worth the wait, I think." Annie sniffed again. "Our renovations haven't been universally popular in the hamlet. There's been a lot of hostility, maybe partly because Simon is from London." She sighed. "To be honest, it's him who insists we weather it out here, but I've hated it from the minute we moved in. There's a weird vibe, you know? It's just not very friendly, and you need that where you live, don't you? If it were me, I'd sell up and move."

"Is there anything else you can remember?"

"When the emergency services arrived, a nice ambulance woman put a blanket round me and gave me a tea from her flask. I was in a right state by then."

"And you didn't see any vehicles or anyone else when you were out running?"

"No. The road was completely deserted. I time my run early, partly to dodge any commuter and farm traffic."

"Okay, thank you, Mrs Hepworth. That's all for now. Again, I'm so sorry you had to go through that. Here's my card. If anything else comes to mind, call me, okay?"

"There was one other thing." Annie glanced over her shoulder. "Could you shut the door?"

"Sure." Walker did as Mrs Hepworth asked, and returned.

"When Martin was here fitting the kitchen, he…
er…"

"What?"

"He propositioned me."

"He tried it on with you?"

"He didn't actually, you know, touch me or do anything gross like that, but he asked me out, more than once. It was all a bit of a joke at first, but when I realised he was serious, I told him to back off."

"Did you tell your husband?"

"God no, he'd bloody kill him." Annie stopped. "No, really, he knows nothing, and I would prefer if it stayed that way. Anyhow, I feel bad speaking like this about someone who's… It's not right. He might have been a bit of a womanising git, but he didn't deserve to die."

"You think they're related?" Walker asked.

"No, I mean, no one deserves to die."

"Did he have a bit of a reputation, then?"

"Yes, but Miss Naïve here only found out after he'd finished our kitchen. That's what he does, or did, apparently. He woos female clients with his craftsmanship and charm. It's so superficial."

"Do you know any other women he propositioned or went out with?"

"No, sorry. I kept well away after that."

"Okay, Mrs Hepworth. Don't forget my card. If you think of anything else, you can ring me directly on that number."

Mrs Hepworth tried to read the card, but her hands shook. "I'm a bag of nerves."

"You'll need lots of rest. You're still in shock."

The door opened, and Mr Hepworth returned.

"I'm all done here for now. Thank you, Mrs Hepworth."

"I'll show you out, Detective," Mr Hepworth said. "Sorry to lose it earlier. I've had better starts to a day."

"Your wife's been through a pretty serious trauma," Walker replied. "It might not be such a bad thing to be around for her this morning."

"Of course, Detective, but I'm afraid when my entire livelihood is dependent on a meeting I can't attend, then life is a little more complicated than that."

"Just a quick question before I go, sir. Where were you between ten last night and seven am this morning?"

"You think I was out prowling in my car looking for victims?" He shook his head.

Walker continued to stare at him, poker-faced.

"I was out cold. I'd been in a series of meetings all day. Twelve bloody hours straight with no lunch. I got back around nine. I drank the best part of a bottle of red wine, Burgundy, the bottle is in the recycling if you'd like to check, and then I crashed around ten-thirty on the sofa, fully clothed, TV on. Annie woke me around five, and I went to bed. Anything else?"

"Do you get on with Mr Burns?"

"Get on? In what way?"

"You know, did you have a friendly relationship with him?"

"He was our tradesman. We weren't bosom buddies. Our relationship was me signing him cheques and him completing the work to our satisfaction. That's it."

"Were you happy with his work?"

"Yes, he did a great job. But hey, kitchens are kitchens. My wife was the one who picked it. I just forked out and kept my mouth shut, as always. Hold on. Is he the one involved in the accident? Has he knocked someone down or has he been knocked down?"

"We're trying to piece together what happened."

"Well, before you ask, I wasn't pathologically furious with him because he used the wrong colour of paint on the doors. His work was excellent. No complaints, other than how long it took him to finish it. Would you like to check our car, perhaps? It's sitting out there. Or maybe you think I had the damage repaired in the middle of the bloody night."

"Thanks, sir. I understand this must be very distressing for you both."

"If that's all, Inspector, I really need to get back to my desk and try and salvage this deal before the shit hits the wall."

"That's fan, sir."

"Sorry?"

"Shit hits fans. We'll let you know as soon as the road is open." Walker walked off, cursing under her breath. When he shut the door, she turned back and checked the front and rear of the Audi parked next to the house. She ran her hand along the pristine bumper.

She spotted Harper at the top of the hill.

He came running over. "I've got the trace on the bike, ma'am. It's registered to a Ms Diane Moffatt—"

"A woman?" Walker interrupted in surprise.

"That's the name registered on the system, ma'am."

"And the address?"

He checked the notes on his phone. "Fourteen Balloch Drive, Kilwinnoch. Are you okay?"

"You know how some folks have faces you just want to lamp with a spanner?"

"Oh yes, I do." Harper nodded.

"How about you? Are you feeling any better?"

"Yeah. I'm sorry again."

"Don't be daft. It never gets any easier. We just swallow a bit harder than you. I'll put a word in with the DCI to up your crime scene experience so that the contents of your stomach stay where they are in future."

"Thanks. Have you seen that, by the way?" He turned and pointed across the gorge to a boarded-up, near-derelict, Gothic-style mansion peeking out above a line of trees. "Creepy, isn't it?"

"Bates Motel. This place is weird."

"Yup."

"Right. Follow up on the bike. The boss wants us back at the station by ten."

"Okay, will do, ma'am. How will you get back?"

"I'll nick one of the squad cars."

They returned to the square.

Walker noticed a light on in the Clachan Arms. "Looks like the landlord is up. I'll catch you later."

"Okay," Harper said, and he jumped in his car.

FOUR

The young service station assistant looked surprised when Bone flashed his lanyard.

"I wasn't on last night. That was Mrs Black. Did somebody drive off without paying again or something?"

"No, nothing like that," Bone replied.

"I didn't think so. When Jean's on, nobody would dare try anything." He sniffed.

"Is Mrs Black around this morning?"

"No, she'll be in at seven again tonight. She does the evening shift, seven to one."

"Is your manager in…" Bone studied his name badge. "Cliff?"

"Er, no. She rang to say she's running a bit late but should be here in half an hour or so. I'm holding the fort." He nervously glanced over Bone's shoulder at the forecourt. "What's going on with all the police vehicles and stuff up the lane?"

Bone ignored his question. "What's your manager's name?"

"Sarah O'Connell. This sounds serious." Cliff attempted a smile, but his mouth refused to cooperate.

"Do you have a contact for Mrs Black?"

"Yes. I have her number on my phone. She lives up in the Craigfallon Flats in Campsie."

Bone handed the lad his card. "That's quite a hike to here?"

"She's wangled a taxi out of the company. I've no idea how she does it. She's a right one." Cliff laughed. "So what's happened then?"

"And who's on after her?"

"Calum Ferguson, one to seven, then I'm in."

"Could I have his details as well?" Bone asked.

"Sure."

"And I presume you have CCTV on the forecourt?" Bone continued.

"Aye, of course. And in the shop." Cliff pointed to a camera behind his head.

"Can we have a look at last night's footage?"

"Of course, yeah, but I'm not sure I can leave the till until the manager gets here. And also I'm not allowed to touch it."

"When did you say the manager's due in?" Bone asked.

"Right now," a woman directly behind them interrupted. "I'm Sarah O'Connell, the duty manager.

44

What's the problem?" She scowled at the young assistant.

"There's been an incident just up the lane," Bone said, "and I'd like to take a look at your CCTV footage."

"Says who?"

"Sorry. DCI Duncan Bone from Kilwinnoch Police Station."

"Oh right, sorry. Ha. The look on Craig's face made me think you were some kind of nutter."

"I do get that a lot," Bone joked.

"What's happened?"

"An accident, and we're just trying to piece things together, find out if there are any witnesses, that sort of thing."

"Oh, well, you'd better come through. The footage will still be in the system. It usually gets wiped after forty-eight hours, but if it was last night, then…"

She went around the counter, squeezed past the assistant, and unlocked the office door.

"Do you want me to come with you?" Craig asked sheepishly.

"Oh aye, let's leave the shop empty and make fuel and food free for the rest of the day." She rolled her eyes.

Bone followed her through into a cramped, stuffy room with boxes stacked up on either side.

"Your assistant said a Mrs Black was on late shift last night?"

"That's right, from seven to one, I think, though she often stays a bit later. She's very conscientious, sometimes a wee bit too much, but she definitely puts the young ones to shame."

She sat by a thin black machine resting on a side table next to a portable monitor. Rows of tiny yellow and green lights flickered every time they moved.

Bone scanned the room. "You have a camera in here as well?"

She pointed to a camera in the corner. "And there." She nodded to one on the opposite side. "The safe's in here, so it's top of our security priorities." She leaned in to the box. "Let's see what we have here. It's been a while since I did this. It usually just refreshes itself."

She prodded a few buttons. Nothing happened.

"Ah, wait a moment." She reached down and plugged in the monitor. The screen came to life. "That's more like it. Right." She hit the play button, and the footage started to roll.

"Can I sit?"

"Of course."

Bone pulled over a chair, close to the screen. "This is from two days ago."

"Yes, hold on." She tapped a button, and the footage skipped forward an hour or so, then she paused the tape. "This is the forecourt at nine p.m. last night."

All was deserted.

"Can we see the other camera footage at the same time?"

"Yes, I think so, but they might be quite small." She fiddled again, and the screen split into three sections with the forecourt, shop floor, and a shot from behind the counter now visible.

Mrs Black moved in and out of various shots, stocking shelves, cleaning the counter screen, and emptying the forecourt bins.

"We definitely get our money's worth out of Mrs Black. She never stops," the manager said.

"Can you go on a bit further?"

She turned the small toggle on the front of the machine. When the timestamp reached ten thirty-three, a car appeared in the forecourt and three young men in tracksuits and hoodies jumped out.

"Any idea who they are?" Bone asked.

"Young boy racers. They use the lane as a bloody race track."

The men entered the garage shop, and gathered around Mrs Black. She waved her arms at them for a moment.

"She's giving them an earful."

"Aye. That's Mrs Black. Take no prisoners."

"Can you freeze the image on their faces?"

The manager tapped the machine and caught one of the three in full shot.

"He looks about twelve," Bone said.

"They always do. They need to raise the minimum age allowed to drive. Idiots like them get themselves killed every bloody day. "

"You wouldn't be able to print that, would you?"

"Sorry, but I can send you the footage. We've had to provide recordings to the police before for fuel thefts."

"Do you get a lot of that out here in the middle of nowhere?"

"We used to quite a bit, but we had a crackdown a few months ago, and you folks helped us with that. Since then, we've had very little. I'll have to get in touch with head office to get the nod to send it over, but I'll sort that this morning."

"Thanks."

"Shall I carry on?"

Bone nodded.

The boys left the shop, climbed back in the car, and drove out of the garage. The manager stopped the footage again when the car exited.

"Sorry, I think the top of the pumps' roof is blocking the view of the car," she said. She continued. Just after half-past eleven, a figure in a coat just disappeared out of the forecourt.

"Can you rewind that slightly?" Bone asked.

She adjusted again, and a figure in a wide-brimmed grey hat appeared at the shop counter. Mrs Black moved into the shot, and she ran a few items through the scanner. The angle of the hat, pulled low over the customer's face, made it impossible to pick out any features.

"Is there any other camera that might ID this man or woman?"

"I think it's a woman. Isn't that long hair sticking out from under the hat?"

"Maybe. Would Mrs Black be able to identify this person, do you think?"

The manager shrugged. "You'd have to ask her that. Sorry."

"There's no car at the pumps," Bone said.

"No, so probably a local on a late-night food scavenge."

"You get that a lot?"

"Oh, aye. Now that we're open twenty-four hours, the temptation for late-night feasts is too strong for some."

"And when you say local, you mean Cullenbrae?"

"Aye, folks call in from there, but we get customers coming up from Kilwinnoch or even driving over the top from as far as Carrbridge." She stopped. "I'm making it sound like Sauchiehall Street. It's absolutely dead most of the time, and to be honest, I've no idea why the petrol company bothers keeping it open past one a.m. Probably some tax dodge." She gave Bone a sideways glance. "Don't tell them I said that."

She pressed play. The customer packed the goods in a bag.

"What's that they're buying?"

"Looks like crisps and sweets. I told you, midnight feasts."

The customer left, crossed the forecourt between two pumps and exited through a gate near the entrance.

"Where does that go?"

"It's a public path to Cullenbrae. Well, it goes as far as Brae Burn, and then you have to get back onto the lane for the last bit. I wouldn't fancy it late at night. I'd end up on my backside in the burn."

"Are you from Cullenbrae then?"

"No. I live in Kilwinnoch. I only know about the path because we had farewell drinks once in the pub and we made the mistake of trying our luck. And yes, I did end up on my arse in the burn."

"And what about your assistant on the till?"

"He's from Lennoxfield."

"How does he get all the way up here?"

"On a moped. It's round the back."

They returned to the screen.

"Can you slow forward a little closer to midnight?"

She pressed the button, and the tape continued on at four times the speed. An object flashed across the forecourt.

"What was that?" Bone asked.

She paused and rewound.

A young adult deer strolled past the pumps, stopped at the sand bucket, sniffed, and strutted on out of shot.

"Aye, we get all sorts of wildlife up here. The badgers are a bloody nightmare. I'm sure they carry wire cutters in hidden pouches."

At twelve-forty, a hooded cyclist appeared in the forecourt. He locked the bike and entered the shop. Moments later, he was at the till.

"Can you stop that there a sec?" Bone asked.

The image juddered and the man's features shook side to side.

"Sorry, that's not great." She toggled the recording again, and it settled.

50

"What would you say that logo is on the customer's jacket?" Bone asked.

The manager leaned into the monitor.

"I'm not sure. It's very fuzzy. Is it a pair of lips? Ah, it could be the Love Candy logo."

"That's what I was thinking."

"Not that I am too familiar with that company, mind." She chuckled.

The man left the shop with a bag of goods, unhooked his bike, and cycled into the night, in the direction of Cullenbrae.

"Do you know who that is?"

"No idea, sorry." The tape rolled on, but no more customers appeared. At five past one, the next assistant arrived to relieve Mrs Black.

"I'm going to have words with Calum. He should never be that late. Especially when it's Mrs Black."

"Okay. That's fine, thanks."

She stopped the tape.

"If you can get that over to us ASAP, that would be great."

"I will." The manager nodded.

They returned to the shop.

"There's a group of young boy racers on the tape who called into the station last night," Bone said to the young assistant.

"Do they drive a ridiculous souped-up washing machine with spoilers on the back and massive tyres?"

"That's them. Have they been in recently?"

"Not on my shift, but Mrs Black moans about them a lot. They made the mistake once of being rude to her."

"Any idea who the driver of the car is?"

"Sorry, no."

"There was one other person on the tape. A male or female in a wide-brimmed hat, like a fedora or a homburg. Do you know who that might be?"

"Long hair?"

"Yes."

"That sounds like Stu Mason. He's in quite a lot. He used to be mates with my dad."

"Used to be?"

"My dad died three years ago. They shared the same awful taste in music. They'd go to gigs together and stuff."

"I'm so sorry. Do you know where I can find Mr Mason?"

"Aye, he lives in Cullenbrae. Him and his wife are artists. They make pots and stuff like that."

"Do you have his address?"

"His place is at the end of that path out there. See the stile?" He pointed out of the shop's front window.

"How far?"

"It's dead near; ten-minute walk, tops. Might be a bit muddy, though."

"Thanks."

The manager joined them. She frowned at the assistant, and he busied himself at the till.

"Sorry to hold you up. Do you have contact details for Mrs Black?"

"Yes, hold on a second." The manager disappeared again through the back, returning moments later with a slip of paper. "Telephone and address, but you might waste your time calling round as she'll probably be with her sister."

"Do you have an address for her sister?"

"She's in the Palliative Care unit in Falkirk General. Coral, I think she's called. It's so terribly sad. Coral is in her last days, but Jean is an absolute rock. She's up there every day and stays with her until her shift starts. I've organised a taxi to pick her up directly from the hospital. I don't know where she gets her energy from. She's eighty-eight, you know."

"I didn't realise that. She looks nothing like that age on the CCTV footage."

"As I said, she's made of girders." The manager smiled.

"Okay, thanks very much for your help."

"I'll get that footage over to you as soon as possible."

Bone continued out across the forecourt to the gate on the far side. The path wound across a field and disappeared into a cluster of trees. He checked his watch and climbed over.

FIVE

Walker pushed at the Clachan Arms' woodworm-infested front gate and negotiated empty beer barrels on either side of the path. The front door was locked, so she went around the side. Sidling around more barrels and crates, she spotted an open back door and made a beeline.

"Hello?" She rattled the rotting frame. She poked her head through, and her nose was hit by the foul stench of drains. She recoiled and knocked again. "Anyone there?"

"Down here!" a voice called from beneath her feet.

She knelt by the rusty iron hatch on the ground.

"Hello?"

"I'm cleaning out the pumps. Just dump them in the kitchen."

"I'm Detective Inspector Walker from Kilwinnoch. Can I have a word?" she called down between the crack in the door.

The metal clunked, and the hatch juddered. She stepped back, and one of the doors swung open and dropped to the ground with a loud clang. An arm, then a head, emerged.

"Polis?" the grey-haired, late-middle-aged man with a sweaty brow asked. The stench of stale beer and sewage wafted out from the hole.

"Sorry to disturb you, sir. Are you the pub landlord?"

"No, I'm king of the underworld," he said.

"There's been an incident on the lane just outside Cullenbrae. We are conducting door-to-door enquiries to try and establish what might have happened."

"Hold on," the man said, and disappeared back down into the stinking hole.

A few moments later, he was at the back door. Walker approached, but he pushed past her, clutching a bucket overflowing with frothy yellowish-brown liquid, the same rancorous stench following in his wake.

As he passed her, some of the contents landed on Walker's gleaming Doc Marten brogues. She sighed.

He emptied the bucket against a wall at the far side of a tiny, overgrown courtyard stacked up on either side with mouldy picnic benches. He returned.

"Roses love it," he said with a grin that exposed a set of teeth not a dissimilar colour to the stinking liquid he'd just deposited by the wall.

"Has someone been knocked down again?" he asked, dumping the bucket by the door.

"Why do you say that, Mr…?"

"That lane is a bloody death trap. Young drivers and neds come up here from toon, get tanked up and then end up in a field or knock someone into a field. Happens all the bloody time."

"You shouldn't allow your patrons to be drink-driving, Mr…?"

"None of my business what they do," the landlord huffed. "I mean, I do check, and they tell me they've walked it. How am I to know where the hell they've stashed their cars and motorbikes?"

"What's your name?" She was annoyed that he'd dodged her previous attempts.

"Dave Gronin. You're no' going to shut me down, are you?"

"Can I come in for a minute?"

"It's not a pretty sight in there. We're having problems with our drains and…"

"I've seen and smelt a lot worse, Mr Gronin."

The landlord showed her in.

"Come through to the pub for a minute." He led her through an ancient, filthy kitchen with boxes and tangles of disembowelled pipework stacked up in knots that covered almost the entire floor space. In the corner, a cracked Belfast sink overflowed with dirty dishes.

"I'm hoping to get this fixed for opening time, but it's not looking good at the moment. The last thing I want to do is let a dozen men loose in loos that won't flush."

"Probably a health hazard as well," Walker added.

They weaved around the debris and went through to the gloomy public bar. He switched on the lights. The interior was surprisingly attractive, in a rustic country pub kind of way. The usual pub paraphernalia festooned the walls; brass horseshoes, and photo-filled frames displaying the hamlet and pub from a bygone age. Walker's attention was drawn to a life-sized sheepdog, its mouth open and tongue exposed.

"What's this?" she asked.

"That's Hector the Hero."

"Is it stuffed?" She grimaced.

"It was here when my dad took over the tenancy. He was going to dump him, but the locals kicked up a fuss. Apparently, if you pat his head when you leave, it's supposed to bring you good luck, or some bollocks like that. If it brings punters through the door, then a creepy stuffed dog in the doorway is fine by me. I've actually grown to quite like him."

"How old is this place, then?"

"No idea, maybe three hundred years. We're just outside the boundary of the dry area that Kilwinnoch used to be in, so it's a fair old age. Would you like a drink, Detective?" the landlord asked, sliding around the counter. He switched on the bar lights.

"No, you're all right," Walker said. The stench of stale ale and drains still clung to the inside of her nostrils.

She sat at the nearest table. The surface was sticky, and she shifted her chair further away.

"What can I do you for, Detective?"

"There's been a serious incident on the lane just outside Cullenbrae, and we're investigating a suspected hit-and-run."

He sat next to her. "That bloody lane is a death trap. I'm forever telling my punters not to even think about walking back to Kilwinnoch at closing time."

"Have there been a few incidents, then?"

"Over the years, oh aye. The council's promised better lighting for years, but they never bother. Luckily, no one's been killed, but it's only a matter of time." He shook his head. "I tell you what, though. If someone has been knocked down, the first person you should be speaking to is Gary Speed." He stopped. "I know, you couldn't make it up. Him and his mates tear about on that lane like it's the Monte-Carlo, day and bloody night."

"Do you know where I can find this Gary Speed?"

"Hold on. I just said it off the cuff, like. I'm not actually accusing him of anything. I don't want any trouble at the pub."

"Just an address. That's all I want."

"I have no clue."

"And what car does he drive?"

"Address and car. You're pushy, aren't you?"

"That's my job, sir."

"Some ridiculous souped-up pensioner's car. Probably nicked it off his granny."

"Honda Jazz, Corsa, Citroen Saxo?"

"Saxo, that's the one. Know your cars then?" He smiled, exposing the teeth again.

"Are you familiar with Martin Burns?" Walker ignored his veiled sexist remark.

"Martin? Why are you after him? I say after, but you know what I mean." He laughed, then his face fell. "He's not involved, is he? Or has he been knocked down?"

"I would like to speak to him."

"Er, right, aye. He's just up the Brae at number twenty-eight. Is he okay?"

"So you know him?"

"It's hard not to know everyone round here, detective." Gronin sneered again. "He used to do a few shifts at the pub, back when we were busy." He rolled his eyes. "And he'd do the odd job. He's a carpenter by trade, makes furniture and kitchen cabinets that sort of thing. But he's a good fixer upper. I could do with him now to sort out these bloody drains."

"Did he make any furniture for you?"

"You're joking, aren't you? His stuff is out of my league. It's the posh brigade like those in the goldfish bowl up there."

"The Hepworths?"

"Aye them."

"So you're not friends then?"

"With those snobs? Aye righto. They've been bad news since the minute they arrived in Cullenbrae. Lord and Lady muck, up in the fucking showhouse." He glanced up. "Pardon my French."

"Did you see or hear anything unusual last night?" She carried on.

"When are we talking? I shut the pub early as it was totally dead, and my drain problem wasn't helping the cause."

"When?"

"Oh, about..." He scratched his stubbled chin. "Half ten?"

"And Gary and his mates?"

"It was way earlier than that. Maybe around tea time. Six o'clock, something like that. But they left about nine. Then dead as a dodo."

"Did they say where they were going?"

"To me? Are you joking? They usually go up to the old airfield at Cumnock and try to kill each other or themselves up there. You lot need to clamp down on that. They are complete pains in the arse, but sooner or later one or more of them is going to get topped. You didn't answer my question. Is Martin okay?"

"We're just following up on the incident at the moment, sir."

She stood and sidled cautiously around the sticky table. "Okay, thanks. If you hear anything else, please ring the station or you can contact me directly." She handed him her card. "By the way, what's going on with that derelict house on the outskirts of the hamlet?"

The landlord stared at her for a second or two.

"The Brae Hill House?" he said.

"The one all shut up; looks like it's been that way for years."

"Surely you must know about that?"

Walker shrugged.

"That's the Sneedons' house?"

"Who are they?"

"Seriously?" the landlord replied in surprise. "I was only a kid, but it was all over the national news."

Walker sat back down.

"My old man was running the pub back then."

"When are we talking?"

"Back in the seventies. I was about twelve. It must have been seventy-six, something like that. Henry Sneedon and his parents lived up at that house. They'd been there forever with their son, who never managed to leave either. My dad used to take the piss out of him, as he was probably in his thirties by then." He stopped to think for a moment. "He was a farm labourer, quiet. My dad said he seemed like a harmless kind of simple bloke who everybody liked, but…"

"Go on," Walker pressed.

"Turned out Henry Sneedon was sick, very sick, in the head. One night, he came back from the farm where he worked, on his tractor. But instead of parking up and downing a quick pint as he usually did, he ploughed into a couple of locals in the square. He carried on up to his house, took a shotgun to his parents and then himself."

"That's grim. Were the residents he hit in the square killed?"

"One was killed, and another had life-changing injuries. Lost both their legs."

"Horrific."

"That's not the end of it. When the police went to the property, they found Sneedon's next-door neighbour in the cellar. He'd been fish-hooked and was strung up by his gullet." The landlord shivered. "Absolute raving monster."

"Did the police get to the reason why Sneedon killed his neighbour?"

"It was so long ago. It was something as daft as a border dispute between the parents and the neighbour, or the neighbour's dog that barked day and night." He exhaled. "Christ."

"Must be hard for a tight community like this to get over something like that," Walker said.

"It's not been easy, but the best part of fifty years helps to get rid of the stain of it."

"Why is the house still like that? Isn't that like a permanent reminder?"

"Two relatives have been fighting over its ownership for years."

"Do they live in Cullenbrae?"

"Oh, good God, no. Sneedon's sister, I think, is now in Bristol. Moved to get away from the nightmare of it all, no doubt. I don't know where the brother is, though. He might be dead by now." He looked up again. "You know, I haven't thought about this horror story for years."

"Sorry to dredge it all up again," Walker replied.

"Anyhow, that's why that eyesore sits there slowly rotting away, like the Sneedons' evil wanker of a son. Apologies. This shite touches a nerve."

"No problem. Would I be able to speak to your father about this?"

"You could try if you know a reliable medium. He's been dead for twelve years."

"Sorry for your loss. Is there anyone else who might remember more, still here in Cullenbrae?"

"Most of the oldies have either died or their kids have farmed them out to care homes. There's mad-as-a-brush Donald Fagan, who lives opposite Brae Hill House. He might know more about what's going on. He's a conspiracy theory nutcase and has about a thousand cameras all over his property. But to be honest, you're more likely to get sense out of a Vileda mop. He's a right pain in the arse. When he comes in for a drink, I have to keep a beady eye on him as he winds up my punters with his crap about UFOs and bloody Area 51. Jesus. It's hard enough trying to get folk through the door without that headbanger scaring them off."

Walker stood again. "Thanks, Mr Gronin."

The landlord unbolted the front door and showed her out.

"Thanks."

"Just to warn you, though. I'd be very careful talking to people about Henry Sneedon. It was a long time ago, and nobody wants reminding of what that monster did."

He slammed the door shut.

Walker stepped out into the square and took two or three deep breaths to clear her nose of the rancid stench.

One of the PCs came over from the other side. "I've just checked with some of the neighbours, and none saw or heard anything last night."

"Have you tried number twenty-eight, Brae Hill?"

"Is that up there?" He pointed up the lane.

"That's right."

"I knocked, but there was no reply."

"Okay. Can you ensure an officer stays up there and keeps the building secure, no one in or out?"

"Even the owner?"

"Unlikely."

"Is he the poor sod on the road?"

"Keep an eye on it, okay?"

"Ma'am." The PC left.

SIX

Once Bone was past the woods, the path widened and wound down the hill towards the hamlet. Halfway down, he came to a cluster of ramshackle buildings and outhouses. He was about to knock on an old wooden front door when it flew open. A flustered-looking young woman in a pair of tatty dungarees and tie-dye T-shirt almost ran right into him.

"Oh!" She stepped back in surprise.

"Sorry to alarm you, ma'am. DCI Bone from Kilwinnoch Police Station."

"Police?" she said, her eyes widening.

Bone held up his lanyard. "We're investigating an incident on the road on the outskirts of Cullenbrae."

"Oh God. I haven't heard. What's happened?"

"A cyclist was knocked off their bike. Does Mr Mason live here?"

"That lane needs lights on it. I've been saying it for years."

A long-haired man in a faded Pink Floyd T-shirt appeared behind her. "What's going on?"

"Mr Mason?" Bone asked.

"Aye, who wants to know?" Mason replied suspiciously.

He clutched the woman's sides and leaned around her. She shifted sideways, and he dropped his hands.

"This is DCI Bone from Kilwinnoch Police Station. There's been an accident on that road," the woman said.

"We're trying to develop a clearer picture of events. Could I come in for a moment?"

The woman glanced over her shoulder. "Sure. I mean, of course."

They showed Bone in. The man went on ahead and shut the first door before Bone reached it.

Large, colourful, modernist abstract paintings that reached from floor to ceiling decked the hallway, and seemed out of place on the ancient lime-plastered walls.

Bone paused to admire one. "These are great."

"My beautiful partner is very talented," Mason said.

He tried to take his partner's hand, but she pulled back again.

"What's your name?" Bone asked the stressed woman.

68

"Caitlin."

"Is that what you do, Caitlin?"

"Call me Cait. I used to, but it doesn't make any money, so now I make ceramic art for the tourists."

"We find that pottery is an easier route to a living," Mason cut in.

"So he says." Cait scowled.

"Sorry. I'm not in the middle of something here, am I?"

Mason smiled. "Oh no, don't worry. It's nothing. Just a row about dinner. Nothing serious. I mean, we're not going to kill each other or anything," he said and stopped.

The hallway fell silent for a moment.

"Not yet anyway," Cait said finally.

"Glad to hear it." Bone smiled.

The pair laughed nervously.

"So are you both artists, then?"

"I'm an electrician by trade, but I now make the light fittings for Cait's pots."

"They're not pots. They are tourist tat. Come, I'll show you."

They took Bone out the back of the kitchen, across a small courtyard, into an outhouse. The inside was very warm and dry.

"Excuse the mess and the temperature. The kiln's on full." Cait nodded to a vast iron oven in the far corner.

Bone unbuttoned his coat and looked around. Shelves stacked up with ceramic, white-washed cottages and farm buildings mounted on plinths

69

encompassed the room. Some of the pieces were set within mountain-shaped, snow-peaked panels.

"Is that Cullenbrae?"

"Are you serious? No, it's some imaginary Brigadoon crap that the American and Japanese tourists love to buy."

She went over to one and flicked a switch on the back. The tiny cottage windows lit up.

"See what I mean?"

"They look very quaint. They are actually charming."

"But it's not art."

"We sell at craft fairs and supply tourist shops dotted around the Highlands," Mason said.

Bone approached a workbench at the rear of the studio, lined up with pots and plates of various shapes and sizes, some half-finished, others complete with elegant Art Deco-style pastel-coloured line drawings.

"These are elegant." Bone picked up a jug with a sculpted, deep-purple tulip handle curving up and around the body.

"A new range. I'm hoping they do well," Cait said. "I need to exorcise my frustrations."

"Hence the row," Mason interrupted.

"Don't put your shit on me, Stu," Cait snapped back.

Bone glanced behind the workbench. A tall rack with a dozen lightbulbs leaned against the wall. "What do you do with these?"

"Photography lights for promotion shots," Mason said.

"I've just been over to the Star Service Station at the end of your path. Mr Mason, you called in there last night around midnight, is that correct?"

"Did I?" Mason said.

"One of the assistants recognised you on the CCTV footage."

"You've been through their CCTV?"

"The incident occurred only a few hundred metres from the garage, so we're trying to establish what exactly happened and speak to potential witnesses."

"Right, aye. I think I did. That's right. We had a big meal and a few glasses of red, and I was ordered out for some snack supplies."

"I didn't order you out. I went to bed," Cait said.

"Did you drive over?" Bone asked.

"No, our van's knackered. I used the path. It's a bit muddy and dark, but clearly it's a lot safer than the lane."

"Did you see or hear anyone out on the path or the lane when you walked over?"

"No one on the path. It was very late. I didn't see any cars, and the path veers off quite a bit away from the road."

"And you went straight there and back?"

"God, aye. It was bloody freezing."

"And did you see or hear anything unusual last night, Cait?"

71

"Apart from him snoring his head off? No, nothing. It's like a mortuary out here." She glanced at Bone. "Sorry, I'm not sure that was appropriate."

"Could I have a quick look at your van?" Bone asked.

"It's at the garage. Basically the arse fell out of it. I'm waiting for them to tell me it's not worth fixing."

"More bloody expense," Cait said.

"Which garage is that?"

"Kilwinnoch Motors. You know it? They're very good, but an arm and a leg." Mason stopped. "I hope you don't think I had anything to do with this incident. You still haven't told us what's happened."

"As I said, our investigations are ongoing. If you think of anything else, please don't hesitate to ring me directly." Bone handed Mason his card.

Mason stared at the Police Scotland logo on the front.

"Sure, aye," he said finally.

"Thanks for showing me round," Bone said.

"I hope they're okay," Cait said.

"Who?"

"Whoever got hurt on the lane."

On the way down the hall, Bone noticed the first door near the entrance was slightly open. He slowed and glanced in on the way past. It looked as though a mini tornado had swept through the front room; broken glass scattered across the sanded floorboards, an armchair upturned, and the large flat-screen TV above the inglenook fireplace hanging off its wall brackets at a precarious angle.

"This way, Detective," Mason said, urging him to proceed to the front door.

"Thanks again," Bone said.

Mason smiled nervously and went back in.

SEVEN

When Harper reached the eighth floor of Hillview Heights, on the south side of Kilwinnoch, he stepped out onto the open landing and paused to take a breath.

He leaned on the railing and gazed across the town towards the Campsies rising behind it. A cluster of cumulonimbus cauliflower clouds rolled over the peak, and the hills quickly disappeared.

"Glorious." He smiled and carried on.

At the end of the corridor, he stopped at number thirteen and knocked. Moments later, the door rattled and swung open. A small dog dashed out between a young woman's legs and ran down the corridor, yelping loudly.

"Catch him!" the woman yelled.

They both gave chase. The dog, which seemed to be a cross between a Jack Russell and an oversized guinea pig, hightailed it down the stairs, almost tumbling off the first step as its frantic, tiny legs failed to reach the bottom.

"Don't let him get to the road!" she screamed.

Harper leapt down the stairs, two at a time, but somehow the miniature mutt seemed to maintain the gap. At the bottom, it tore out through the close and into the car park.

"Quick!" the woman shouted.

On the far side of the car park, a black cat appeared from under a van. The dog barked and took off towards it.

"Oh, God!" Harper quickened his pace.

The dog tore straight at the cat, who seemed completely unfazed by the incoming hamster. As Harper veered towards the pair, the dog stopped. The cat sidled over. The dog bowed its head, and its foe licked the dog's neck. Harper scooped up the dog, and the owner appeared behind him.

"Thank God for that," the woman said, taking the dog from Harper's tight grip. "That's Potty, my cat. He's always looking out for him. Come on, you two," she said to her pets. She turned to go back to the flats, and the cat followed by her leg.

"Diane Moffatt?" Harper puffed.

"Aye, do I know you?" she asked, her dog wriggling furiously in her arms.

"I'm Detective Constable Harper from Kilwinnoch station. Can I have a word about your bike?"

"My bike?" Moffatt said in surprise. "You must have nothing better to do down there if a detective sergeant is assigned to chasing a bike theft."

They went back into the close, and she started up the stairs again. Harper paused.

"Are you okay?" Moffatt asked.

"Just a bit of déjà vu. I have this funny feeling I just climbed these things."

Moffatt laughed. "I know. You get used to them. I put in that complaint months ago. I thought you lot weren't going to do anything." She carried on.

"You reported the bike stolen?"

"Not exactly, no. I reported that the leech of an ex-boyfriend refused to return it."

"I couldn't trouble you for a glass of water, could I?"

"You'd better come in then."

Harper followed her back to her flat, and she took him through to her kitchen. She dropped the dog down on the floor. It rolled over, and Potty resumed his dog-grooming regime.

"It's pet porn, day and night," she scoffed. "Quite sweet really, if a little disturbing."

Harper winced.

She poured him a glass of water, and he gulped it down.

"Thanks," he said.

"Another?"

"No, you're all right. So who is the boyfriend who borrowed the bike?"

"Martin Bloody Burns, and it's ex-boyfriend. Is he saying the bike's his or something? That wouldn't surprise me at all." She sat at the kitchen table.

Harper removed his phone. "I'm just going to make some notes. Is that okay?"

"It will be when you tell me what this is about."

"And you said you reported that he took your bike without your consent?" he continued, ignoring her comment.

"He can be very persuasive and convincing. I'd watch him if I were you, Detective. He can charm the pants off anyone who wears them." She stopped. "Has something happened?"

"Your bike was found on the lane leading into the hamlet of Cullenbrae."

"That's where he lives."

"You said he took your bike. When was this?"

"Has he been in some kind of accident?" She wouldn't let it go. "Is he okay?"

"We're just information-gathering at this stage, Ms Moffatt. When did he borrow your bike?" Harper persisted.

"When we were going out."

"And when was that?"

"We split over four months ago."

"And he refused to return your property after?"

She continued to stare at Harper's book.

"Ms Moffatt?" Harper prompted.

"We were in and out of each other's houses. When we split up, I left a few things over there, including my bike, but when I asked for my stuff back, he refused."

"What else did you leave at his?"

"CDs, makeup, nothing big, but I bloody loved that bike, and he just wouldn't give it back."

"Do you have Mr Burns' address in Cullenbrae?"

"Aye, twenty-eight Brae Hill. Have you not spoken to him yet, then?"

"When's the last time you saw or spoke to Mr Burns?"

"Maybe a couple of months ago. I rang him to let him know that if he didn't return my stuff, I would go to the police and report him for theft."

"How did he take that?"

"Another blazing row. He turned on me. He was absolutely horrible."

"And you've had no contact since?"

"After what he said to me, are you serious?" She tutted.

"When did you report the theft?"

"It was late in May. The twenty-first, something like that? I can't remember. I called the non-emergency number and filled in one of those online forms, but you never got back to me."

"Sorry about that. Can I ask why you split up?"

"Why is that important?" She stood, her agitation increasing.

"Sorry, I'm not trying to pry into your personal life. As I said, we are trying to build a picture of what's happened."

"You still haven't told me what's happened, Detective." She sighed. "Well, if you must know, he's a foul, disgusting, womanising sleazebag." She laughed. "You know he tried to pass it off as an addiction, his string of… said it was just a sex thing. What a coward, but by then the creep had me, just like all the others, no doubt, and it was too late."

"Too late?" Harper quizzed.

"He smarmed me until he was sure he could break my bloody heart." She exhaled and slumped down at the kitchen table.

"Can I ask why Mr Burns didn't want to return your bike and the rest of your property?"

She brushed a tear briskly from her eye. "I think with the other stuff, he was just being a nasty, controlling, spiteful bastard. He had something on me to wind me up and it saved him buying another one. Ah yes, I forgot that one. He was a tight-arsed bastard as well."

"Where does he work?"

"He's a cleaner at the Love Candy factory in Kilwinnoch. The sick, perverted irony of that never ceases to make my stomach turn. But he's a carpenter as well. He makes his own bespoke furniture and sells it to mugs who'll pay through the nose for his tat."

"And how did you two meet?"

"Sadly, that was how he hooked me. See that cabinet?" She pointed at a freestanding oak unit in the corner of the kitchen, the double doors beautifully carved with a floral design.

Harper went over. "That's very skilled."

80

"Oh aye, he's good with his hands. That's all part of his charm. I only asked for a basic storage cupboard, and he turned up with that and a bunch of compliments. Next thing you know, he's inside your head with his bloody hammer and chisel. I should take a hammer to the bloody thing."

"Was he abusive then?"

"No fists, but betrayal and denial set on repeat, then rage at even suggesting he was in the wrong. Industrial-scale misogynist. I call that abuse, Detective. What would you call it?"

"Okay, thank you, Ms Moffatt. Just one more question. Where were you last night between the hours of ten p.m. and seven a.m.?"

"In bed, why?"

"Alone? Sorry, I have to ask."

"If you must know, then yes, I was." She huffed. "And that's how it's going to be from now on. Men can take a running jump as far as I'm concerned." She looked at Harper. "No offence."

"None taken." Harper smiled. He pushed his glasses up his nose.

He fished in his pocket and retrieved one of his cards. "We may be in touch again, but in the meantime, if you think of anything that might help us with our enquiries, give me or the station a ring."

"I know I've told you I can't stand the creep, but please, Detective, has something happened to him?"

"Our investigations are ongoing. Do you own a car?"

"No, I don't have a licence. That's why him taking my bike was a deliberate retaliation for dumping him. I use it to get me about. Now I'm reliant on unreliable buses. But if I did, he'd have probably nicked that as well."

"Okay, that's all for now. Thanks for your time." Harper went back into the hallway.

The dog disengaged from the cat's attention and ran ahead of them. Ms Moffatt picked her up before she could escape again, and she opened the door.

Harper turned. "Sorry, just one more. Do you know if he has a current girlfriend?"

"Ha!" Ms Moffatt said. "I'd use the plural there, Detective. You think I have any interest whatsoever in his love life; sorry, sex life?"

"Okay, thanks again."

The dog barked, and she shut the door before it wriggled free.

EIGHT

In Kilwinnoch Police Station foyer, Brody, the desk sergeant, wrestled with a large, rainbow-coloured, inflatable unicorn.

"What the hell?" Bone said, avoiding impact.

"Sorry, sir, I can't control this bloody pump thing I bought to blow the bastard up. Pardon my French."

"Are we having a Mardi Gras later or something?"

"It's my daughter's third birthday party this afternoon, and I thought I'd have a wee go at this auto-inflator garbage I bought online. I can't turn the bloody thing off."

With a sudden, loud bang, the unicorn shot from his arms and rocketed across the foyer, bouncing off the walls and the reception screen until it finally dropped to the floor, semi-deflated and pathetically wheezing its last.

"Looks like your unicorn's no longer with us," Bone said.

"For God's sake. I've butchered her present," Brody said He picked up the limp, flattened remains.

"You'd better turn that off before it blows up the station." Bone pointed to the inflator, its rubber hose hissing and writhing around angrily in the corner. "There's more than enough hot air in here already." He grinned. "See what I did there?"

Brody shook his head and jumped on the wild rubber beast.

"I know where this is going!" Brody said, yanking the mechanism from the wall and dumping it unceremoniously in the bin, along with his deceased mythical creature.

"Plan B then?" Bone smiled.

"C." Brody sighed.

"Speaking of hot air. Is the boss in?"

"No, he's over at head office," Brody replied. "You think I'd be executing an inflatable monstrosity if he was around? He said he'd be back within the hour."

"Right, well, you'd better get My Dead Little Pony cleared up before he comes back and blows you up."

"Ha. I see what you did there." Brody chuckled.

"What?"

"The wee joke about getting blown up. That was a reference to you, wasn't it?"

Bone scowled at him. Brody's face fell.

"I'm so sorry, sir. I didn't mean to bring that up again. Me and my big fat bloody gob."

Bone smiled. "Of course it was, ya numpty. You are so easy."

He left Brody to collect the tattered body parts of his daughter's obliterated birthday present and went upstairs to the incident room.

On his way in, Walker caught up with him in the corridor.

"I'm not late, am I?" she asked, pushing an errant red curl from her flushed face.

"No, I've just come in myself. How did it go?"

"Interesting, to say the least. I left shortly after the PCs arrived. They're on door to door."

"What about Will? Where's he?"

"We have an ID on the bike owner. He's chasing that up."

"Right, let's get on with it then," Bone said.

They went in. DS Sheila Baxter was at the incident board, setting up the new investigation.

"Morning, sir." She adjusted her tweed suit jacket and continued to write on the board.

"No DS Mullens, then?"

"Not yet, sir."

"Or coffee, I see." Walker held up the empty percolator.

"Sorry. I've been busy." Baxter turned to Bone. "What should I call this case?"

"Hit-and-run, for now," Bone said.

The door flew open, and Mullens stumbled through.

"Glad you could join us, Detective Sergeant," Bone started, then spotted his attire. "What the hell are you wearing?" He gawped at Mullens' impossibly tight Lycra running shorts.

"Don't," Mullens said. "The guy in the shop persuaded me to buy these, as he promised it would keep everything in one place. But they're so fucking tight, the RSPCA'll be after me for double haggis abuse." He grabbed his crotch and adjusted the bulge.

"For God's sake, Mark. Put that away," Sheila complained, covering her eyes.

"Honestly, have you tried running in these bastards? It's like being constantly kicked in the nuts by a Clydesdale horse. I'm going to sue that first-class fud who sold me them."

"But why?" Baxter asked, averting her eyes.

"Why what?"

"Why are you even wearing them?"

"Ach, blame Sandra. She persuaded me that running to work would keep my ticker, well, ticking. She's still convinced I'm a lard arse, even though I'm a lean, mean haggis torture machine now." He grabbed his parts again.

"Sexual harassment at work. It's a thing, you know?" Baxter said.

"Okay, enough of the haggis, Mark," Bone said. "I suggest you put the poor beasts out of their misery and wear something more appropriate for work, i.e. a bloody suit."

When Mullens returned, Bone gathered everyone around.

"So last night, there was a hit-and-run incident just outside the hamlet of Cullenbrae. A male cyclist was struck by a vehicle and found dead in the middle of the road by an early morning jogger. The victim had suffered severe skull and facial injuries. The victim was also wearing a fleece jacket with a company logo on the breast pocket, Love Candy."

"The dildo factory?" Mullens asked.

"The sex toy company, Mark," Walker said.

"He's one of their employees, or just a frequent flyer?" Mullens grinned.

"Right, before we go any further," Bone said, "I can predict where this is likely to go, and I'm talking directly to you, Mark. We are dealing with a probable murder here, so respect for the deceased at all times, okay?"

"I'll button it, sir," Mullens said.

"Good."

"Did it look like someone panicked and fled the scene?" Baxter asked.

Bone shook his head. "Cash and his team discovered that there's more to it than that. He believes the victim had been moved and then stabbed through the eye socket. The eye itself had been gouged out or pulverised."

Mullens folded the wrapper over the top of the Snickers bar he was discreetly eating, swallowed uncomfortably, and slid the bar into his suit pocket.

"Couldn't the impact with a speeding vehicle cause an injury like that?" Baxter asked.

"That was my first thought, too, Sheila. But while we were at the scene, forensics officers found a corkscrew discarded in a ditch nearby. I requested Cash send images over to Will. Hopefully, he'll be here shortly."

"I'm here," Harper said, entering the incident room. "Sorry, sir, I called in on the owner of…"

"Yes, no worries, Will. Rhona filled me in. Your timing is excellent. Can you check if the forensic photos have landed in your inbox yet?"

"Let me check now." Harper went over to his desk.

"Do we have an ID on the victim?" Mullens asked.

"Not officially, but a local by the name of Martin Burns has cropped up a few times."

"That's the name the bike owner gave me," Harper said.

"Hold on, Will. Let's do this systematically," Bone interrupted. "You carry on looking for the images." He turned to Walker. "What have you got so far, Rhona?"

"Okay, so this morning I interviewed the witness who found the victim, Mrs Annie Hepworth, a Cullenbrae local. She was out jogging and came upon the deceased at around seven-thirty a.m. She believed the victim may be a Mr Martin Burns."

"There he is again," Mullens said.

"She reported no traffic or anyone else on the road during her run. Her route takes her past a farm, and the farmer was out, but she didn't think he saw her.

88

She seemed pretty shaken up, but the husband, Simon Hepworth, was possibly the most irritating person I've ever met, and believe me, my list is very long, so no mean feat. All he was interested in was getting the road opened as soon as possible so he could get to work. No sympathy whatsoever for his poor wife who'd just witnessed a horrific killing, or for the possible victim."

"So they knew the victim?" Baxter asked.

"Burns built and fitted their kitchen, which I have to say looks amazing. Their house has been completely modernised, from a quaint wee bungalow to basically a massive glass box on a hill. She said their renovations had ruffled a few feathers in the hamlet."

"Someone with a grudge against Burns for helping them?" Harper suggested.

"It's possible," Bone replied.

Baxter noted down the information on the board.

"Anything else?"

"She said he propositioned her a few times, and in the end she had to tell him to do one."

"The dirty dog," Mullens said.

"How did the husband feel about that?" Bone asked.

"According to Mrs Hepworth, he doesn't know. But to quote her words exactly, she said he'd 'bloody kill him' if he found out. I buttonholed him after my interview with her, and while he was completely obnoxious, I don't think he was aware of Burns' behaviour. But I'd say stick him on the board, Sheila. I also got Burns' address, twenty-eight Brae Hill. But as you'd expect, there was no one in and the house was locked up. I also called into the local pub, the Clachan Arms."

"A bit early, even for you, isn't it, Rhona?" Mullens said.

"And I interviewed the landlord, a Mr David Gronin. The pub is absolutely hanging, along with its landlord. He was a fairly obnoxious man. He told me the pub was quiet last night, so he shut up shop early, around ten-thirty. But he told me that there were boy racers out on the road in the early part of the evening and they called into the pub at around six-thirty. He named one of the lads as Gary Speed but then clammed up."

"Speed, you say?" Baxter said. "If it's who I'm thinking of, I might have represented his father, Kenny Speed, back in my advocacy days."

"Did you win?" Mullens asked.

"Of course not. Irrefutable evidence, but the arse insisted on pleading his innocence."

"What crimes?" Bone asked.

"You name it. But now he's serving two life sentences for killing a prison officer while in for armed robbery. A nasty piece of work, and it sounds like the son is going the same way."

"Could you see if you can get an address for the son?"

"Should be fairly straightforward. And even if the family has moved since, I would suspect Gary Speed has already accumulated quite a few run-ins with our uniformed colleagues downstairs."

"Okay, hold that for a sec. Anything else, Rhona?"

"Yes, the landlord went on to recount an interesting wee tale. Apparently, a notorious murder took place in the hamlet there in the mid-seventies."

"Of course," Baxter said, clicking her fingers. "The Sneedon Killings. You've been in Kilwinnoch forever, Mark. Surely you must remember Henry Sneedon?"

"I know I've had heart surgery and have already died twice, but believe it or not, I wasn't even a twinkle in my old man's eye in the mid-seventies. But now you mention the name…"

"Go on, Rhona," Bone urged. He leaned against the nearest desk.

"Henry Sneedon, a resident of Cullenbrae, ploughed his tractor into two residents, killing one and leaving the other with life-changing injuries, then drove up to his parents' house on Brae Hill and shot them both, then himself. When police investigated, they also found the next-door neighbour in the cellar, throat cut and hanging from a meat hook. "

"Good grief," Bone said.

"When was this?" Harper asked.

"Nineteen seventies," Walker said.

"Seventy-six," Baxter clarified.

"The weird thing is…" Walker continued.

"And that's not weird?" Mullens interrupted again.

"Mark." Bone scowled at him.

"The house is still there, untouched, as it's in some kind of legal dispute between Sneedon's relatives. Mr Gronin mentioned that there's an old man, Donald

Fagan, or as he described him, mad as a brush, who lives opposite, who has taken it upon himself to keep an eye on the property. He didn't seem that enamoured with the guy, called him a pain in the arse. It sounds as though Mr Fagan may have some out-there views about the world."

"A pub isn't a pub without at least one," Mullens said.

"You don't think that horror story is related to the hit-and-run, do you?" Harper asked.

"Maybe, maybe not, but from my first impressions, Cullenbrae is a pretty miserable place, and there's not much community spirit, put it that way," Walker replied.

"That's all we need." Bone sighed. "McKinnon and his family of woodlice will have a bloody field day with this one."

"The forensic shots have landed, sir," Harper said.

"Before that, how did you get on?"

"Ah, yes. I interviewed the bike owner, and she claims…"

"A woman?" Bone asked. "So, is the bike nicked?"

"Yes, well, no. The owner, a Ms Diane Moffatt, claims that her ex, Martin Burns, refused to return it along with more of her property when they split up. She also claims that she reported the theft on…" He checked his phone. "The twenty-first of May this year, but it wasn't followed up by the police."

"Oh dear," Bone said.

"But she also basically trashed his character. She said he was a womaniser and a cheat, and a few other things, too."

"Mrs Hepworth more or less said the same thing," Walker said.

"Yes, she was pretty angry."

"Does Moffatt have an alibi?" Bone asked.

"She said she was at home alone last night, went to bed early. She didn't appear nervous or unwilling to cooperate, just angry that he'd nicked her stuff and that we'd not followed up. She seemed pretty legit, to be honest. And, judging by the horrific injuries sustained by the victim, seems a little extreme for a stolen bike."

"Get you, Agatha Christie," Mullens said.

"Open minds, Will," Bone said. "Right, it's looking very likely now that our victim is Martin Burns."

Mullens laughed. He looked up. "Sorry, sir."

"On my way back," Bone said, "I interviewed the manager and her assistant at the Star Service Station on the outskirts of Cullenbrae. It's open twenty-four hours, with a convenience store tagged on. So it's well used by Cullenbrae residents. The manager confirmed that a Mrs Jean Black was on the seven p.m. to one a.m. shift last night but may have stayed a bit later while she waited for the next shift to arrive."

"Have you spoken to her yet?" Walker asked.

"No. Apparently, she has a terminally ill sister and spends her days up at the Palliative Care unit at Falkirk General. I'll go find her after this. I checked the

CCTV footage, and a hooded man on a bike called in at twelve-forty a.m."

"Burns," Mullens said.

"His face was obscured, but it looks that way. He bought some shopping and carried on, heading in the direction of Cullenbrae."

"Any vehicles following?"

"Nothing on the tape, but I stopped it just after one a.m. and it'll need the fine-tooth-comb treatment. I've asked the manager to send it over to you, Will."

"I'll run it through my magic eye."

"I think you might want to rename that." Mullens sniggered.

"I don't get it," Harper said.

"Don't explain, Mark. Just don't," Walker interrupted, before Mullens could speak.

"Also, a group of lardy-arse youths called in to the garage at ten-thirty, in a sports-adapted Citroen Saxo."

"That ties in with the landlord's story, but ten-thirty is a lot later."

"Indeed. So what were they up to during those four hours?" Bone asked.

"And the two hours after," Harper said.

"The assistant identified a long-haired, wide-brimmed hat wearing local Cullenbrae resident, who was captured on the CCTV as Mr Mason. He bought some snacks at eleven thirty p.m. The assistant said he calls in regularly as there is a path that leads all the way from the garage down to his house on the edge of Cullenbrae. I checked it out and walked over. It's a surprisingly quick route considering how windy the lane is; less than ten minutes. I interviewed him and his partner, Caitlin. They are artists, though he's an electrician by trade."

"Could the killer have used the path somehow?" Walker asked.

"Possibly, but it's very narrow and a mud bath at points. I don't know how he negotiated it in the dark. I suppose once you know it…"

"So if he walked over, is he ruled out then?" Baxter asked.

"I'm not ruling anyone out. He told me his van was in for repairs."

"Very convenient. Which garage?" Mullens asked.

"Kilwinnoch Motors. There was something not quite right about them, though. The two of them were in the middle of some sort of barney. Their living room looked like a bomb had gone off. They'd clearly been tearing strips off one another."

"Sounds like me and Sandra." Mullens chuckled.

"Stick him on the board, Sheila." Bone turned to Harper. "Okay, Will, forensic photo gallery time."

Harper winced. "Let me fiddle with the files for a sec." He tapped at his keyboard, and the monitor on the wall flashed to life. "He's sent a few."

"Go through one by one."

Harper tapped again, and the first image appeared; a wide shot of the victim spreadeagled on the road.

"Nasty," Mullens said.

The second shot was a close-up of the victim's mutilated face. Harper averted his eyes.

Bone went over to the screen. "You can see here where the eye has been obliterated almost completely."

"It's the 'almost' bit that's turning my stomach," Baxter said.

"Okay, Will, move it on," Bone ordered.

The third image showed the tyre marks on the road.

"Anything on those yet, or the flecks of paint?"

Harper checked the email. "No."

"The vehicle would have to be going some to make that length of a mark," Walker said.

"Traffic should be able to give us an approximate speed on that soon," Bone said. "Keep going, Will."

A close-up of the corkscrew appeared, the handle protruding from its muddy resting place in the ditch.

"Can you zoom that in a bit more?" Baxter asked.

The monitor went black for a second, and then the object almost completely filled the screen.

Baxter approached the monitor. "That's not a corkscrew, it's a tapered reamer," she said finally.

"A what?" Bone asked, squinting at the screen again.

"I know because I've had to traipse round ironmongers with my husband buying all these specialist types of bloody tools for his mandolins."

"He plays the mandolin?" Mullens sniggered. "In full medieval jester outfit, I hope."

"He makes them."

"I didn't know that," Bone said.

"He doesn't want anyone to know, for the very reason Mark has just demonstrated. He took it up when he retired. He said it was either mandolins or whisky."

"One would drive me to the other," Mullens said.

"Are they any good? The ones he builds?" Bone asked.

"I've no idea. It keeps him out of my hair, that's the main thing, and as long as he doesn't try to play them for me, then who am I to complain?"

"So what makes you sure?"

"I recognise the make. See that wee logo on the side of the handle? That's a famous instrument tool-making company. I can't remember..." She stopped. "No, I'd have to look that up or ask Jim."

"Any more, Will?"

"Just the one." He clicked the keyboard. The screen flickered again, and the bike frame flashed up with the serial number clearly visible.

"Ah yes, that takes us back to Ms Moffatt," Bone said.

"Hold on." Harper flicked back to the first image. "Yes, I thought so."

"Spit it out, Will," Bone urged.

"When I was at the scene, even though the frame was completely mangled, it crossed my mind that it looked like a step-through, but then I..."

"Got distracted?" Bone smiled at his young colleague, saving his blushes. "Could you print up these images and stick them up on the board?"

"Is this officially a murder inquiry now, then?" Baxter asked.

"Most certainly, but we'll need to wait for the official word from Cash and co. on cause of death, so it remains suspicious for now." Bone stood again. "Okay, Sheila, can you run some checks on Martin Burns and the residents of Cullenbrae? Find out if Burns has any relatives that we may need to contact. Dig out a bit more on this multiple murder that took place up there in the seventies, along with identifying the brand of that— What did you call it?"

"Tapered reamer."

"Is that your porn name?" Mullens asked.

"Remember what I said, Mark," Bone interrupted. He sighed. "I'll probably regret this, but could you and Will go find out if Mr Burns was employed over at the Love Candy factory?"

"You want me to go with him to a sex toy factory?" Harper asked.

"Call it a test, Mark. See if that button can remain tightly shut."

"Please don't do this to me, sir."

Mullens looked over at Harper and grinned.

"In the meantime, Rhona, if you head back to Cullenbrae and continue the search, I'll go and find Mrs Black at Falkirk General, then I'll rejoin you," Bone said.

"What about the Super? Should we update him?" Walker asked.

"He's over at head office, probably locked in another budget streamlining meeting, so he won't be in the best of moods."

They grabbed their coats and left.

NINE

When Walker arrived back at the crime scene, the body had been removed and the SOC team were now concentrating on a forensic search of the immediate area. She waited for a few minutes until a scene-suited officer waved her through the roadblock.

She parked at the top end of the square and walked up to Burns' house. Another uniformed officer appeared from behind an outhouse, close to the lane.

"Any joy?" Walker asked.

"Not a sausage. My colleague is keeping a watch on number twenty-eight like you asked. I don't envy him up there." He shivered.

"Everything all right?" Walker asked.

"That house at the top gives me the willies."

"Brae Hill House. You know about its history then?"

"My granddad worked on the investigation."

"What's your name, Officer?"

"Constable Greaves, ma'am."

"And your grandfather, is he still alive?"

"Oh aye, ninety-eight now and still causing trouble." He smiled. "He used to talk about Henry Sneedon and what he did. Stuff like that sticks, you know?"

"Thanks, Constable. Carry on with the house-to-house."

"Ma'am." The PC nodded and, spotting a second officer at the bottom of the lane, he carried on down to meet him.

Halfway up, Walker stopped at Burns' property, a modest whitewashed cottage at the end of a ramshackle terrace. She tried the door and peered through the low-level sash window adjacent. She glanced around, leaned into the frame, examined the lock, and frowned.

"Replacement windows." She sighed.

She continued up the hill towards Brae Hill House. The once-whitewashed façade of the towering building was covered in green and black mould. Windows and doors had been boarded up with steel panels bolted onto the frames, and the grounds were enclosed by a high wire fence with a barbed crown and a plethora of signs warning thieves and trespassers to keep out. A glint of sunlight flared and she glanced up. A small dormer window in the roof was uncovered. A shadow flitted across the pane. She rubbed her eyes and squinted again. A crow cawed loudly behind her. She jumped back.

"Jesus!"

She squinted up again but the window was black. She approached the front. Donald Fagan's cottage was directly opposite. She noticed several cameras on the roof and another on a telegraph pole by his garden gate. At the perimeter fence, she shook the rusting gate. The padlocked chain rattled. Kneeling, she studied the lock type.

"What do you think you're doing?" a voice called from behind her.

She stood. An elderly, dishevelled man in a vest and pyjama bottoms approached, brandishing a baseball bat.

"The property is out of bounds. If you're tampering with that lock, I'll have the polis on you." He raised the bat.

"Hey, stop right there," Walker said in surprise. "I *am* the police. DS Walker from Kilwinnoch station." She held up her lanyard.

The man lowered the bat. "Well, I don't care if you're Inspector Bloody Clouseau, no one is permitted in there."

"We are investigating an incident on the lane outside Cullenbrae."

"What's going on?"

"There's been a hit-and-run."

"Doesn't surprise me. The lane is a bloody death trap. It wasn't a local, was it? Are they okay?"

"We are making initial inquiries in the hamlet. What's your name, sir?" Walker asked.

"Donald Fagan.

"And that's your house?"

"Aye."

"A police officer knocked on your door earlier. Why didn't you answer?"

"I don't answer the door unless I know who it is. What are you doing snooping about the Sneedons' for?"

"You knew the Sneedons?"

"Mr Sneedon put me in charge of security. I am his eyes and ears when it comes to that." He pointed the bat at the fence.

"Which Mr Sneedon is that?"

"Craig Sneedon, the owner."

"Is he a relative of Henry Sneedon?" Walker asked.

Fagan's face fell. "We don't talk about him," he replied. "Mr Sneedon inherited the property after the—" He stopped again.

"So is the property vacant?"

"Aye." Fagan replied.

"It's just that I thought I saw someone up at that top window." She pointed.

"You're seeing things. The house has been empty for years."

"So what's with all the cameras?"

"My eyes and ears. I take my job very seriously."

"I can see that," Walker said. "Are you paid by Mr Sneedon, then?"

"Not at all. He paid for all the equipment, though. It makes me feel safe as well, so happy to help him out."

"When's the last time you spoke to Mr Sneedon?"

The old man scratched at his balding, chaotic hair. "Three, maybe four months ago. There was a break-in. Some wee neds looking to nab the lead off the roof. But eagle-eye over there clocked them, and they knew better than to mess with this." He lifted the bat and swung it wildly over his head.

"Okay, maybe just set that down before someone gets hurt."

"They'll only get hurt if I want them to get hurt, Detective. I'm well versed in sorting out wee numpties from the estate, believe me. I served in Afghanistan. I know quite a few wee tricks, and they all know it."

"I don't doubt it," Walker said. "But all the same."

The man lowered the bat.

"Do you have a contact for him?"

"Aye, but he never answers his phone. He rings me once a month or so."

"If you have the number, though, that would be great."

"It's inside, hold on a minute."

"I'll follow you in, if that's okay? I'm quite interested in your setup." Walker nodded, feigning enthusiasm.

Fagan shuffled up the path. "It's an absolute midden. My cleaner's on holiday."

"You have a cleaner?"

105

"Oh aye, and a butler, a dresser, and a chauffeur." Fagan shook his head. "This way."

The hallway was stacked on either side with teetering towers of newspapers and magazines, with barely enough room to squeeze through. When they made it to the end, Fagan put his shoulder to a door. It slowly opened with a loud creak, and he edged around the gap. Walker followed.

There was more chaotic mess in the living room, the walls plastered with cut-outs of newspaper articles and photos.

"As you can see, I like to do a lot of research," the old man said.

He shifted a chest from the doorway.

"Is that your setup?" Walker gestured to a rack of black and grey video recorders and monitors on a dining table at the rear of the room.

"Aye," the old man said.

They picked their way around the debris.

"How many cameras do you have, then?" Walker asked, eyeing up two more recorders under the table.

"Five in total, though one is down at the minute."

"And Mr Sneedon pays for all this? It must cost him a fair packet?"

"Whatever I ask for, he supplies."

"Aside from the two cameras set up on the side of your house, where are the others?"

"There's one on the telegraph pole on the lane by Mr Sneedon's house, another on the security fence at the back, and the last one is above the front door of the property. That one is a night camera. I also set up a couple of sound devices on the fence that pick up intruders, but that's usually either foxes or deer, or the neighbour's cat. So those are a bit of a pain in the arse, to be honest."

"And they are all wired into these units here?"

"Aye. I was in the signals with the army, and they paid for me to do a degree in electrical engineering, so I know my way round the wiring up."

"As well as a baseball bat, eh?"

"Oh, aye!" Fagan smiled.

"And your cameras picked up the intruders, then?"

"Caught before they could even fart at the fence."

"Did you report it to the police?"

"I did, yes. But they were long gone when the squad car arrived. Useless shower." He looked at her. "I mean, it can't be easy with all the cutbacks and so on."

"Have there been any other attempts or actual break-ins in recent days and weeks?"

"No."

"And why the Fort Knox? Has he got gold bars in there or something?"

"No, Mr Sneedon just wants to protect his family's asset from scum."

Walker examined a few of the clippings Sellotaped to the walls. "What kind of research are you doing, Mr Fagan? Are these UFOs?"

"Not UFOs. I hate it when people use that term. They are IFOs."

"IFO?"

"Identified Flying Objects. The US military has been studying and running experiments on many of these recovered objects for years and years."

"You think they actually have some of these UF... sorry, IFOs in their possession?"

"I don't think. The evidence is concrete and substantiated. We have to be prepared."

"For what?"

"The invasion. It will come. They are waiting."

"Fascinating," Walker replied. "I hope they've brought plenty of Lemsip. That common cold could wipe them out before they even get their laser guns out."

"You might joke, but this is no laughing matter, and the invasion won't be with lasers but with viruses. Biological warfare. It will be a new fatal strain of the cold that wipes *us* out."

"I have learned that ownership of Brae Hill House is in dispute." Walker steered quickly away before the conversation turned any weirder.

"Aye, her."

"Who is that?"

"Bernadette Sneedon, Craig's sister."

"So there's some kind of feud between them?"

"War, more like. She has absolutely no right to that property. She was a witch to her poor parents and she's a witch to her brother now as well. Craig actually showed me the will."

"She lives in Bristol, is that correct?"

"As far as I know, aye, though Mars wouldn't be bloody far enough away."

108

"Did you know her then when she lived here?"

"She was never here. Always off to India finding herself or living in a drug squat with some loser or other, wasting her parents' generous allowance."

"She was into drugs?"

"The works. What wasn't she into? Mr and Mrs Sneedon were at their wits' end with her."

"Black sheep then?"

Fagan tutted. "That's not how I would describe her."

"Do you have Craig Sneedon's contact number?"

"Ah, yes." Fagan shuffled over to a side table and, yanking at a drawer, he reached in and fumbled around. The table rocked back and forth and almost toppled a stack of files to the floor. Finally, he retrieved his hand, clutching a shoddy notebook. "Let's see. I put it in my address book." He flicked forward and stopped. "Here it is. Let me scribble it down."

"If you give me the book, I'll put it into my phone." Walker reached across, and Fagan handed the address book over.

"You see it, Craig Sneedon?"

"Yes." Walker retrieved her phone and tapped in the mobile number. "And what about Bernadette Sneedon?"

"Are you serious?" Fagan said. "If I had her number, I'd be on at her every day. Giving her a piece of my mind, the nasty cow."

Walker was about to hand the book back when she noticed an entry below. "You have Henry Sneedon's number in here. Did you know him?"

"I told you, Inspector, we don't talk about that man."

"Was he a friend?"

"Unfortunately, he was a neighbour."

"So did you see or hear what went on over there?"

Fagan frowned. "I don't want to go back there."

"It must have been an awful time for you and the rest of Cullenbrae."

"The absolute worst of times. I had no idea what was going on over there, and when we found out what he'd done to his parents and the residents who lost their lives to his madness... It was absolutely shocking for all of us."

"Were you home that night?"

"I heard the gunshots. They woke me up. Then I heard sirens and..."

"How long did you know the Sneedons?"

"For as long as they lived here, which was probably about thirty years. I knew Henry when he was a wee laddie." Fagan exhaled. "Inspector, I am in no mood to go through this. I've had my fill of morbid curiosity and I have no desire whatsoever to go back to that dark time."

"Sorry, Mr Fagan. We are conducting house to house enquiries and I just need to confirm that the house is vacant."

"That's the second time you've asked me that." Fagan sighed. "I can't see why you're making me go over this again. You know, I had the world's press parked outside my door for weeks?"

"I can imagine it must have been horrific."

"Yes, it was, so you can understand why I don't want to talk about it."

"That's fine. Thank you for the number."

"But I would say that not one single person in Cullenbrae knew what Henry Sneedon was capable of. So when you go through your records and files, as I'm sure you will, for whatever pointless reason, any notes or reports that suggest otherwise are one hundred percent wrong. He shocked all of us."

"We called in earlier to number twenty-eight, just down the lane, but he wasn't in."

"Aye, Martin Burns' place."

"You know him?"

"I've spoken to him a few times, but I tend to keep myself to myself."

"You didn't see him out and about last night on his bike, or anyone else for that matter?"

"When are we talking?"

"Between say, eleven and one a.m. Maybe your cameras picked something up?"

"If they did, then I'd have woken up. I have an alarm by my bed but I slept through the night. First time in bloody weeks. The foxes must be on holiday. Has Martin been knocked down then?"

"Why do you say that?"

"You know, with the hit-and-run. Was he knocked off his bike? It's bloody dangerous walking or cycling up there in the pitch-black, and those idiots driving about don't help either."

"Do you know a young lad called Gary Speed?"

"Is he one of the brainless morons who roars about? I stay well clear. And if any of them come near my place or the Sneedons', they'll soon know all about it."

"Would you be willing to share your footage of last night with us?"

"Why? I told you the eagle eyes picked nothing up."

"Just in case you missed something. We have technology to carry out a forensic examination of the footage."

"Believe me, I miss nothing. You'll be wasting your time, Inspector."

"Okay. I'll get out of your hair now," Walker said and scrambled across the chaos to the door.

Fagan showed her out. "I hope Martin or whoever it was that got knocked down is all right and you catch the idiots who did it."

"If you see or hear anything else you think might help our enquiries, just give me a ring, okay? Here's my direct number." She handed him her card.

Fagan studied it a second. "What exactly am I supposed to be looking or listening for?" he asked.

"Eyes and ears, eh?" Walker waved at the two cameras peering down at them.

Fagan huffed and shut the door.

On her way back down to the square, Walker stopped and peered up at Brae Houses' exposed dormer window again. Something just didn't sit right with Fagan's responses. She found her phone and called Bone.

TEN

Harper jumped into the passenger seat of the pool car.

"Right, before we go any further, if you start with your smutty, nine-year-old euphemisms, you are on your own. I can't believe the boss would..." He stopped. "What is that smell?"

Mullens' hands were buried in a large paper bag. He looked up sheepishly. "What smell?"

"Curry. Is that what's in the bag?"

"Ach, that was from last night."

"Show me what's in that bag," Harper insisted.

"It's just a salad morning roll," Mullens protested.

"Show me."

Mullens slowly withdrew a foil container of rice, followed by a second full to the brim with thick, creamy red sauce, then two naan bread, one half eaten.

"Good God!"

"Mid-morning snack. I'm bloody starving. All I had last night was a kwinhoo salad. Sandra's latest fucking obsession."

"A what salad?"

"Kwinhoo, kennowaywa, keenqu…"

"Stop!" Harper exclaimed.

"Ach, that shite tastes like desiccated toe jam."

"Quinoa, you mean."

"Aye, that. The Devil's smegma."

"I like it. It's full of protein."

"That's what I'm worried about, especially when it sticks in your teeth."

"I'm going to be sick." Harper stared down at the oily mess of food in Mullens' lap. "You shouldn't be eating that, Mark."

"That's what makes it all the tastier. It's like danger food." He turned to Harper. "Please don't tell Sandra or anyone, partner."

"Don't pull the 'partner' bribe. If you're going to sit here and trough your way through that, I have double reason to bail out."

"But then they'll ask questions. Just let me take a quick dip and then I'll put it away."

"Go on then."

Harper averted his eyes while Mullens folded the naan in two, took a massive dip of the masala, and shovelled the contents into his eagerly waiting mouth.

"Oh, it's better than humping, this."

"Oh, good God," Harper moaned. "Why was I posted to this station?"

"You love me really, young Skywalker," Mullens mumbled through the food. He took another quick scoop and then returned the cartons and bread to the bag. "Missing you already," he said and placed the bag on the back seat.

"You'll get oil all over the upholstery," Harper said.

"At least it's not the usual blood or vomit."

"There will be blood in a minute if we don't get going."

"Ooh, handbags. I like it when you get all assertive."

"And we haven't even got to the dildo factory as you so elegantly put it."

Mullens tittered.

"Oh, dear God." Harper rubbed his forehead.

Mullens started the car and with a roar, drove out of the station car park.

The Love Candy reception was surprisingly austere, considering their brand. The walls were bare and grey, and the front desk looked like a basic flat-pack from IKEA. The only hint that the detectives were in the right place was a large pair of illuminated crimson lips with the company name in a curly neon signature in the open mouth. Mullens approached the receptionist, who was busy with a plastic container full of parcels.

"DS Mullens and DC Harper from Kilwinnoch station. Could we speak to someone about a possible employee of yours, a Mr Martin Burns?"

The receptionist spun round. Her mouth fell open, a pale facsimile of the huge pair above her head.

"Miss?" Mullens said.

"You're here for Carol's birthday, aren't you?"

"What?"

"Are you the karaoke stripper guys?"

"The what? No."

They held up their lanyards.

She smiled and winked at them. "Very good. I have to say, you do look the part."

"We are police officers, ma'am. We are investigating a serious incident and would like to speak to one of your directors."

The receptionist's smile dropped. "Oh, right. So you're not singers then?"

"He might be, but you don't want to hear this sing," Mullens said. He tapped his chest.

"Or strip," Harper added.

"Let me just check and see if Richard is around." She picked up the phone.

"The managing director is called Dick," Mullens whispered in Harper's ear.

"He'll be through in a minute." She carried on scanning parcels with a handheld machine.

"Are those some of your products?" Mullens asked.

"Oh, jeez." Harper sighed.

"These are returns," she said.

118

"Returns? You mean folk return stuff, used?"

"We do require all goods to be returned in original packaging, but we do get the odd one that customers haven't been er… satisfied with." She winced.

"That's minging."

"Tell me about it. Thankfully, if there's any sign of that, they go straight in the bin. Believe me, you get all sorts of feedback."

"I bet."

A middle-aged man in a T-shirt and jeans emerged from a door at the back of the reception. He approached the pair, smiling.

"Richard Croft, Love Candy MD. How can I help?"

"We're looking for information on one of your employees, a Mr Martin Burns."

The MD glanced over at the receptionist.

"He's our night watchman, Rich."

"Ah yes, that's right. I'm a bit out of it at the moment as we have auditors arriving any time now and we're having a complete nightmare that I won't bore you with. It might be better to speak to our HR manager, but I warn you she'll be tearing her hair out this morning. Fiona, can you let Sue know we're on our way?"

They followed the MD down another drab corridor.

"So where does all the action take place?" Mullens asked, wide-eyed.

"Packing, you mean?" the MD said.

"Well, you know."

"Ah, you mean our products. It's all very boring on the shop floor, just boxing, bagging, and shipping. Here we are." He stopped at a door and knocked gently.

"Come in," a high-pitched voice called from the other side.

A flustered woman perched behind a tidy desk at the rear of an equally organised room.

"Hey Sue, sorry to disturb. Two detectives are here and want some information on one of our employees."

"With me, right now?"

"DS Mullens and DC Harper, ma'am. It should only take a minute or two."

She exhaled. "So sorry, Detectives. It's madness here. They've literally given us three days to get our ducks in a row, and our system is down." She glared at the MD.

"We're working on it, Sue. In fact, I better get back and help out." He shut the door.

"Help out. The guy just swans around. He's barely bloody here. Off spending his millions in his second or third home." She stopped. "Sorry, that was very unprofessional of me. I'm a little flustered. Which employee is it you want to speak to?"

"Martin Burns."

"Who?"

"We have reason to believe he works here, as a night watchman?"

"Ah, yes, of course. Sorry. My head's all over the place. Let me just check." She turned to her computer.

"Isn't your system down?" Harper asked.

"Accounting system, conveniently." She rolled her eyes. "Sorry, unprofessional again."

She tapped at her keyboard. "I believe Mr Burns started with us three years ago. I don't have much to do with him as he works overnight, obviously." She peered at the screen. "Yes, he started with us in 2018."

"Has he always worked nights?

"What's this about? Has something happened? Is he okay?"

"We're investigating an incident out at Cullenbrae."

"Involving Mr Burns?"

"As I said, our investigations are ongoing."

"Right." She scanned the screen. "Yes, that's what his record states. He does six until midnight, Thursday to Sunday inclusive."

"Are you happy with his work, then?"

"He's worked here for three years, but it hasn't been without incident, if I remember correctly. Let me have a quick scan of his record." She paused to read. "There are a couple of warnings for tardiness. Hold on." She scrolled forward. "Ah yes, that's right."

"What?"

"About five months ago, he was caught on camera bringing a young lady onto the premises."

"On his night shift?" Mullens asked.

"I was all for dismissal, but Richard insisted on a warning. He's too soft on the staff."

"Do you have this recording?"

"No, I wouldn't think so. That's too long ago, and I remember Richard ordering for the tape to be scrubbed before it ended up on the internet. The last thing a sex toy retailer needs."

"And no more bother after that?"

She checked his record again. "No, all fine. I think he must have learnt his lesson, though when it comes to his love life, somehow I don't believe it."

"Does Mr Burns have a bit of a reputation then?"

"I really shouldn't say anything. That would be very…"

"If you think it might help our enquiries."

"Well, the women in the office call him the heartbreaker."

"Do you know who he dated?"

"I'm not sure that's what the unfortunate women would call it, but I couldn't give you names. That would be a breach of confidentiality. I'd be instantly dismissed. I'm head of HR, after all. I mean, how would that look?"

"Perhaps you could put the word out that we'd like anyone who was or is acquainted with Mr Burns to come forward. How about that? And also if anyone might know who the woman caught on camera was. But I'm afraid we might reach a point where we may need to interview all employees."

"I'll make sure they are made aware and encourage them as best I can to speak to you."

"How many employees are we talking about here?" Harper asked.

"I know of one who sat where you are a few months ago bawling her eyes out, but there could be more. There are times in life when a pair of sheep shears might come in handy," the HR manager said. "To be honest, I don't know what they all see in him. He's not exactly George Clooney, you know?"

"Do you have a telephone number for him?" Harper asked. "And a photo?"

"Let me just check." She tapped at the keyboard. "Oh, I'm afraid not. There doesn't seem to be any record here. Hold on, yes, that's right. We've asked Mr Burns a few times to provide a contact number, but he says he doesn't own a phone."

"So how do you get in touch with each other if, for example, he's sick and can't make it in to work?" Harper asked.

"He's never actually missed a day's work. Late, yes, but no absences. I think if he has any issues, he comes in the day before and speaks to a supervisor."

The photocopier on the other side of the office sprang to life.

"That's the picture we have on file," she said.

Harper retrieved the black-and-white head-and-shoulder shot of Burns. He was wearing the company fleece, staring straight down the lens of the camera, smiling.

"We'll let you get on now. Here's my card. Give me or the station a ring if anything else comes up," Mullens said.

"Will Mr Burns be coming into work tonight?"

"I'm afraid I don't know that," Mullens replied. "Though you might wish to think about organising cover."

"Well, if he's done something wrong, throw away the key for me. I'll show you out."

"No, no. you carry on," Mullens interrupted.

"I need to speak to Richard again, so follow me, gents." She emerged from behind her desk in an electric wheelchair.

The detectives moved out of the way to let her through, and they followed behind.

"He might be all over the place when it comes to the accounts, but he's been very good when it comes to access."

"I couldn't get a quick look at your operations, could I?" Mullens asked.

Harper shook his head.

"Yes, I was going to take a shortcut through there anyway."

They went up a ramp, through a sliding door, and into the main factory. Conveyor belts moved boxes and parcels from one side of the vast floor space to the other. Workers in company overalls lined up along workbenches, packing brightly coloured sex toys of varied shapes and sizes. As they passed, one employee battled to pack a two-foot-long blue phallus into a box.

"That's a big 'un," Mullens said.

"One of our top sellers. I think it's the Scottish flag markings that do it."

Mullens laughed. "That puts a whole new spin on *Braveheart.*"

"This way, Detectives."

They carried on through a set of plastic screen doors to a second, smaller area.

"This is our prototype testing room," Sue said.

A few employees in white overalls were dotted around tables, busy working on unidentifiable objects. Mullens spotted a man kneeling by a space hopper with a giant protruding appendage.

"What the hell is that?" Mullens asked.

Sue stopped and turned her chair.

"What are you working on, Josh?" she called over. "That's Josh, he's head of testing."

"Are you like a porno Q?" Mullens joked.

"Mark," Harper said, his embarrassment escalating by the second.

Josh picked up a box from the adjacent worktable and joined them.

"I'll show you." He aimed the box at the space hopper, and it shuddered. "Just a moment while I adjust the range." He fiddled with the buttons on the front. The space hopper shook again and then bounced towards them, the protrusion on the end flapping up and down.

"Brilliant," Mullens said.

Josh stepped out of the way, turned the dial, and the rubber creature charged directly at Mullens. He pulled back, but it rammed up against his leg.

"Jesus, he's keen, isn't he?" He retreated further, but the space hopper persisted. Mullens took off across the room and the horny bouncing ball gave chase.

Harper bellowed with laughter.

"Okay, joke's over. Turn it off," Mullens cried out.

When the space hopper had Mullens pinned in the corner of the room, its rubbery appendage whacking against the side of his leg, Josh finally hit the off button, and the toy rolled onto its side as though exhausted.

"Looks like you have an admirer," Harper said between giggles.

"Bloody hell, mate, that thing's lethal," Mullens said, glancing over his shoulder in case his new admirer fancied seconds. "You did that deliberately, didn't you?"

"Sorry, no." Josh concealed a grin. "We need to make some minor adjustments, but I'm very pleased how this one is turning out."

"Pleased? I'd have the thing locked up. It's a bloody sex pest."

"Yes, that's kind of the point."

"I really do need to get on, Detectives," Sue said. "Though I could leave you if you wish, Detective Mullens."

"With Randy Andy over there, I'm out of here."

At the end of another walkway, they reached the exit door. Sue leaned out of her chair and tapped in a code.

"Here we are."

They followed her out into the main car park.

"Thanks for the tour," Harper said with a grin. "Good luck with the audit."

"We'll need more than luck, I'm afraid." She about-turned and rolled the chair across a raised pathway back towards reception.

"I feel used," Mullens said.

They climbed into the car.

"Bloody hell, that stench of garam masala is overpowering," Harper said.

"All that shock has made me bloody starving."

"Post-coital hunger?" Harper snorted. "Strangely enough, me too."

"Share it?"

"Oh God, now you've bloody got me. Okay," Harper conceded.

"Fantastic. To a lay-by, we go!" Mullens started up.

"I'm sure there's probably enough for three. I could go back in."

"You wouldn't even make it to the door." Mullens belted up, hit first, and they accelerated out of the car park.

ELEVEN

"If you take a seat, Inspector, I'll go and see where they are. Sometimes Jean takes Coral out into the gardens," the nurse at the Palliative Care reception desk said.

Bone glanced around the waiting room. It was painted in soothing pastel colours with serene landscape prints dotted around the space. Even the furniture looked comfortable and inviting.

"They should make all the wards like this," he said.

"You're not the first to say that." The nurse slid around her desk.

She went through into the main ward.

Bone sat and smiled at a young couple reading magazines. One mouthed a hello. Bone nodded. A few moments later, another older couple emerged from the ward, holding each other up. The woman was in tears, and the man was stern-faced. A nurse followed behind, and she took them down a corridor and into a room at the end.

The nurse reappeared with an elderly woman by her side.

The woman approached Bone. "You want to see me?"

"Mrs Black?"

"That's right, yes."

"DCI Duncan Bone from Kilwinnoch station. Sorry to interrupt you."

The young couple both looked up again in surprise.

"Has there been some sort of bother at my house? Not a break-in, surely?"

"No, no. Perhaps we could go somewhere a little more private?" The couple returned guiltily to their respective magazines.

"Will it take long? I'm here with my sister."

"Yes, your manager at the garage told me. I'm so sorry."

"Ach, we're prepared for it. We're just making the most of it all while we can."

"It should only take a few minutes."

She went over to the reception and then, after a few words, came back.

"We can use family room two. This way."

She marched off, and it took Bone a few seconds to match her pace.

They went in.

"Hold on a minute," she said.

Bone stood in the doorway, unsure what she meant.

She went over to a small Hi-Fi unit resting on the table. She reached over and turned off the mains. Soft, soothing music that Bone had barely been aware of, suddenly stopped.

"Can't abide all that New Age claptrap. Right, let's get on with it." She eyeballed Bone. "Are you going to sit doon then, or does your police training extend to draught excluders as well?"

Bone approached a sofa and three chairs. He went for the sofa but changed his mind and sat on an armchair. She was making him a little nervous.

"I just wanted to check a few things with you, Mrs Black. You worked at the filling station last night between seven p.m. and one-twenty a.m., is that correct?"

"Well, you've already spoken to my manager, so that much you already know."

"This morning a cyclist was found on the Brae Lane approximately a quarter of a mile from the Star Service Station, close to Cullenbrae."

"Alive or deid?" she asked abruptly.

"I'm afraid he was dead at the scene."

"Hit by a car then? It's a bloody death trap, that road."

"We are still investigating the cause, but we haven't ruled out a hit-and-run."

"So no driver, then? I bet it was those bloody joyriders who tear up and down that lane like they think they're at bloody Brands Hatch."

"We believe the victim may have been hit late last night at some point shortly after midnight."

"It couldn't have been that close to the garage, I'd have seen it happen."

"So you didn't see anything suspicious?"

"I didn't say that. I said I didn't see the hit-and-run."

"So you did see something suspicious?"

"Agatha Christie must be awfa worried wae top sleuths like you competing with the likes of Poirot."

"If you don't mind me saying, you seem quite… er… old to be out there on your own in such an isolated location," Bone persevered.

"It doesn't bother me. The manager couldn't find anyone to fill the shift, and I volunteered. I've been through the war, and believe me, I've had to deal with a lot more than a few wee toerags trying to steal petrol or raid the shop."

"It may not be quite as simple as that, Mrs Black."

"When I'm on, nobody messes me about, simple as that."

"If you don't mind me asking, how old are you?"

"I'm eighty-eight this August. Fancy your chances, do you, Inspector?" She winked.

"Well, I'm impressed."

"That I'm still breathing?"

"That you have such a youthful outlook."

"Well, when I moved here, I was just sitting in my flat rotting away like an auld horse, ready for the knacker's yard, or worse, a bloody care home. I even started watchin' daytime TV. Bloody *Place in the Sun* wae awe they beached whales lookin' at some dump on a ring road for a two bob thrupenny bit. That was the last straw. So when I saw the job advertised in the *Courier*, I went straight over there and told the manager to give me the job."

"And that's what she did." Bone smiled.

"I think she felt sorry for me at first, but I soon shook that out of her. But she is very good to me. When I told her I had to take three buses to get to work and no way of getting back home, she persuaded the company to pay for my taxis."

"That's generous of them. They must value you."

"Or bloody terrified; one or the other." She smiled.

"We went through the CCTV footage for last night, and you had one or two customers, is that right?"

"Aye, Monday nights are like a bloody graveyard usually. Let me think."

"A group of young lads in a souped-up Saxo car were in the shop at about ten-thirty?"

"Ah yes, that's right. I put them right in their place, let me tell you."

"I could see that on the footage. Did they give any indication where they were going?"

"I wouldn't be surprised if they're the ones who did your hit-and-run."

"And were they back at all, or did you see them on the road again later on?"

She shook her head. "No, I think I scared them off."

"Then at eleven-thirty, a person came in on foot, I think, and bought some goods from the shop. They were wearing a wide-brimmed hat."

"Now, I do know him. That's Stuart Mason. He calls in now and again and buys snacks, chocolate bars, crisps, that sort of rubbish. I think he's on the whacky backie. Has that glaikit look about him like he's off his trolley, but not boozed up. Believe me, that's a hell of a lot worse. The times I've had folks wae the entire contents of their pockets oot on my counter searching for a two-pence bit. Makes you want to spit. He was just bleary-eyed with that permanent stupid grin on his face. But I do not like his rat tail. That is not a good look on a man."

"How do you know his name?"

"I've known him for years. He used to live in Campsie. When he was a wean. He went to the same school as my granddaughter."

"Does he drive to the garage?"

"No, no, as you said, he usually traipses over. I'm not sure he even owns a car, to be honest. He used to be an electrician but now he makes these wee pots that light up, for tourists and craft fairs and the like. I'm not sure they make a lot between them, him and his partner. She's an artist as well." She stopped. "And then there was Martin Burns. He was in shortly after."

"Was that at about twenty-to-one?"

"Correct. When I should have been on my way home. He was in for his usual supplies of health food."

"Someone else you know then?"

"Oh aye, and I wish I didn't. He's a right sleazy so-and-so. Treats women like they're dirt on his shoe. I can't stand men like that. I hope you're not like that, Inspector."

"Wouldn't dare," Bone replied. "How do you know this?"

"I've had a few of his exes in after he's dumped them, stocking up on self-medication. Sometimes in floods of tears or ready to rip him a new... I've no idea what they see in him, bloody Poundland Paul Newman, though I'd rather buy bin liners than waste a pound on that. So, yes, I know all about that parasite. Sometimes I think we should change the name of the garage to Burns' Exes Counselling Service."

"Was he driving?"

"No, he rides his bike. He stops on his way home from his work, out at that new sex toy factory. Good God. What the hell will they think up next? In my day, you were lucky if you could get your hands on a quarter of sherbet lemons, never mind anything wae batteries and flashing bloody lights."

"Indeed," Bone said, feigning an understanding of what she meant.

"The whole world's bloody sex daft. It gives men like him permission to do their worst."

"So, do you see him most nights then?"

"No, he's usually in after my shift ends, so I don't have to put up with his smug face. My replacement was late last night, so I had the unenviable task of having to serve him." She looked up. "It's not Burns you've found on the road, is it?"

"Our investigations are ongoing, Mrs Black."

"Oh God. If it was a cyclist, it's got to be him. Are you sure it was an accident, because there's an army of angry women who'd queue up to run him over? You'd be hard-pressed to stop me doing the same, to be honest." She caught Bone's expression. "Don't worry, Inspector Poirot. I don't have a car and haven't driven since the war. I'd need to hijack a tank to run his arse over."

"Could you tell me what he bought?"

"It's always the same. Three bridies. I mean, who eats two of those lard bombs? Even the thought brings on my chronic heartburn. Crisps and some roll-up tobacco and papers. The diet of champions, eh?"

"And you didn't see any cars passing the garage after he left?"

"Not that I remember. I was in at the safe for a few minutes, depositing some of the takings, so those boy racers could easily have roared past."

"That's fine. Thank you, Mrs Black." Bone stood. "I won't keep you from your sister."

"Ach, she's no' going anywhere. I'm quite enjoying this now." She smiled.

"We might call again, but just ring me if anything comes to mind." He handed her his card.

"Anything?" She winked at him again.

Bone stepped back.

"Don't worry. I'm just teasing you."

He made a hasty retreat out of the room, looking forward to the relative safety of the hospital corridor. On his way through the door, he collided with Gallacher, walking at a pace in the opposite direction.

"God, sorry, sir. I didn't see you there."

"What are you doing here, Duncan?" Gallacher asked, picking up some papers scattered on the floor.

"Visiting a witness. I thought you were up at head office." Bone went over and helped Gallacher retrieve the documents.

"Walk out with me, Duncan," Gallacher said.

Bone followed him up the corridor to the entrance.

They cut across the car park and into a square enclosed by concrete tubs filled with faded flowers and weeds and benches at the side that had seen better days. Gallacher sat on the nearest.

"What's going on? Have they finally pulled the plug on the Rural Crime Unit?" Bone sat beside him.

"It's Denise." Gallacher sat back.

"What's happened? Is she okay?"

"A couple of weeks ago, she found a lump."

"Oh shit."

"We had the results back yesterday. It's malignant."

"I'm so sorry, sir. That's just bloody awful. Are they going to operate?"

"The works and chemo, but…"

"What?"

"It's stage three, Duncan. They are concerned it might have spread, you know, lymph glands and possibly organs. She's undergoing these horrific tests." He ran a palm across his over-lacquered hair and sighed.

"Denise is an absolute bruiser, Roy. She'll beat this into bloody submission."

"I'll tell her you said that. It's not every day she gets compared to Rocky."

"You know what I mean. She's tougher than the whole RCU put together. She'd need to be, married to you." Bone smiled.

"You know it must be bad when they don't tell you what her chances are. All they say are things like, *we are working as hard as we possibly can* and *she's in the best possible place,* and other trite bollocks like that."

"She *is* in the best possible place." Bone glanced around the desolate, neglected garden.

"I had to insist on coming with her today. She wanted me to go to work. She said I'd just be in the way. She's some bloody woman."

"You did the right thing, sir. She might say that, but she needs you."

"No, she definitely means it. She said work will stop me brooding and being a pain in the arse." He chuckled, but his face fell again.

"Well, you haven't missed much, so don't worry about it," Bone said.

Gallacher turned and studied Bone's face. "You're a very bad liar, Duncan. Don't ever contemplate a life of crime. I called the incident room a few hours ago and Baxter filled me in. So where are we now? You said you were here visiting a witness."

"Are you sure, sir? After that bombshell, it doesn't seem quite right to yabber on about this stuff."

"Just get on with it."

"So you know the hit and run at Cullenbrae hamlet has escalated to a murder investigation?"

"Yes and you were in the process of trying to identify the victim."

"We now believe him to be a local Cullenbrae resident, Mr Martin Burns."

"Believe or know?"

"Ninety-eight percent sure. A number of witnesses in the hamlet have confirmed his identity, though we're still waiting for an ID from forensics. There is no question now that this is a murder investigation."

"Okay, right. So there will need to be some kind of public statement. Have the vultures landed yet?"

"Yes, they already made an unwelcome appearance at the crime scene."

"Including your friend?"

"Strangely, I haven't seen him yet."

"That's not like Mr McKinnon."

"There's a cordon in place around the village, so hopefully we'll keep them out for as long as we can."

"For now, physically at least, but there is such a thing as social media and telephones."

"Correct. That's why we need to alert residents, especially as some of the older ones were caught up in the media bun fight during the Sneedon murders."

"There can't be many of them left, can there?"

"You'd be surprised."

"Please don't tell me you think there could be a connection?"

"Open mind at the moment. But you know the house is still there, and it puts Dracula's castle to shame when it comes to horror film locations."

"This could stoke up all sorts of memories."

"And not just with the locals."

"Aye, I can imagine McKinnon rolling around in the Sneedon story like a pig in shit right now." Gallacher sighed. "That statement is urgent, then."

"Maybe if we let the residents know first, then we might be able to keep the lid on it a bit longer."

"Right. I'll sort that out. Anything else?"

"Press conference. Are you up to that? I could step in."

"Statement will be sufficient at this stage, so leave that with me."

"We'll need to search Sneedon's property as Walker thought she saw someone at one of the windows."

"Someone hiding out?"

"Possibly."

Gallacher thought for a moment. "Probably best to request a warrant and keep things as simple as we can."

"We also have some toerag boy racers in the frame and a conspiracy theorist with more cameras trained on the street than Oscar night on Sunset Strip. Apparently, Sneedon's brother has employed him to look after the house while he tries to get his hands on the deed. We also have a pot-smoking hippie who was feeding his munchies near the scene around the time of the killing and about a thousand angry ex-girlfriends of the victim, all potentially baying for blood."

"That's quite a haul in less than twenty-four hours."

"Never a dull moment."

They sat in silence for a moment.

The wail of a passing ambulance shattered their peace.

"I hope she's okay, sir. And you, too," Bone said.

"One day at a time. That's what we always do."

"Send her my very best wishes, but please don't tell her what I said. Despite evidence to the contrary, I'm still quite fond of my tackle."

"And how are you, tackle aside?" Gallacher asked.

"Oh, forget about me. I'm doing fine."

"PTSD?"

"Calm, sorted. Really, nothing to worry about with me. What happens next?"

"Operation's first thing tomorrow morning."

"Jesus. At least, as you say, they are all over it."

"Obviously I won't be in tomorrow, so you'll need to hold the fort. But she won't let me hang about, so it'll only be a day or two."

"No problem at all."

"But I'm on the end of the phone, day and night."

Bone nodded.

"I mean it, Duncan. Regular updates, please."

"Sir."

"And keep this to yourself for now, until we know for sure what's going on."

"Of course."

Gallacher stared at Bone for a moment, then came to again. "Haven't you got a murder to attend to?"

Bone got up and left. At the car, his phone rang.

"Sheila?" Bone said.

"Sir, forensics has just confirmed that DNA taken from the body is that of Martin Burns. Apparently, he's on our books."

"What for?"

"Handling stolen goods, eight months, six years ago."

"We're going to have to force the door on his property."

"Also, I have Gary Speed's home address."

"Are Mark and Will back yet?"

"Not yet, no."

"Okay, can you ring Mark and divert them? But tell them to be careful. This sounds like a family not to be messed with."

TWELVE

"That's honestly the funniest thing I've seen in years," Harper said, clutching his sides in pain. He'd been laughing all the way from the Love Candy factory to Speed's house in Northview Avenue, and his ribs hurt.

"Don't. The bloody thing had me pinned against a wall. It was worse than my Aunty Muriel. She'd nobble you at Christmas and demand a full-on winch."

"Please!" Harper said.

"Including our dogs."

"Serves you right for taking the piss out of the tester guy."

Mullens parked alongside a row of run-down ex-council houses. "What a dump. Do you think they get famous garden designers in to do their fronts?"

"What?" Harper asked.

"The disembowelled, stained mattresses, and the mangled shopping trolleys. Or maybe they're art installations by what's-her-face."

"Tracey Emin?"

"That's the one."

"Do you ever stop?"

"Just trying to make our day a little lighter, young Skywalker."

"Oh, I think you've ticked that box already, Mark."

They got out and crossed the street.

"Check out the car," Harper said and stopped by a lurid purple Citroen Saxo, complete with oversized wheels, huge rear spoiler, and a driver's seat fit for the next NASA mission to Mars.

"For God's sake. What a waste of bloody time and money all that shite is. At the end of the day, it's still just your deid Granny's old mobility vehicle, isn't it?" Mullens moaned. "Do they think the girls will love it or something?"

"Extensions of their insecurity," Harper replied. "Check out the plates."

"TIGER1," Mullens said. "I bet he's got a can of Lynx deodorant in the glove compartment, as well."

Harper went around the back of the car and knelt by the bumper. "See this?"

Mullens joined him.

The corner was torn off, with an exposed section of fibreglass dangling precariously underneath.

"And scrapes along the side here, too." Harper ran his finger along a deep gouge in the paintwork.

"Is that blood or dried-in mud?" Mullens asked.

"Hold on." Harper ran back to the pool car, rummaged in the boot, and returned with a sample bag. "Have you got something to scrape this off?"

Mullens searched his pockets. "Will this do?"

"A fork?" Harper exclaimed, staring at the utensil.

"My best curry fork, that." Mullens shrugged.

Harper carefully saved some of the debris.

"Let's see what James Bond has to say for himself," Mullens said.

At the front door, Mullens stopped. "You smell that?"

Harper sniffed the air. "Skunk?"

"You can almost see it." Mullens wafted his hand in front of his nose. He rapped the rusty knocker.

A few moments later, the door flew open, and a cloud of smoke rolled out. Two boys, in mid-conversation, almost ran into the two detectives on the doorstep.

"Mr Speed?" Mullens asked.

The boys pulled back in surprise.

"Aye, er, I mean, he's no' in," Speed spluttered and then giggled.

His mate joined in.

"Police," Mullens said.

They held up their lanyards.

"Can we have a word?"

"Fuck!" Speed exclaimed and rammed past them.

Mullens spun around and snatched at Speed's tracksuit top, but he swerved and ran on. The second lad dashed back inside.

Mullens chased the first, and Harper the second.

Before Mullens could reach him, Speed jumped into his car, and with a massive backfire, he tore up the street. Mullens ran to the pool car and screeched after him.

The Saxo sped through the junction at the end of the road, sparks flying off the low-level spoiler on the front. It carried on to a set of lights.

Mullens turned on the car's sirens.

"Stay red!" he shouted.

But they changed just as he approached and the boy's car careered through. Once through the High Street, it took a right, then a sharp left onto The Crow Road, heading for the hills.

Mullens rammed his foot down on the pool car, but the boy racer's souped-up engine was more than a match.

"Bloody useless Vauxhall," Mullens grumbled.

He crunched it into second and started up the steep incline. When he reached the top, the road straightened, and Mullens pushed the car as fast as it would go. The distance between the two cars narrowed until he was within touching distance of the Saxo's mangled rear bumper. He swerved out to overtake and force the boy to stop. But a tractor pulled out of a gate onto the road a few yards away.

"Shite!" He hit the brakes, yanked the steering wheel and careered onto the verge.

The tractor roared past within a hair's breadth of taking the side off his car. The farmer waved an angry fist at him. Mullens exhaled and raced on, but when he took the next blind corner, the Saxo had vanished.

"Where are you?" He scanned right and left, then braked again. The car skidded to a halt.

He spotted the Saxo tearing across a field. He slammed the car into reverse, swung around, and drove across a cattle grid onto a farm track. He raced on until he was parallel with the Saxo. It suddenly stopped, the wheels stuck in the muddy, ploughed earth. The driver's door flew open, and Speed tumbled out. Mullens pulled over and chased after him. The boy ran, stumbling across the field towards a line of trees and the river.

"For God's sake, give it up!" Mullens hollered at him.

But Speed sprinted on. Reaching the trees, the boy stopped. Mullens slowed to a marching pace.

"Come on, Gary. There's nowhere to go," Mullens wheezed.

Speed gave him the finger, and jumped.

"Moron!" Mullens hollered.

He raced over. The edge of the field gave way to a sheer drop into the river. Speed was on the bank, knee-deep in mud, the fast-flowing water within a few feet of him.

"What are you doing?" Mullens called down.

Speed tried to free himself, but his legs sank further.

The boy groaned and panted. "Get me out. I'm sinking." His voice shook as panic set in.

"I'm thinking I might just leave you for a bit."

"Please! I'm going doon."

"That water's definitely getting nearer." Mullens smiled.

A couple of cows plodded along the bank and cautiously sniffed the air close to Speed.

"Get them away fae me. I hate fuckin' coos."

"You could have just used them, you tool." Mullens gestured to a set of wooden steps a few feet away.

He descended and stopped on the bottom step. The cows ran off when they saw him lumbering towards them.

"Quick!" the boy screamed.

"Dear oh dear, so what brought on that wee unexpected tour of the fells?"

"Come on! It's sucking me in."

"Gary Speed, I'm arresting you for the—"

"It's no ma gear. Somebody brought it wae them to the hoose."

"Oh, let's start again then. Gary Speed, I'm arresting you for—"

"Just get me oot of this stinkin' shite first, please!"

Mullens reached over, grasped Speed's arm, and yanked the boy out. His muddy, foul-smelling legs emerged with a loud slurp. He dragged him over to dry land.

"Aww, thank fuck!" Speed said with relief.

Mullens grabbed his muddy tracksuit jacket and hauled him to his feet.

"Keys," Mullens ordered, keeping a tight grip on him.

"They're still in the car."

"Right!" Mullen frogmarched the boy up the steps and back across the field.

"Cows coming!" he shouted, just before they reached the pool car.

Speed dropped to the ground as though he was expecting them to dive-bomb him from above.

"Get up, ya bloody eejit." Mullens pulled him to his feet.

He opened the door.

"Now sit there, and if you make one move, I'll throw you back in the bog with the cows."

He pushed Speed onto the back seat, his reeking clothes splashing mud all over the upholstery. "If this was my car, I'd have thrown you in the river first." He slammed the door and locked it. Speed whimpered in the back.

Mullens called Harper.

"Are you okay?"

"All good here. Second runner apprehended and on his way in. Found another guy hiding in the house. Where are you?"

"Tell you later but the cow shite clown is also nicked, finally, and reeking out the back of this once spotless pool car. And for once I'm not to blame."

"What?"

"Never mind. Shall I swing past and pick you up?"

"Don't worry. I'll hitch a lift in the wagon. See you shortly back at the carbuncle."

Mullens hung up and climbed into the driver's seat. "Jesus Christ, you're going to have to change your aftershave mate." He opened his window. "Now, where was I? Oh yes," he said. "I'm arresting you on suspicion of murder—"

"What?" Speed yelped. "I've no' murdered naebody," he blubbered.

"Don't interrupt. Fleeing the scene of a crime..."

"Aww, come on, what is this?"

"Aww, now you've made me lose the thread. Murder, scene of crime, ah yes, driving with intent to injure or kill a police officer..."

"That's bollocks. I was just parking up!" the boy protested.

"Look, if you're going to keep interrupting, we could be here all day. Just shut your face and let me finish."

And so it continued until Mullens completed his arrest, and Speed slumped back in his sludge-soaked seat and sobbed like a toddler all the way back to the station.

THIRTEEN

When Bone and Walker returned to Burns' house, the First Response team were already waiting for them.

"We're just about to go in, sir," the response officer said.

"Okay. I hate to ask this, but do you have any protective gloves and shoes we could borrow?"

"Aye, sir." He went over to the vehicle parked opposite and returned with the gear.

After a brief battle with the elastic, the detectives were ready.

"After you," Bone said to the officer.

He joined his colleague, who wielded a battering ram. Bone and Walker stepped to one side, and an officer smashed it into the door above the lock.

Wooden splinters flew in all directions. The door swung open and thumped against the inside wall. The uniform cleared out of the way, and Bone peered into the gloomy hallway beyond.

"You smell that?" he said.

"UHU," Walker said.

"Hello to you, too."

Walker sighed. Bone leaned through the gap, reached around, and fumbled for a light.

The entrance hall was stacked up with lengths of cut wood of various shapes and sizes that reached almost to the ceiling.

"Bloody hell. It's like B&Q in here," Bone said.

He squeezed past a thick bundle of two-by-twos leaning against the wall and went in. Aside from the spoils of the Amazon rainforest, the hallway was spartan, the walls covered in ancient magnolia-painted Anaglypta wallpaper and a bare light bulb hanging from the ceiling.

Walker picked up some letters balanced on top of an upended bookshelf.

"Red bills," she said, and put them back.

Bone turned and checked through the pockets of a coat hanging on the back of the door. He removed a slip of paper from one and held it up to the dim, yellow light.

"A receipt for…" He squinted again. "Two fish and chips, a pint, and white wine."

"Meal for two, and I know it's not like me at all to make sexist assumptions, but white wine suggests female company to me. Does it say where?"

Bone screwed up his eyes again. "It's very faded."

"Let me." She took it from him. "The Methuen Arms, Clachan."

"Where's that?"

"Not sure. Shall I bag it?"

Bone nodded. Walker removed a fist-sized evidence bag from her bag and dropped the receipt in.

They carried on to the living room. A moth-eaten sofa chair was positioned in the centre, opposite a bulky valve TV that balanced precariously on a side table. Next to the chair, sat a side table loaded up with empty cans of cider and an overflowing ashtray. Bone picked out one of the butts and sniffed.

"Weed."

Aside from a framed print of a faded Scottish mountain scene above a tiled fireplace, the walls were bare and covered in the same Anaglypta paper.

"No sign of a phone?" Bone asked.

Walker shrugged.

They about-turned and continued down the hall. The pokey fifties-style kitchen at the end was in a state of chaos; dirty pots and plates piled up in the sink and on whatever space was left on surrounding worktops, and cider cans and newspapers strewn across a kitchen table rammed up against the wall. Walker pointed to a second full ashtray.

"A man who likes a wee puff," she said.

Bone went over to the back door. He unbolted it and stepped out.

"Come see this," he called back.

Walker followed.

153

The yard was filled to the gunwales with more wood, some of the piles half-covered with filthy tarpaulin, the corners flapping around in the wind.

"What's in there?" Walker pointed to a shed at the rear.

Bone approached and tried the door. It creaked open, and a strong stench of glue escaped. He held his nose, stepped in, and switched on the light. Two fluorescent strips above their heads flickered to life, illuminating a long narrow workshop filled with half-completed furniture, carved decorative panels, three-legged tables, and seatless hardback dining chairs. Around the workspace, tools hung on hooks, shelves stacked up with more wood and boxes of screws, nails, and other assorted ironmongery.

Walker went over to the long bench in the middle of the room. A mahogany cabinet was on its side, its door lying next to it along with various carving tools, pots and tubes of glues, adhesives, fillers, and pastes. Walker picked up a litre-sized open pot of glue with a brush sticking out the top.

"I think I've found where that lovely smell is coming from," she said.

"There's a drum of the stuff over here as well." Bone rapped a large plastic container pushed against the rear wall, and it boomed like a marching band drum.

"These are beautiful," Walker said. She knelt by a row of cupboard doors lined up along the side wall, and ran her finger along one of the delicately carved floral designs.

"That's real craftsmanship," Bone said.

"Furniture maybe, but certainly not personality, by all accounts."

Bone stepped back. "But still no phone. Right, let's set the SOC team loose on this and we'll see if they can find any more for us to work with."

Walker followed him out.

"Hopefully, Will and Mark will have more from Burns' work."

Bone checked his watch. "Right, I think that's just about enough in Amityville. I'll drop into the Clachan on my way back and chase those receipts, then I'm going to call it a day. If you could check in with the team for updates, then I suggest you and the team go home too. Another early start and long day tomorrow.

"Okay. I'll ring you if there are any more developments."

"See you tomorrow." Bone nodded a weary farewell.

"If I don't see you first."

"No offence, Rhona, but I do hope not." He smiled, and they parted.

FOURTEEN

Gary Speed slumped at the interview table, picking the varnish off the surface with his nail. Mullens and Harper sat down opposite.

The young ned sprang back in his seat.

"Mr Speed, good morning." Mullens checked his watch. "Sorry, afternoon."

"I huvnae done nothin'." Speed held up his hands.

"Double negative, Gary. That means you've done everything," Harper said.

"Whit? I mean, I don't know what any of this is about. I'm freezing my arse off sitting here in this shit." Speed pulled at his muddy tracksuit trousers. "It's an infringement of my human rights."

"Absolutely," Mullens said. "And we'll sort that out for you as soon as you help us with a few questions. It shouldn't take too long. We're both acquainted, of course, but you haven't met my colleague yet, DC Harper, have you?"

"Don't give a fuck." Speed folded his arms.

Mullens set up the recorder.

"You're turnin' that on?" Speed asked.

"For our records, and seeing as you're under arrest, it's what we do."

"This is a joke. I huvnae done nothin'… anything, I mean."

Mullens pressed record and started going through the intro.

"You pushed me in. Assault, that is. I could have died. It was sucking me under."

"You have a right to a solicitor, and we can arrange that for you," Mullens carried on.

"A lawyer? I don't know any lawyers. I'm skint."

"We can sort it. Would you like us to? Though as a word of caution, it will take us a few hours for the duty solicitor to attend."

"Hours?"

"I'm afraid so." Mullens pulled a face.

"Sitting in this reekin' cow keich?"

"Shall I arrange that for you?"

"Aww, just get on with it." Speed sighed.

"So you are happy for me to proceed without legal representation?"

"Aye!"

"Why did you run away when we called at your house?"

"Ah didnae run away. I just fancied a wee drive."

"So you failed to notice me with my sirens blaring and lights flashing right behind you?"

"Correct."

Mullens slapped his hand on the table. "Cut the bollocks, Speed. Your so-called mate is chewing off his fists in the custody cells as we speak, and I'm sure they'll have plenty to say about why he ran off as well."

"They're here?"

"Oh yes. My colleagues reported a rather potent smell at your property."

"My brother has been on to the council for ages about the drains. They absolutely reek."

"No, it's a more exotic, chemically enhanced sort of smell than that."

"Oh?"

"Oh indeed. Are you cultivating skunk on your premises?"

"Skunk? You mean cannabis?"

Mullens sighed and tapped the table.

"No, never. I don't do drugs. They'll mess you up." Speed sneered.

"You really don't want to mess with me, numbnut. Officers are all over your house right now, and they will find your wee farm, so if I were you, I'd admit to it before things get a hell of a lot worse for you."

"No idea what you're talking about." Speed shrugged.

"Are you working for your old man, is that it?" Mullens sat back. "Now there's a colourful character, eh, DC Harper?"

"I'd say more low-life scum than colourful," Harper said.

Mullens glanced over at his colleague.

"Hey, don't bad mouth ma da. He's got nothing to do with anything."

"Ah yes, because he's in prison for double murder," Mullens said. "It must be so hard for you, living in the shadow of such an illustrious low-life scumbag."

"It's for my own use."

"Ah, now we're getting somewhere." Mullens said. "So you can smoke your way through five hundred kilos in what, a day? And I suppose the two grand in fives and tens that officers confiscated from the premises was your paper run money?"

"I got that out of ma savings to buy some gear for ma car."

"Ah yes, your car. That brings us to the next hot topic of the day. Were you out driving last night in said spin dryer?"

"What? Last night?"

"Come on. This is getting painful." Mullens sighed.

"Er, I can't remember."

"Your car was spotted speeding around Cullenbrae. You and a group of your friends were in the pub around six-thirty p.m., then later CCTV footage recorded you at ten thirty-three hassling the garage attendant at Star Service Station in Cullenbrae."

"Oh aye, now I remember. We went up there for an early drink before the game."

"What game?"

"Football. European Cup. Celtics were playing AC Milan, away leg. You don't know that?"

"When did you leave the pub?" Mullens continued to press.

"Must have been just after nine. The game started at nine forty-five."

"So what were you doing at the garage at ten-thirty?"

"Halftime. Do you no' watch football then?"

"You went all the way from the Northlands Estate to the Star Service Station in Cullenbrae for a family pack of Monster Munch?"

"Fancied a drive oot."

"Who was with you in the car?"

"Just my mates."

"Is that Robert Delaney and Joseph Crampton? Our guests along the corridor?"

"Del and Cramps, aye, but they'll just tell you the same. It was halftime, and we went on the hunt for more slosh." He looked up. "And before you ask, I was the nominated driver."

"Aye, right."

Speed sat back. "Look, Officer. Okay, right, we might have been smoking a bit of weed when you lot called round, and I suppose I might have panicked a wee bit. I have been cautioned before for possession, so I was worried that I'd be charged this time. I don't want to go to prison. I'm only eighteen." His mouth tightened.

"DC Harper, can you show Mr Speed the photos, please?"

Harper produced an iPad.

"For the purposes of the recorder, DC Harper is showing Mr Speed photos of a Citroen Saxo, registration plate TIGER1."

Harper turned the screen. "Can you confirm that you are the registered owner of this vehicle?"

"I am, aye."

Harper flicked the images forward. "Now showing Mr Speed a second photograph. Can you explain how the rear of your car appears to have sustained substantial damage to the spoiler?"

"It looks so awful in that photo. I can't believe it. Those spoilers cost me three months' wages."

"Well?" Mullens pressed.

"On the way back from the pub, I hit a deer. Came out of nowhere. My driving instructor, though, told me never to swerve but aim straight at them, otherwise you might lose control and all end up deid."

"A deer?"

"Aye, a fuckin whore of a size it was too."

"Did the animal survive?"

"No idea. It ran off or hobbled away. Probably snuffed it." Speed looked up. "I wisnae drunk or stoned or anything, if that's what yer thinking."

"So not a cyclist, then?"

"A cyclist? A person, you mean?"

"Unless deer have developed skills I'm unaware of, yes, a man on a bike."

"No, of course not. I would have reported that. It was a deer, I'm telling you. Big stripy bastard. Fuckin' hell. Is that what all this is about? You think I clocked someone on the road and did a runner?"

"You have form, Gary, as you've just demonstrated."

"That was for possession, no' killing somebody." Speed exhaled. "This is fuckin' over the top."

"I put it to you, Mr Speed, that you struck the male cyclist either accidentally, or perhaps even intentionally. Maybe you and your mates thought it would be a bit of a laugh to just knock the guy off."

"No way, man."

"Maybe you were so off your face you didn't see him."

"I wasn't on anything. I was driving. I love my car. I don't want to lose my license."

"You drove off. But then, a little further along, did skunk paranoia get the better of you and you panicked? 'What if he clocked my plate?' 'He'll go to the polis.' And your mates might have jumped in as well. 'We'll all get nicked, banged up.' 'We need to sort him out.' Is that how it went?"

"Total bullshit. It was a deer."

"Did you go back and find him still alive? Maybe he recognised you. Making things even worse. Was it then you decided to keep it simple, and you finished him off?"

"I couldn't do anything like that."

"Your so-called mates won't be saying that. They'll all be dropping you right in it to save their own skins."

"This is a fucking nightmare. I hit a fucking deer."
His face crumpled, and he whimpered. "I just grow a
bit of weed for my friends."

"What friends?"

"Ma mates, and a few folks around the place, you
know, that helped me out. I don't sell it, it's personal
use. But that's it. I didn't fucking tank somebody and
drive away."

"Do your mates include anyone in Cullenbrae?
Martin Burns or Stu Mason, for example?"

"I'm not landing anyone in it."

"It would definitely help if you cooperated, Mr
Speed."

"I'm no' a grass, end of." He wiped the tears from
his face.

"I'll give you a few minutes, Mr Speed, and I
suggest you take up our offer of a solicitor." Mullens
reached for the recorder. "Interview paused while DS
Mullens and DC Harper interview more persons of
interest in the Cullenbrae murder investigation."

"I didnae do this shite you're talking about."

In the corridor, Mullens and Harper went out into
the stairwell.

"Any news on the blood sample taken from the
car?" Mullens asked.

Harper checked his phone. "Not yet."

"Okay, let's leave him to cook for a bit while we
interview the others." Mullens stopped. "Wait, what
day is it?"

"Wednesday, why?"

"What time is it?"

164

"Look at your own watch."

"Shit," Mullens said. "I take my da out to the chippie every other Wednesday. I totally forgot."

"If you need to go, that's fine. I can handle the interviews."

"You, on your own? I don't think so."

"No, with Sheila, or if the boss and Rhona get back, we'll share it out."

"Are you sure?"

"It's either corroboration or not, and we have them for cultivation at least anyway, so what can possibly go wrong?" Harper grinned.

"You're turning into a bit of a smart arse, you know."

"I learnt from the master."

"That's what I'm talking about."

"Well, if you're going to insult me, I might not do you—"

"Okay, thank you, young Jedi. I owe you."

"Even Stevens?"

"That new-born baby howl is worth way more than this, but noted."

"Go on, get lost," Harper said.

Mullens legged it out the back door.

FIFTEEN

After a few wrong turns, Bone finally located The Methuen Arms, hidden down a lane behind Clachan's village church. He drove into a tiny car park located alongside the beautiful eighteenth-century pub building and parked between a top-of-the-range Mercedes and a Range Rover almost double the size of Bone's Saab.

"Don't let them intimidate you, Bertha," Bone said.

He tapped the dash and got out. He gazed up at the ivy-covered front of the pub. It seemed somehow familiar, but he couldn't put his finger on why. He crossed the car park and went in.

"Fuck off!" a high croaky voice cried out close to his ear.

Bone spun around. A mynah bird, perched in a cage, cocked its head and glared at him.

"What do you want?" it squawked.

"Morris!" a second voice called from beyond the entrance.

"Morris!" the mynah bird repeated. "Fuck off!"

There was a roll of laughter.

"Good evening to you, too," Bone said to the bird.

It tilted its head again and scratched its beak.

"Pint of 80!" it parroted.

Bone approached the grinning barman, who leaned over an elaborately carved mahogany counter.

"Sorry about him, sir. He's got a mouth on him like a slurry pit."

"I know someone just like that," Bone said.

"But if he swears at you, he must like you."

"Yup, that, too."

"What can I get you?"

Bone glanced around. Golf memorabilia covered every inch of wall space: antique golf clubs, framed, signed photos of golfing stars, cups and trophies, and directly above Bone's head, a moth-eaten tartan golf bag hung from a beam. Three wooden clubs stuck out of the end.

"Sir?" the barman prompted again.

"Sorry, just admiring your décor. What's the bag?"

"Those are Old Tom Morris's clubs."

"Fuck off!" the mynah bird cackled from the doorway.

"Not you, Morris!" the barman hollered.

Two men at the end of the bar laughed again.

168

"What do you want?" the bird called back.

"Who?" Bone continued.

"You don't know who Tom..." The barman stopped and glanced over at the bird. "Who he is?"

"Sorry, I'm not a big golf fan."

The pub fell into silence, the clientele turning to stare.

"I wouldn't say that too loud round here. Ye'll find yourself six feet under the bunker on the thirteenth hole." The barman smiled.

"I'm DCI Bone from Kilwinnoch station," Bone said.

"Police station?"

Bone held up his lanyard.

"Oh God. You know I was joking about the thirteenth-hole thing."

"Ya clown!" the mynah bird cawed.

"No bother. I'm looking for some information on one of your customers." Bone opened his rucksack, removed a photocopy of the receipt, and laid it out on the counter. "Mr Burns and a second customer had dinner here on the first of September. Can you remember who he was with that night?"

"That's over a month ago. We take a lot of bookings, and that was around the time we had Bubba Watson and his American entourage staying."

"I assume that's a US golfer?"

"You're having a laugh, aren't you?" The barman scanned the receipt. "That's a pub meal rather than the restaurant. Let me check the bookings." He disappeared out the back.

"Ya numpty!" the mynah bird squawked.

"What do you want?" one of the men at the bar shouted back.

But the bird remained silent.

"He doesn't like *you*, then?" Bone joked.

The man scowled at him and resumed his heated conversation with his drinking companion.

Just then the front door opened, and three golfers entered, dressed in lurid checked outfits, one in tweed plus-fours clutching a massive golf bag stuffed full of bobble-hat-wearing clubs. The mynah bird leapt around its cage, cackling with excitement like an old witch.

The men approached the bar.

"Who the fuck does he think he is?" one said to the group. "That's two extra rounds for the same bloody money."

"Fuck off, not again!"

"Fuck off!" the mynah bird repeated.

"I see where he gets it." Bone nodded to the men.

"Whit?"

"The sweary doorman."

"Oh aye, Morris," the first said and rolled his eyes at his friends.

"Tosser!" the bird cawed.

They retreated over to a table, and after a moment, the man in the plus-fours came back.

"Were you out this afternoon?" he asked Bone. "The wind was horrendous." He turned to his friends. "Definitely not Florida, eh, lads?"

"No, I don't play golf." Bone smiled.

"Lucky you. It's the Devil's game."

"So are you a caddy, then?"

"Sadly, aye. All of us losers. It's a mug's game these days. The money's just nothing like it used to be. You'd think that all these big stars would flash the cash, but it's the bloody opposite. Moan, moan, moan. Not to mention their tight-arse agents. Back in the good old days, we were respected. I caddied once for Lee Trevino, and he invited me and the family over to his ranch in Florida. Generous, kind man. Not now. Sharks and sphincter-faced scrooges."

The barman returned. "Sorry, Inspector. The book had gone walkabout, but I found it. He laid it down next to the receipt."

"You a copper?" the caddy asked.

"I'm afraid so, aye."

"Hear that lads, Pepsi Max all round." He grinned at Bone.

"The usual for everyone then, Jim?" the barman said. "I'll bring them over in a minute."

"Don't worry, Officer. I was only joking. We've all lost our licenses."

The group laughed loudly, and the caddy returned to his table.

"Right, let me have a look." The barman opened the book.

"It was the first, wasn't it?"

"Yes."

"Who did you say it was again?"

"Martin Burns."

The barman turned the pages and stopped halfway through. He ran his finger down the diary dates spread across the two pages.

"Here he is." He tapped the book. "He actually stayed for one night. Hold on." He flicked back a few more pages. "And again three weeks before that."

"One-night stays?"

"Aye."

"Double room?"

"Correct, yes."

"Can you remember who he was with?"

"Let me just go and get the boss a minute." He disappeared out the back again.

Moments later, he returned with a diminutive woman by his side who looked uncannily like Nicola Sturgeon.

"This is my wife, Martha, Inspector. The detective wants information on one of our guests, Martin Burns."

"Hello, gorgeous!" the mynah bird yelped when it saw the landlady.

"Hello to you, too." She blew the bird a kiss.

"Cupboard love, Inspector, pure and simple," the landlord said.

"DCI Bone, ma'am. Can you remember taking the bookings for Mr Burns? He's booked a double room a few times."

"Yes, I do." She turned to her husband. "He's that guy, you know?" She nodded at him.

"I know what?" the barman replied, looking vacant.

"You know, with different girlfriends every five minutes."

"Oh him! That's him?" the barman said. "Sorry, Inspector, I do know him."

"Perhaps we should go in the back," Martha said.

The couple at the nearest table both stared at them.

"This way." She lifted the side counter.

Bone followed her through the back to an office halfway down a narrow corridor.

"Watch your head on that beam," she said.

But Bone ducked too late, and head-butted the tree trunk in front of his face. He yelped and rubbed at his forehead.

"I did that nearly every day for months after we moved in," she said.

Bone studied her size and wondered how.

They carried on to the end and went into a messy office.

"I didn't want to say anything out there as it's worse than bloody *Emmerdale* in this village." She cleared a space on a chair next to her desk. "Sit down a sec."

Pushing papers to one side, she opened the diary.

"So Mr Burns booked a room on…" she turned the pages. "the first of September."

"Hold on, let me grab my notebook."

"I'll write them down for you." She rummaged around the desk, plucking a pen and notebook out from the debris in front of her. She searched through the entries. "So the twenty-third of August is his first stay of this year."

"He booked last year as well?"

"Possibly, but those will be in an older booking diary. Would you like me to check?"

"Maybe later. Carry on."

She scribbled down the first date. She checked a little further on. Then, the seventeenth of September, the second and tenth of October. She tore out the page and handed it to him.

"That's quite a short gap. Do you remember who he was with?"

"It was a different woman every time. It didn't go unnoticed." Her eyes widened. She looked back at the book. "But these two in October, it was the same person. And that last one was—er—eventful."

"Go on."

"I remember they had a right barney. The two of them going at it in the room. Our flat is at the back of the pub, and unfortunately, I booked them into the room that backs onto our bedroom. It went on for hours, and then in the morning he had breakfast on his own."

"Did she join him after?"

"She'd already gone. Legged it in the middle of the night. I heard her car tearing out of the car park."

"Do you have a name?"

"Sorry, no. Only his. She was blonde, very attractive, wealthy-looking. No idea what she saw in him."

"Would you recognise her if you saw her again?"

"I would think so, aye."

"Can you remember the make and model of the car she was driving?"

"Oh, it was posh. A big BMW Series something or other. Silver or grey, I think, though not sure. I remember Barry, the big Heffalump in there, saying he fancied one, and I thought he meant her." She laughed. "Hold on a minute, I will have jotted down the reg number. We had a terrible time with one of our customers a while back when they said their car had been damaged and they wanted to sue us. It turned out it was another car, and they were trying it on."

"Some folks, eh?"

"You've no idea, Inspector. Anyway, now I keep records of all guests' vehicles, and we've put signs up to remind them that they use our car park at their own risk. Sorry, I'm blethering on." She ran her finger down the entry. "There it is." She turned the book again.

"That's brilliant, thanks. If she left in the middle of the night, how did Mr Burns get home?"

"He asked where the nearest bus stop was and walked. I don't know what was going on between them, but I'm sure that four-mile walk and three-hour wait for the number three focused his mind a little." She smiled.

"What about his previous companions?"

"No fireworks or midnight exoduses. All lovey-dovey as far as I remember."

"Was he always driven here?"

"No, I think previous times he drove. His car wasn't posh. A bit of a wreck and filthy. That's his plate registration number there."

"And they've not been back since?"

"Nope. Love on the rocks, eh?" She closed the book.

"Okay, thanks again."

On his way out, he waved to the caddies huddled around, conspiring in the corner.

"Fuck off," the mynah bird cackled as he left.

"Fuck off to you, too, cheeky." He smiled at the bird.

It cocked its head and eyeballed him, sizing up the opposition.

Bone retreated to his car before it launched into its next verbal assault, and called Baxter.

SIXTEEN

Mullens rushed into his dad's care home and ran up to the front desk.

"Hi, Julie. I'm so sorry I'm late."

"No bother. Your dad's been quite happily playing Scrabble with his mates in the lounge while he waits for you. I think he's in his coat, ready to go."

"Ta."

Mullens dashed through and spotted his da at a long table with his usual cronies.

"No, no, no, that's not how you spell wanker, Jimmy," his da roared.

Mullens went over.

"Sorry I'm a bit late, Da. Are we ready to go?"

"Tell him, Mark. It's W-A-N-K..." He stopped. "Hold on."

Mullens glanced down at the board. His da had spelled out a whole range of expletives, some accurately and others less so, but all totally offensive.

"I think you might be the only one playing this game, Da," Mullens said.

The residents gathered around George, and stared vacantly at the board or the walls beyond.

"Aye, they're at it. Game play. Poker-faced wankers. E-R. That's it. I told you, Jimmy, not A-R. It's wanker, E-R. Ya wanker." He laughed so loud it made him cough.

"Let's go, Da, before you start a fight."

"Oh, that would be good. Better than sitting here waiting to bloody keel over."

Back in reception, Mullens waved to the duty manager.

"See you Friday," the manager called over.

"Saturday, you mean," Mullens said.

"No, we've moved it because the weather is absolutely atrocious on Saturday. I sent you an email last week."

"Friday? This week Friday?"

"You haven't read it, have you?"

"So sorry."

"What's he done noo?" George piped up from his chair.

"Is it the same time?"

"Aye, four until six p.m. If it's too much hassle now, don't worry. We've got plenty going on."

"No, no, I'll muster the troops. Just leave it with me."

"Only if you're sure."

"It's my stupid fault. I'll sort it."

"That'll be great. I'm sure they'll all really appreciate it."

"You reckon?" Mullens pulled a face.

"Troops? Are we off to Arnhem?" George interrupted again.

"Chippie, Da. Don't tell the manager." He glanced over and winked.

She waved a disapproving finger at him and smiled.

Mullens pushed his dad around the side of the building, down a ramp, and through the back gate.

"Good God, son, are you trying to shake ma bowels oot ma arse?" George complained, bobbing about in his chair.

They carried on to the Burngreen and headed towards the bandstand. Some late summer flowers were still in bloom, lining the pathways on either side and in circular beds in the centre of the well-groomed lawns.

"The council excelled themselves this year, eh, Da?"

George grunted.

Mullens squinted down at him. "All right? You're worryingly quiet."

"We're not all empty barrels, you know," George said, feigning a Newton Mearns accent.

Two teenage boys appeared ahead, one with rampant eczema consuming almost every centimetre of his face.

"Jesus," George muttered as they approached.

"Da. Behave," Mullens ordered.

"Think you've overdone the pepperoni there, son," George called out.

Mullens winced. "Da!"

"Whit was that?" the ned asked.

"Don't bother with him, lads." Mullens smiled. He rolled his eyes.

"I didnae know Pizza Express wiz deliverin' by foot noo," George continued.

"Listen, Jabba the Hut. Ye want tae try me?" the boy retorted and stepped forward.

Mullens flashed his lanyard, still hanging around his neck.

"Do one!" he growled at him.

The second lad, who clutched a bottle of Buckfast, furtively tried to hide it behind his back.

"And bin that now!"

"Waste a good juice that," George piped up again.

"What Jabba says," the second boy said.

"Now!" Mullens cut back.

The boy dumped it in the nearest bin, and the pair walked on. Mullens turned, and they both gave him the finger.

"Da, please. If you don't behave, I'll take you straight back." Mullens sighed.

"Good as gold, me." George shuffled in his wheelchair.

A pencil-thin, scruffily dressed young woman emerged from around the bandstand. She pushed a pram laden underneath with shopping and she dragged a reluctant, flush-faced toddler along beside her.

"Look at the pins on that!" George chuckled.

"Oh, God help me." Mullens blew out his cheeks.

"Haw hen, is that rickets, or have you had so many weans your pins are now in permanent tunnel formation?"

"Right, that's it. Enough." Mullens took a right and pushed his da at speed out of the green and up the lane.

"Oh, come on. That was funny."

"No, it was just fucking rude."

"Enough of that foul-mouthed fucking language, my boy. You're not too old for a skelpit leathering."

Mullens sighed and held his breath for the last section of the long and tortuous journey to the chippie.

At the entrance, he stopped.

"Now best behaviour in here, and no Mafia jokes, okay?"

George shrugged.

When Mr Sandino spotted them, he paused stirring the fryer and came around the counter to greet them.

"Mr George and Mark. I wondered if maybe you don't come in today."

"Sorry we're a bit late. We had an altercation with two no-marks in the Burngreen. Or I should say, George here did."

"Ah, George, you are such a funny man."

"No' so funny with a black eye," Mullens said.

181

"See, even Don Corleone appreciates my sense of humour."

"Da!" Mullens thumped the chair. "So sorry, Mr Sandino."

"Haha, your father makes me laugh. Don Corleone." He knelt. "Shall I make you an offer you can't refuse?"

"Aye, wae plenty a salt and vinegar," George replied.

"So, how are you keeping this week?" Mr Sandino asked.

"They're trying to poison me in there."

"They look after you well, George. Mark is always saying."

"The Gestapo? Are you kiddin'?"

"Ha, Gestapo. That's a good one."

"And they play that incessant fucking... What do you call it, Mark?"

"Music?"

"Aye, fuckin' disco or some garbage that Bonzo here listens to in his room at full pelt. I tell him over and over to turn the racket down, but does he?"

"You no' fancy a wee dance then?"

"Wae you? Are you on the turn, Marlon?"

"Da, for God's sake." Mullens shifted uncomfortably on the balls of his feet.

Mr Sandino glanced up and winked at him.

"You know, George, my Grandfather Guiseppe, he fought with the partisans to stop that dafty Hitler and his Gestapo. He got a medal for it, too. I show you next time, eh?"

"Hero," George said. "No' enough of them these days..." He twisted his neck to frown at his son.

"You call me Carlos, remember?" Mr Sandino said.

"I knew Guiseppe," George said.

"You met him?"

"Aye, he worked on the buses with me until he got sacked for shaggin' the boss's daughter."

"Ha, that's no' the same Guiseppe. My grandfather came over after the war with just his coat and the address of a friend of the family who lived here."

"Da, let Mr Sandino finish," Mullens said.

"He started selling chips out of a wee cart he pushed round Kilwinnoch. He built it all up from nothing to this." He threw up his arms and beamed with pride.

"How many fucking Guiseppes are there? It was him, I'm tellin' you."

"Okay, Da. Fancy your tea now?" Mullens intervened.

"I'll just go and sort it out for you, just the way you like it, George."

"Wae broon sauce, and nae skimpin' on the salt like you usually do." He licked his lips.

"Where's Marco this afternoon?" Mullens asked.

"He's off at some music festival with his girlfriend," Mr Sandino replied.

"He has a girlfriend? That's great to hear."

"Aye, another one. I can't keep up. The next thing he'll be telling me, I'm going to be a bloody grandfather. The boy's brains are in his trousers, and they are always bloody falling doon." He laughed.

183

"We're only jealous, eh, George? Oh, to be young again."

"Me and your mother were at it like rabbits back in our day," George said.

"Da, no!" Mullens said.

George shrugged. "I'm only sayin'."

"Well, don't." Mullens took Mr Sandino to one side.

"Just the bridie today. I'm on strict orders from the care home as his cholesterol is up."

"I put a bridie in the oven, as usual."

"That's great, thanks. Deep fried would probably kill him." Mullens stepped back. "God, I missed an open goal there."

Mr Sandino elbowed him.

"And you'd better stick a few of those vegetable fritters to make it look like it comes with chips. Otherwise, we might be looking at World War Three."

"Coming right up." Mr Sandino returned to the fryer and resumed stirring.

Two elderly men in flat caps came in.

"Good God, don't tell me that's George Mullens in that contraption," one of the men said and came over.

"Why me?" Mullens muttered.

"Who the fuck are you?" George said.

"Ah yes, same old George." The man chuckled. "Don't you remember me?"

"My da has dementia. So you might get an earful."

"Well, he must have had dementia for an awful long time." The old man laughed again. He leaned over the chair.

"Sandy McRorie, George. We worked together up at Muirhead Machine Tools."

George stared at the man for a moment, then smiled. "Ah, Sandy of Crow Road."

"That's the one. It's good to see you."

"I remember you."

"Yes. Six years we were up there. Must be seventy-three to—"

"You're the cunt who used to snaffle my sarnies every fucking day, ya greedy wee snivelling bastard."

"Sorry, Sandy," Mullens said, now almost completely exhausted.

"Selective memory, I see, George, eh?" the old man said.

"So how many times was it I kicked your arse?" George continued.

"You didnae kick ma arse." Sandy turned to his mate and shrugged. "He didnae."

"Have you dementia or something? Barely a week went by without me kicking or punching some part of your face or arse. I'll kick it for you noo, if you like." George wriggled around in his chair. "Get me out of this, Mark, so I can put my boot to this thieving wee ratbag's bony backside."

"I'll leave you to it," Sandy said and retreated to the entrance. "I'll get my chips later, Carlos."

Mr Sandino waved and concealed a grin.

"I'm lost for words, Da," Mullens said.

"There's a first for everything, I suppose," George said. "He was going to nick ma chips."

185

Mr Sandino returned with a warm wrapped bridie, fresh from the oven.

George tore at the paper. "Where's ma chips?"

"Oh no. Wait a moment, George." Mr Sandino dashed back to the fryer, filled a bag with a few veg fritters, and handed them to George.

"A wee poke a chips, my good friend."

"Let's eat them in the park, eh, Da?" Mullens snatched up the bag before George could check the contents.

"Hey, sir, and you keep your mitts oot as well," George said.

Mullens paid Mr Sandino and pushed his dad to the door.

"I'll see you in two weeks, George," Mr Sandino said with another warm smile.

"Aye, say hello to Mrs Corleone for me," George said.

"Haha, you are a very bad man."

Mullens gave Mr Sandino an apologetic wave goodbye, and with the now familiar deep sinking feeling returning to the pit of his stomach, he pushed his dad back to the Burngreen.

SEVENTEEN

When Bone finally made it home to his wife's farm holding, Michael was out in the front of the farmhouse, hosing down his upturned bike. As he pulled the Saab into the yard, the boy waved and carried on washing the wheels. Bone pulled up and climbed out.

"Hey, son," he said, approaching.

The boy turned and aimed the hose towards him, a spray of water splashing on the gravel just in front of him.

"Don't even think about it." Bone smiled. "Where's that been?" He stared at the mud-caked frame.

"Off-roading with my mates," Michael replied.

"So no hugs, then?" Bone extended his arms.

"Dad!" Michael exclaimed.

187

They fist-bumped each other, the ten-year-old's current choice of greeting.

"Be careful on that," Bone said. "I hope you always wear your helmet."

"Yes." Michael sighed.

"And stay off the main roads."

"We go *off-roading*, Dad. That's the point," Michael scoffed.

"Your mum around?"

"At the hens." He looked over Bone's shoulder.

"Okay." Bone started to walk away but spun around, snatched the hose from his son, and gave him a quick spray.

The boy yelped and giggled at the same time and tried to grab the end back, but Bone dropped it, and a cascade of water splattered against the wall. The boy stopped.

"Who's that?" Michael said, looking over Bone's shoulder.

Chronicle reporter, Colin McKinnon, lingered by the gate.

"Turn off the hose, son." Bone approached McKinnon. "What are you doing?"

"Could I ask you some questions about the hit-and-run up at Cullenbrae?"

"No. What are you doing here, on my property?"

"I'm not on your property. This is a public highway, and seeing as you are avoiding us yet again, I thought I'd come to you."

"You are stepping way over the line. I'm off duty now. This is my home. This is an invasion of privacy."

"Have you found out who the driver was yet?"

"I'm telling you, McKinnon, if you persist, I'll have uniformed officers down here and have you arrested for harassment."

"I don't think that'll hold water, do you? Come on, Bone. Give me something, otherwise, I'll be forced to dig up the past."

"This has got nothing to do with any previous cases."

"How can you be so sure?"

"I'm warning you…"

"How is your witness, Mrs Hepworth, taking it? She must be pretty distraught."

"How did you find out her name?"

"A wee bird told me." McKinnon sneered.

"Right, I'm calling now." Bone found his phone.

"Okay, I'm going."

"If I see you anywhere near my house or my family again…"

"Perhaps if you kept me up to date, I wouldn't feel the need to come looking for you. The public has a right to know."

"I'm so tired of your 'public interest' excuse to print salacious bullshit and lies."

"That's slander," McKinnon said.

"See you in court, cockroach. Now, are you going to leave? I have the station number right here."

McKinnon saluted him and sauntered off. Bone resisted the temptation to kick his backside. He exhaled and returned to the yard. Michael was gone. He cut around the side of the house and down the path to the hen coop. Alice was inside the cage, clutching a large cockerel and inspecting its leg.

"Hey, love," Bone said, approaching the wire, his heart rate slowing immediately.

"You're back at last," Alice said.

He opened the gate and squeezed through before the birds could escape. He leaned over the bird and kissed his wife on the side of the head.

"He's got an abscess." Alice gently turned the cockerel's leg.

"Oh dear. Poor Mark. What's caused that?"

"Not sure. Might be from a bit of squabbling."

"Hen-pecked husband?" He smiled, but she didn't reciprocate.

Two hens ran over, clucking and pecking around Bone's feet.

"Evening, Sheila and Rhona," he said with a smile and bent down to greet them.

"I'm not sure I like you naming them all after your team," Alice said.

She put the cockerel down. It shook out its feathers and strutted off to the far side of the coop.

"Oh, come on, they even look like them, don't they?"

Alice sighed. "So anyway, great news about the scan."

"It was a relief," Bone said.

Alice suddenly threw her arms around him. "I was so worried this time. I don't know why. I just had this sinking feeling something wouldn't be right."

"No, it's all fine. Why did you think that? Have I been behaving strangely?"

"No more than your usual irritating self." She let go. "Maybe it's all the restless dreams you've been having or something, and you have been a little quieter than normal."

"Result!" Bone exclaimed. "For you, I mean. He finally shuts his ranting cakehole."

"You would tell me if there was anything else, wouldn't you?"

"Of course I would."

He hugged her again, and she squeezed him tight.

"Can't breathe," he joked.

The hens gathered around and pecked at Bone's feet.

"Your team's jealous." Alice laughed. "Mark, in particular, seems besotted."

The cockerel flicked at Bone's shoelace.

"Perish the thought," Bone said.

"Come on, I'll get you something to eat. You're bloody emaciated." Alice locked up the coop, and they went back to the kitchen.

Bone slumped down, exhausted, at the table.

"So what did the consultant actually say then?" Alice asked and handed him a mug of coffee. "That's decaf, by the way. You need your beauty sleep." She smiled.

"Everything is fine. Nothing untoward going on in the scan." Bone took a sip and sighed.

She sat opposite. "Tough day?"

191

"A lot of toing and froing, the usual. I'm just feeling a bit weary."

"I hear an 'of' in there."

"Of the constant bloody carnage. I know we are murder and serious crime and all that, but sometimes I'd just like to rescue cats from trees, you know?"

"That's the fire brigade." She sipped her drink. "God, this is awful. Sorry."

"That's what I wanted to be when I was a kid. I should have followed my dream."

"What did you want to be?" Michael interrupted from the doorway. He shuffled over.

"Hey, son. I thought you were heading out on your bike."

"Nah. I got to level six in *Sporadica 5*."

"Wow, that's great. Oh, and by the way, what the hell are you talking about?" Bone asked and grabbed his son.

"Get off." Michael pulled away. "On my game box, you know?"

"I'm only teasing, and level six is for wimps. I could easily get to ten."

"It only goes up to nine, Dad." Michael frowned.

"That's how good I am. They need to invent a whole new level for me," Bone joked.

"Yeah, right."

"And *you* need to get off that now and finish your homework, Michael," Alice said.

"It's all done."

"Well, I want to see it."

"Aww, Mum. It's finished. Do I have to?"

"I'd like to see it, if that's okay?" Bone asked.

"It's maths. You won't understand, Dad."

"Cheers. I'll have you know I was the class maths champion when I was at school."

"That's not true."

"It is true."

"How the mighty have fallen," Alice cut in.

"Why don't I come up in ten minutes and you can show me what you've done?"

"And can I go on *Sporadica 5* until then?" Michael pleaded.

"Go on then. But that'll be it for the day, okay?"

"Deal." Michael went to shake his dad's hand but snatched it away and ran off, giggling.

"You're too soft," Alice said.

"And that's why you love me, or is it my algebra skills you're secretly lusting after?"

"Oh, now there's a word I vaguely remember." Alice raised her cup, then changed her mind.

"Soon remedied." Bone smiled.

"I thought you were exhausted?"

"I am capable of a second wind."

"Yeah, whatever." She got up and opened the fridge. "What do you want for dinner?" She spun around.

He was behind her.

"Don't answer that."

They laughed and embraced.

"I wish you rescued cats as well," she whispered. She ran her finger along the scar on his temple.

"You're not hiding anything from me about this, are you?"

Bone paused, considering whether to tell her about Peek-a-boo's adventures around his skull, but then changed his mind. "It's all fine. Nothing to worry about."

She pushed him away. "Right, go and sort out that pre-teen upstairs, and I'll try and work out what the hell we can make with fourteen eggs, half a tin of baked beans, and three mouldy potatoes."

EIGHTEEN

For the third time that night, the buzz of a motion sensor woke Donald Fagan from restless sleep. He jumped out of bed, grabbed his dressing gown, and went downstairs.

He fumbled with the alarm until it stopped beeping, slumped down by the monitor, and switched it on. The screen stuttered to life, filling the room with grey light. He tapped the keyboard and selected the night camera view of the street outside. All was still.

"Another bloody fox," he muttered.

He flicked channels to the camera perched on top of the telegraph pole by Brae Hill House opposite. He leaned in closer. The gate appeared to be open. He rubbed at his sleepy eyes and squinted again.

"Bollocks!" He jumped up, and from a cupboard in the hall, he picked up his baseball bat and a flashlight.

He dashed out the front, across the street, and stopped at the open gate that creaked back and forth noisily in the wind. The chain and padlock lay on the ground. The lock had been forced open. He turned on his torch and directed the beam at the derelict house and overgrown garden. The light swooped back and forth across tangles of bushes and old twisted trees, but he couldn't see an intruder. He aimed the torchlight at the front door, but it was shut. He raised his baseball bat and cautiously proceeded.

Halfway up the path, a faint noise came from around the side of the building. He stopped and held his breath. The sound of music faded in and out on the breeze. He turned his head. It was coming from the back of the house. He veered off the path, pushed through the thick tangle of shrubs to the side wall, and slid through the overgrowth.

At the rear corner, he stopped again. The music was louder. He peered around the corner. Darkness shrouded the rear garden, but at the furthest edge, a faint glow of light poked through the foliage. He turned his torch on the ground, located the path, and crept forward towards the light, careful to avoid contact with the high wall of nettles crowding in on either side. When he reached the line of trees at the back, he weaved through, and at the edge, he crouched.

The light and the music came from an old brick well tucked in close to the boundary wall. He raised his bat again and moved forward.

"You are trespassing!" he called out.

He glanced around the clearing and back to the house, but there was no one there.

"I'm armed and fucking dangerous!"

He approached the well. The music grew louder. Frank Sinatra's soft crooning voice singing 'Some Enchanted Evening,' lilted out from the hole.

"Right, stop taking the piss!" he said.

A narrow branch straddled the hole with a thick rope tied around its centre. He leaned over the side. The rope dropped down into the gloom. A small, illuminated box swung from the end. Sinatra and his band's tune bounced off the walls and soared up towards him.

He was about to turn his torch beam down into the well when he was struck on the back. The blow jolted him forward. He snatched at the brickwork to save himself, but a second blow sent him over the low wall.

His head smashed against the rim, and the sharp, buckled serrated edge of the lock snagged his neck, slicing through skin and muscle and puncturing his jugular. He tumbled down, but his feet got snared around the rope. Crashing towards the bottom, the radio, tied to the end, spun wildly around his ankles, locking them together. The rope tightened. His body jolted and bobbed wildly from side to side, his arms swinging down over his head, a few centimetres from the bottom.

He moaned through a semiconscious blur, but blood poured from the wound in his neck, and he choked as it haemorrhaged over his face, into his eyes, and up his nose. Sinatra's smooth crooning rendition of 'Some Enchanted Evening' echoed all around him.

He blubbed and gagged, unable to breathe, drowning in his own blood. He tried to swing his torso, to escape the torrent, free his legs, reach for the ground below, but a searing pain shot across his chest. He convulsed, his body contorting like a fish on a hook. With one final, bloody splutter, his heart stopped, his limbs relaxed, and his battered, lifeless shell swayed gently from side to side, in metronomic time with the final few bars of Sinatra's song.

NINETEEN

B one woke to the faint sound of music coming from the living room downstairs. He glanced over at Alice, who was lying on her front next to him, her face buried in her pillow. He slipped out of bed. On the landing, he peered down into the hallway. Light squeezed out from under the living room door. He moved cautiously downstairs, careful to avoid the creaking stair near the bottom.

He gently pushed the door. The red-headed boy was by his Dansette. The French doors were wide open, and moonlight illuminated the expanse of loch beyond the decked terrace.

Bone tried to speak, but his voice refused to obey.

'Delilah' played quietly on the turntable. The boy pointed to the record player. The volume intensified.

The boy lifted the arm and scratched the needle across the surface of the LP and dropped it back on the opening line. He repeated the move again and again.

Bone neared. He tried to stop him. The screech of the needle tearing through the grooves in the record intensified. The speed and pitch of the song increased. The boy smiled and continued. Bone reached out. But the boy remained just beyond his reach.

Bone held his ears, and finally, his voice returned. "Stop!"

A hand gripped his arm. He spun around.

"Duncan. It's okay. Duncan." Alice's soothing voice penetrated the white noise soaring inside his head. "Duncan. Wake up."

He opened his eyes. Alice stood next to him, holding his face in her hands.

"You're dreaming," she whispered. "It's okay."

Bone looked around. The boy, the Dansette, and his cabin's living room had dissolved. He was back in the farmhouse.

"Come back to bed," Alice said.

She led him slowly back upstairs.

Bone lay down on the bed and within a few seconds was asleep.

The next morning, when Alice asked him what had happened, he couldn't remember at first, but then the memory of his waking dream slowly returned.

"Was I sleepwalking?" Bone asked. He sat on the edge of the bed and pulled on his socks.

"Yup, and pretty weird it was, too. Is that something new, then?"

"So sorry for scaring you like that. Yes, unfortunately, it's probably another manifestation of my PTSD."

"I thought you were feeling a lot better?"

"Okay, I haven't been entirely honest with you."

"What?" Alice cut back. "I knew there was something you weren't telling me."

"It's nothing to worry about, but the fragment lodged in my brain has moved. Not much, and it isn't causing any damage, but the consultant said it may alter the effects of my PTSD."

"Sleepwalking." Alice shook her head.

"I have these dreams about a red-headed kid who seems to be following me about now, instead of Frankenstein's monster."

"What kid?"

"I don't know, but what I do know is it's bloody strange."

"Oh, Duncan. Why didn't you tell me?"

"I didn't want to worry you, and it's only just started happening."

"So what was this kid doing?"

"I was back at the cabin. The boy was playing 'Delilah' on the Dansette."

"Tom Jones's Delilah?"

"Long story, but he was yanking the needle back and forth. Scratching it across the LP."

"Is that why you shouted 'stop'?"

"Did I? Oh, sorry to scare you like that."

"Is it getting worse, then?"

"I haven't sleepwalked before, at least not that I know of."

"Did you mention these new hallucinations to the consultant?"

"Yes. He said it was to do with how the fragment was pressing on a new area of my brain, or something like that."

Alice frowned.

"But he insisted that there is absolutely nothing to worry about." He got up and tried to hug her, but she pulled away. "Sorry I didn't come clean."

"Don't keep anything from me, Duncan. I thought we'd agreed that if we were going to try and make this work, we'd be one hundred percent honest."

"Yes, you're right, and I'm sorry."

"Have you brought this up at your counselling sessions?"

"Not yet, but I will now."

"And your boss?"

"That's complicated."

"No, Duncan. You need to be honest with him, too. That's the deal."

"His wife is ill."

"No!"

"She found a lump, and the doctors are worried. She's going under the knife today."

"Oh, that's awful for her, for them both."

"That's between us, though, okay?"

"Of course. When did she find out?"

"Only in the last few days. You can see why I'm reluctant to lay my own shit on his desk."

"But you have to, Duncan."

"I know. I'll pick a moment."

"Make it very soon, okay? And no more lies. Otherwise, we'll head straight into the same mess we were in before."

"Deal." Bone nodded.

"How old is the boy you see, by the way?"

"Looks about nine or ten, the same age as Michael." Alice shivered.

"I know. It's a bit creepy."

"A bit?" She shivered again. "You are bloody strange sometimes."

"Sometimes?" He laughed. "Right, I'd better get my act together. There are cats out there needing to be saved."

"Promise me you'll take it easy and back off if you feel you have to."

"You sound like the Super."

"I mean it, Duncan."

"I know you do. Vigilance. Vigilance. Vigilance. It's our counselling motto."

"Well, pay attention to it." Alice nudged him.

He gave her a peck on the cheek. "Thanks for being here for me again."

"Oh, get to work before you have any more funny ideas."

She pushed him away, but he wrapped his arms around her.

She laid her head on his shoulder. "I wish you'd stop scaring me with that mental head of yours."

"I do too."

His phone on the table screamed to life. And almost rattled off the edge.

He continued to hold her. The phone fell onto the floor.

"Answer the bloody thing," Alice said.

"Do I have to?" He picked it up. "Sergeant Brody, what can I do for you?" he said and smiled at Alice.

"Morning, sir. Sorry to call so early. There's been a report of a break-in at number nineteen Brae Hill, Cullenbrae."

"That's Donald Fagan's place, isn't it?"

"Correct, aye. That's why I thought I'd better ring you."

"Okay, can you call Rhona and tell her I'll meet her up there in twenty minutes?"

"Sir." He hung up.

"Sorry, Alice. I have to go."

"Of course you do. You haven't had any breakfast."

"I'll grab something on the way," he lied.

He went in search of his shoes.

TWENTY

When Bone and Walker arrived at the scene, two PCs stood outside Fagan's open front door.

"Morning, sir, ma'am," one of the PCs said as the detectives approached.

"Are you the officers who called it in?" Bone asked.

"Yes, sir. We started our shift at seven and when we did a quick scoot round, we spotted the door like this. And then when no one came out when we called, we went in to find the place ransacked."

"And the property owner is nowhere to be seen?" Bone asked.

"No, sir."

"Okay, let's have a look."

"There's also that." The second PC pointed across the road to the abandoned house. The gate was wide open, the chain and lock strewn across the path.

"Have you been in?"

"I went as far as the front door, but it seemed to be still secure."

"What's your name, son?" Bone asked the first PC.

"Constable Mellon, sir."

"Right, Constable Mellon, you come with me. Rhona, you check Fagan's house."

"Sir."

Bone crossed the road with the PC following behind.

"This is where those murders took place, isn't it, sir?" he said anxiously.

"Correct."

"It's like something out of a horror film. Gives me the heebs."

"It's not exactly The Ritz, no," Bone said. "So you said you tried the front door?"

"It was secure, yes."

Bone checked the chain lock. "It's been forced."

He pushed the gate, and it swung open with a piercing scream. Officer Mellon shivered.

They pushed through the overgrowth to the front door. Bone turned the handle and shoved, but it didn't budge.

Bone scanned the front windows. The rusty iron panels bolted onto the frames seemed intact, and there was no sign of forced entry.

"Let's go round the back. You go that way, and I'll meet you on the other side."

"Of the house, you mean?" Mellon asked.

"Unless Freddy Kruger gets you first." Bone smiled.

"Who?" The young PC pulled a face.

"Never mind."

"I'm not sure I'll get through all these brambles, sir." Officer Mellon elbowed the tangle of briar.

"Give it your best shot."

Bone zipped up his coat and squeezed along the side of the building. At the corner, a bramble branch pinged back, and the thorns scratched across his face. He yelped in pain.

"Okay, sir?" Officer Mellon called from the other side of the building.

"Bloody brambles!" Bone yelled back and carried on.

At the rear corner of the house, he spotted a gap in the overgrowth and, ducking down, squeezed through into the back garden, which was relatively free of demonic vegetation. He brushed the debris from his coat and scanned the space ahead. A high stone wall ran around the perimeter with a mangle of trees, shrubs, and a wild meadow of weeds and wildflowers sandwiched between.

"Well, that's unexpected," Officer Mellon said.

Bone spun around. "Jesus, don't sneak up like that."

"Sorry, sir."

How did you get here so quickly?"

"The path. It's pretty clear round that way."

"Now you bloody tell me." Bone ran his finger along the bloodied scratch mark on the back of his hand.

"Quite surreal isn't it?" the officer said, scanning the cut square on the lawn.

"Shh. Can you hear that?" Bone interrupted.

The sound of music wafted across the garden.

"Yes, is it a radio?"

"Where's it coming from?" Bone asked. He glanced up at the back of the house. "Not in there. It's definitely over there somewhere near the wall."

"Or on the other side. Maybe the neighbour?" Officer Mellon suggested.

"There aren't any neighbours over there. Isn't it just a burn and gully?"

"Oh aye, right enough."

They started across the grass.

In the centre of the garden, Bone stopped. "Where now?"

"Behind those trees," Mellon said.

"When they reached a twisted, half-dead apple tree, Bone stopped again and peered through the gnarled branches. "Over there by the wall. What's that?"

"Looks like a well." The PC pulled a face.

They carried on. The waterlogged ground squelched underfoot.

They approached the circular brick structure rising about four feet out of the ground. The music volume intensified. Bone stumbled over an object and almost fell into the mud.

"Shit!" he cursed.

A spherical steei plate was half buried under rotting leaves. He levered it up for a closer look. A section of the rim was scratched and bent upwards.

"The cover," Bone said.

They continued to the well. Bone leaned over the top.

"The music's coming from down there." He peered into the darkness.

"What's this?" Mellon ran his hand along a thick, moss-covered branch lying across the centre and stopped at the rope tied round the middle. "The music is definitely coming from here."

"No shit, Sherlock."

Bone fished his phone out of his pocket, turned on the torch, and directed the beam into the void below, tracking the rope's descent.

The beam flashed across an object, but it was so far down, the light was too faint to identify what it was.

"Have you got your torch?" Bone asked.

But the officer had already plucked it from his belt and shone the beam into the well.

"Can you make out what that is?" Bone asked.

The two beams bobbed around the cavity, but the light was still too dim.

"Right, let's pull this thing up and see what we've caught," Bone said.

The PC leaned over the side and grabbed the rope. It pinged out of his grip. "It's really heavy, sir."

Together, they hauled until they had enough slack to step back from the abyss. Mellon wrapped the slack around his waist and pushed his boots into the side of the well for leverage.

"I was tug-of-war champion at Police Training," the PC said, slowly edging the rope up and out of the hole.

Bone assisted as best he could, but his strength was no match for his young burly assistant. The officer huffed and puffed, his face turning a deeper shade of purple with every heave at the rope. Bone picked up Mellon's torch and aimed it into the well. The beam caught a glimpse of the sole of a shoe.

"Oh, Christ," Bone exclaimed.

"What?" the officer wheezed.

"Keep going," Bone ordered.

Mellon groaned and carried on. Trouser legs and a torso emerged from the gloom.

Bone leaned over and grabbed at what he suspected were Fagan's legs. A pair of mud-soaked slippers popped over the lip of the well. The officer almost lost his grip, and Fagan's footwear disappeared again, almost taking Bone with them.

"Keep pulling!" Bone shouted, and when the body was near enough, he yanked at the pyjama top and tried to get a grip around the body's waist.

"Help me get him out," Bone rasped, still grappling with the swinging corpse.

"I don't want to release the rope. Hold on." Officer Mellon let out a deep primaeval roar, and with one almighty tug, the legs flopped over the side.

"I've got him. You grab his waist," Bone said.

The officer edged closer still, and with an outstretched arm, he took hold of a trouser leg. Then, shifting his position, he managed to get both his arms around the corpse's hips. They hauled the body up and over the rim of the well, and it flopped down onto the muddy earth at their feet.

Fagan.

Bone slumped down on the ground, wheezing with the effort. Mellon coughed, gagged, and dashed over to a bush to throw up. He waved his hand at Fagan's head. It was flopped back. A deep open gash across his throat. Fagan's face was smeared in dried blood that clung in clumps to his upstanding hair.

"That, my friend, is what a cut throat looks like," Bone said.

The PC threw up again.

TWENTY-ONE

Walker stepped around Fagan's front door, and the officer started to follow. She stopped.

"No, you go round the side and check the back door. I'll meet you there."

The PC disappeared, and Walker carried on.

"Mr Fagan, hello?" she called out. "It's Detective Inspector Walker!"

At the end of the hallway, she stopped at the living room door and listened. But all was quiet. She pushed it open with her fist. The room had been ransacked. The furniture was upturned, drawers hanging out of units, and by the back wall, all his CCTV monitoring equipment lay on the carpet.

She weaved through the mess. Cables had been severed, and it looked as though someone had taken a sledgehammer to the recording devices. There were components, broken circuit boards, screws, metal panels, and splinters of plastic scattered all over the floor. She continued through to the bedroom. Fagan's recordings were all gone. The shelves were bare, cupboards and drawers emptied onto the bed.

By the bed, she examined the contents strewn across the duvet: clothes, socks, boxers, along with a few papers, instruction manuals, and the usual clutter that accumulates in bedroom drawers.

She returned to the living room.

The PC stood in the doorway. "No sign of the owner, ma'am. But the back door was open."

"Forced?"

"Don't think so."

She went to the kitchen and checked. "Probably went out this way."

She stepped out into the small courtyard garden surrounded by a high moss-covered stone wall.

"Do you know what's over there?" she asked.

"Only one way to find out." He went over, and with one quick leap, he hoisted himself up on top. "There's a narrow path through some trees. Looks like it might go back to the road one way and up the hill the other." He jumped down and brushed the moss from his jacket.

"You could have used the gate, here in the corner." Walker smiled.

"Ah, didnae see that. Ah well, I'll write it off as my workout for the day."

214

She pulled at the handle on the wooden door in the wall, and it creaked open. She stuck her head out, then followed the path along the wall, round the corner, and onto the road. She turned back and followed it up through the trees until it came to a set of makeshift stone steps cut into the ground. Using overhanging branches, she scrambled up and continued through the woods until she reached the top of a ridge.

She cut right, and the trees cleared to reveal a view of the hamlet below, with the chimneypots of Brae Hill House just visible. She followed the path back into the woods and carried on.

Behind her, a branch cracked. She turned and listened, but the only sound was the rustle of trees. She carried on. At the brow, she spotted an old overgrown railway bridge. She walked across and stopped halfway. Fagan's place, Brae Hill House, and the main village square were now in full view, with the Campsie hills looming behind, bathed in full sun.

"Why is it so bloody dreich here?" she muttered and swept her mist-soaked hair from her face.

The old railway line continued to the other side and disappeared around a protruding cliff face. She crossed the bridge and continued along the track until it reached a lane on the clifftop.

A row of three lock-up garages appeared through the gloom up ahead. They were sitting under a low-hanging ridge in the rock face. Each had rusting metal doors of various faded colours and a variety of locks and bolts.

She rattled the first, then checked around the side of the row to look for a window, but the garages were slotted under a deep ledge in the rock.

She moved along the row, trying each door. At the third, she stopped. There were dried-in muddy tyre tracks on the tarmac leading from one. She removed her phone and took a couple of snaps. Kneeling, she examined the lock attached to the centre of the door, but with a shrug, she resisted attempting to unpick it or force it off.

A man in a Barbour coat with a collie came down the lane towards her. The dog ran up, wagging its tail. Walker stood and clapped, but that seemed to excite it even more and it jumped up, trying to lick her face.

"Gip, come here!" the man shouted at the dog, and it immediately returned to his side. "Can I help you?" he asked suspiciously.

"I'm DS Walker from Kilwinnoch Police Station. Do you know who owns these garages?"

The dog sat on her shoe, its tail slapping against her trouser leg.

"I do, why?"

"You own all of them?"

"I use the first and rent the other two. I'm Robert Barrowman. I own the smallholding at the top of the lane, just up there. Is there a problem?"

"Who rents the other two?" She stroked the happy dog's head.

"The second is empty at the moment, and the one you're at is Martin's."

"Martin?"

"Burns. I can show you inside mine if you like."

He went over to the first garage. The dog followed him. He unlocked the bolt and pulled the handle. The door swung up with a loud squeal. The stale stench of fish belched out.

"Sorry about the smell," the farmer said. "I'm off on a fishing trip this afternoon and I keep all my gear in here. The wife doesn't allow it anywhere near the house. It suits me as I can buy equipment and she doesn't need to know." He turned around. "You won't tell her I said that, will you?"

Walker peered inside the gloomy interior, rammed with rods, reels, nets, plastic containers of various shapes and sizes, and all-weather coats and waterproofs hanging up.

"And I can assure you, I'm not a poacher, if that's what you're thinking. I go loch fishing with a club."

"That's fine, thanks. Don't worry. There's been a road incident on the lane into Cullenbrae, and we're conducting enquiries in the hamlet."

"I saw that. I was trying to get to my high field, and they turned me back. I heard someone was killed. Is that true?"

"You said Martin Burns rents the one on the end from you. How long has he done that?" Walker asked.

"Oh, for years now."

"What does he keep in there?"

"I know he used to store some of his furniture in there. He makes cabinets and the like."

The dog whimpered.

"Shoosh, Gip," Barrowman ordered, and with a grump, the dog ran over to Walker and sat.

"He's lovely, by the way."

The dog licked her hand.

"Collies are manic buggers, but he's a good yin. Aren't you, Gip, my boy?"

The collie's tail went into overdrive, and he jumped up and ran around in circles.

"See what I mean? Sit," he ordered the dog, and it complied obediently.

"You wouldn't happen to have a key, would you?" Walker continued.

"For Martin's lock-up? I'm afraid not, no. But that garage has a window at the back. I think there might be enough space to squeeze through for a look inside. I'm sure it's probably furniture, though. Why the interest in his garage?"

"It's all just part of our investigations, Mr Barrowman."

Walker went over to the end garage. "The back, you said?"

"Aye, there should be a wee gap between the wall and the cliff."

She went around the side to the back of the garage. Sure enough, there was a gap with a small window in the middle of the wall, but the space was barely a foot wide, and rainwater poured off the mossy wet cliffside.

"Lovely," she muttered.

She removed her jacket and slowly squeezed into the narrow space, her back scraping along the rock.

She shivered as the water ran under her shirt collar and down her neck. She pressed on, and the space narrowed further. With a final push, she managed to extend her head to enable a glimpse through the corner of the window.

The pane was soaked and filthy. She leaned further and used her shoulder to wipe the glass. There was a car parked inside. She manoeuvred her leg to help her adjust her position. It was an old Volvo estate. She stretched again, but she couldn't move any further, and the licence plate was obscured by the bottom edge of the window frame. She slowly attempted to retreat but soon realised she was stuck. She pushed again, but her torso wouldn't budge.

"Excuse me. Mr Barrowman?" she called out. "Hello?"

"Aye?" Barrowman's voice cut through the sound of running water.

"Can you help me out?"

"Hold on."

Noise rustled behind her, and a hand tugged at her shirt, then yanked at her left shoulder. She twisted her frame to allow the farmer to pull harder. Finally, she slowly slid out and stumbled backwards onto the side path. Barrowman's dog leapt around as though she was playing with him.

"Gip!" Barrowman bellowed again, and the dog settled.

"Thanks," she said, wiping the mud and grime from her face and shirt.

"I've breach-birthed a few lambs in my day, so that was no bother at all." He grinned. "Are you all right?"

"Aside from the impromptu wild swim, I'm fine." She shook the water from her hair and tugged the front of her cold, freezing-wet shirt.

"Did you manage to get a look inside?" Barrowman asked.

"Did you know Mr Burns owns a Volvo estate?"

"Is that what's in there? No, I didn't. I didn't know he drove. I thought he was against all that sort of thing."

"What sort of thing?"

"Modern life. He doesn't care much for the twenty-first century, or the twentieth, for that matter. He's always moaning about how Big Brother uses our phones and the internet to spy on us. Good luck to them, that's all I can say. They're not going to find out many national secrets from me and my dogs. To be honest, though, I can't remember the last time I saw him up here at the garages. But I've never seen him driving about in it."

"And you said the middle garage is empty?"

"Yes, I cleared it out about two years ago when old Mr Forder died, and no one's rented it since."

"Do you have a crowbar or something to prise the lock off Mr Burns' garage?"

"That might damage the door. I'm not sure that's a good idea, and it's his property in there. Do you have the authority to do that?"

"I'm afraid so, yes."

Barrowman tutted.

"You'll be helping us with our enquiries."

"That's great, but you haven't told me what those enquiries are."

"Two nights ago, Mr Burns was struck by a vehicle."

"Oh, Christ. Is he okay?"

"I'm afraid not. So you see why it is imperative I get into his garage."

"Christ, yes, of course. That's bloody awful. He was… was it a car… an accident or…?"

"If you could help me here?" Walker interrupted.

"Aye, just a bit of a shock, ken."

"It is, yes."

"Let me have a look." He turned to his dog. "Gip, sit and stay."

The dog obliged, and the farmer disappeared into the depths of his fishing gear.

"And if you have some protective rubber gloves, that would be useful as well."

Moments later, he emerged clutching a claw hammer and a set of bright yellow Marigolds.

"Would this work? I use the gloves for gutting fish, so they might be a bit manky."

She took the items from him, returned to the garage door and, careful to avoid the tyre tracks, she inserted the claw end of the hammer between the lock, skewered and twisted it in, and then with one swift, forceful lever, she tore the lock out of its socket and it dropped to the ground. She drew back the bolt and lifted the door.

The tracks led all the way to the rear of the car. She stepped inside. A large dent marred the rear corner, the left brake light hanging out of its socket. Removing her phone, she took some pictures of the damage. She knelt. Some dried-in, reddish-brown-coloured matter clung to the torn metal bumper. She continued around the side to inspect the rest of the car. A long scrape ran the length of the front passenger door and the wing mirror had sustained damage. She took another couple of snaps. She put on the gloves, sniffed the fingers, and grimaced.

"It just gets better and better."

She continued to the driver's door and tried the handle. To her surprise, it opened.

More mud dirtied the floor and the pedals, the same reddish-brown stains on the dash and steering wheel.

She searched around the seat and quickly checked the rear. An open toolbox was on the floor under the passenger seat, a collection of odd-shaped tools poking out the top.

She returned to Barrowman, who hovered by the open entrance with an anxious expression on his face. She shut the door.

"I'm going to send some officers over. Can you stay until they get here?"

"Aye, of course."

"I'm afraid you might have to cancel your fishing trip, as we are going to need to cordon off all three garages for the time being."

"I don't think I'm in any mood for fishing now. I'll wait here."

"Good, thanks. They won't be a minute. What's the quickest way back to the main square?"

"Straight down the lane, fork right, and the square is at the bottom of the steep hill. Two minutes."

"Right." She marched off and stopped. "Don't go in, and keep well clear, including the dog."

"Okay," Barrowman called back.

Halfway down the hill, her phone rang. It was Bone.

"Get back here now," he said.

"On my way, sir."

TWENTY-TWO

Walker took a moment to process what she was looking at.

"It's definitely Donald Fagan."

"It is," Bone said.

"So you said he was hanging by his feet?"

"Tied or tangled, still not sure which, and the radio was caught up in the rope. That's what attracted our attention. It was still blaring out music. Throat cut, and looks like he bled out upside down."

"I can see that. Horrific."

"Forensics are on their way, so we'll have to leave him here for now." Bone turned to the PC, who lingered as far as he could from the body flopped out on the grass at the detectives' feet.

"Can you watch him until SOCO gets here?"

"Sir," the officer said and, averting his eyes, he moved a little closer.

"There's something I want to show you," Bone said to Walker.

She followed him back to the bistro table and chairs by the house.

"Has the grass been cut here?" Walker asked.

"I think so, and the ashtray is full of cigarette butts."

She leaned over the table and examined the contents.

"A few in there look relatively fresh," Bone said.

"Someone's been in here."

"Clearly, and that's not gone very well."

"No, I mean using the garden, or this bit at least."

"Possibly Fagan? He was taking care of the property, after all."

"Was he a smoker?" Walker asked. "I didn't see any evidence of that when we interviewed him. I can usually smell the smoke on them."

"I think we have just cause to enter the property, don't you?"

"Absolutely, if that's what you want to do." Walker squinted at the boarded-up windows. She shivered and rubbed at her arms.

"Are you sure you don't want to get out of those wet clothes?"

"I'm fine. My jacket has soaked up most of it." She went up onto the concrete patio and over to the back door. She rattled the steel panel bolted into the frame.

226

"That's completely rusted on. I think you'd need a specialist team to cut that out."

She shifted over to the first window. It was also heavily secured. She carried on around the side of the house and jumped back down onto the overgrown lawn. Further along, she came to a smaller window close to the ground. She tapped the steel panel, and it rattled. The bolts were missing, the rectangle of heavy metal detached and balanced on the windowsill.

"Give us a hand," she called back to Bone.

Together, they lowered the board to the ground. Behind, the window was open.

"Welcome to my humble abode," Bone said. "Let me…"

But Walker was already halfway in, and then, with a moment's pause, disappeared into the darkness beyond.

"Are you okay?" Bone called into the gloom.

"Yeah, it's the basement."

Bone followed her, though with considerably less grace. He flopped over the side and landed with a thump on the floor at Walker's feet. She helped him up.

"It stinks of damp. Is there a light? I can't see a bloody thing," he said.

"I doubt the power's on." Walker removed her phone and turned on the torch. The beam illuminated an almost empty room, but on the far side, there were a number of large, odd-shaped objects covered in canvas tarpaulin and tied with rope.

Walker went over to a switch on the wall. She flicked it, and to her surprise, a strip light directly above their heads spluttered to life.

"Power supply?" Bone asked. He tugged at the ropes tied around the tallest object.

"Mark, is that you under there?" he joked and, yanking at the edge of the tarpaulin, uncovered the corner of a wardrobe. "Furniture."

He turned, but Walker wasn't there.

"Rhona?"

"Up here," she called from beyond an open door at the back of the basement.

He followed her through and climbed a steep set of rickety wooden stairs leading to a musty, cobweb-covered hallway.

"Where are you?" he called again.

"Living room. This way."

He followed her voice again and found her in a web- and dust-covered mahogany-panelled Edwardian drawing room lit by a chandelier that hung from an ornate cornice. Framed, faded paintings of African landscapes decorated the walls, and the mounted head of a gazelle stared down at them from an enormous hardwood fireplace. There was more tarpaulin-wrapped furniture collected together by one of the boarded-up bay windows that stretched the width of the room.

"Bloody hell. I didn't know the Sneedons were so wealthy," Bone said.

"Colonialism lives on in Cullenbrae," Walker said. "Or delusions of grandeur, perhaps."

They carried on through a connecting door that opened onto an equally proportioned kitchen that looked like a museum piece from the nineteen thirties. Walker went over to an ancient rusty Aga stove that was sandwiched between ancient kitchen cupboards. She pressed her hand against the oven door.

"Does that feel warm to you?" she asked.

Bone touched the surface. "It does, yes. Is it on?"

She turned the knob on one of the hobs, and it hissed.

"Electricity *and* gas? I thought this house was abandoned."

Bone approached a mouldy, heavily scratched Belfast sink. A fork lay across the plughole with some food matter collected around the drain.

"I think someone's been eating," he said.

But Walker had gone again.

"Where are you now?" he called out.

He went back into the hallway. Walker stood by a mahogany staircase that wound up through the centre of the building.

"For God's sake, stop doing that," he said.

She raised her hand. "I heard a creak coming from upstairs."

"Of course you did. Where would we be without the obligatory creak?"

A loud thump sounded above, and flakes of plaster showered down on them.

They started up the stairs, stopped on the first landing, and listened again.

A second creak.

"There." Walker pointed to the first door.

They approached cautiously. Bone leaned in and shook his head. He gently pushed the door, and it slowly opened. He edged his head around the frame.

There was a single bed pushed against the wall, a few clothes scattered on the floor, and a pile of plates and mugs stacked up on top of a bedside cabinet.

Walker crept past to an adjoining door on the far side of the room. She tried the handle, but it was locked.

"There was definitely someone or something moving around in here," Walker whispered.

"Something?" Bone asked, his eyes widening.

"You're not scared, are you, boss? You don't think it's your hallucination wandering around up here?"

"I wouldn't put it past him. He has form," Bone said.

Suddenly, a door slammed on the other side of the wall. Bone dashed back onto the landing. A figure rammed past, and he was knocked off his feet. Walker gave chase down the stairs. Recovering, Bone followed behind. At the bottom, the runner had disappeared, and they ran back through to the living room, then on to the kitchen. But there was no sign. Walker raced to the back door, but it was locked. They returned to the hall.

"Did we just imagine that?" Walker asked.

"My sore shoulder says otherwise." Bone rubbed his arm.

Walker spotted the cellar door ajar. "Out through the in-door?"

She yanked it open, and they leapt down the flight of stairs. The figure, an elderly man in filthy overalls, stood by the window, attempting to squeeze through the narrow gap.

"Police. Stop!" Bone shouted.

He rushed over and snatched at the fleeing man's leg. But he kicked out, his boot connecting with Bone's chest, knocking him backwards onto the floor. Walker intervened and grabbed the man's arms, hauled him back in, and wrestled him to the floor.

"Where do you think you're going?" she said.

Bone scrambled back to his feet and sat on the runner's flailing legs.

"Get off me!" the man moaned, his face pushed against the concrete floor. "I don't have any money, if that's what you're after."

They flipped him over onto his back. The man was bearded, with long, filthy, grey-and-yellowing matted hair obscuring his face. He was older than Bone expected, considering the force he'd used to escape and his nimble attempt to climb through the window.

"Take what you want. Just leave me alone!"

"We're police officers. What are you doing in this house?" Bone asked.

He tried to wriggle free again, but the detectives tightened their grip.

"We'll let you up when you calm down," Bone said.

The man exhaled, his limbs finally relaxed, and Bone sat him up.

"Are you going to behave now?"

"Just let me be." The man spoke with a refined West End Glasgow accent.

Walker showed him her lanyard. "What are you doing on this property?"

The man stared at the ID. He closed his eyes and took a deep breath. "No comment," he mumbled.

"Have you broken in? Are you homeless?" Bone asked.

"No comment," the man repeated.

"What's your name?" Bone pressed.

The man dropped his head as though trying to shut the detectives out.

"You know that this is private property. We can arrest you for breaking and entering?"

"No comment," the man muttered.

"Did you have an altercation with anyone at the well, at the back of the garden?"

"No comment."

Bone sighed. "I've had enough of this."

The detectives lifted the man to his feet.

"I'm arresting you on suspicion of breaking and entering the property known as Brae Hill House," Bone said.

The man tutted. "Why won't people just leave me alone?"

"You don't have to say anything, but if you do, then it can be used as evidence in a court of law, do you understand?"

"I understand that I have done nothing wrong!"

"Go get the PC," Bone said.

"Be good, okay?" Walker said to the man. She let him go and climbed back through the window.

A couple of minutes later, she returned with the PC, and together they forced open the basement door a fraction. They pulled the man out into the light, and Bone followed behind.

"We're going to need easier access than this," Bone complained, rubbing at his bruises.

The man spotted Fagan's body splayed out at the rear of the garden.

"What the hell is that?" His mouth opened in shock.

"We're hoping you might be able to tell us," Bone said.

The man dropped his head again. "No comment."

TWENTY-THREE

The team stood stern-faced around the incident board, now covered in a complex network of lines, arrows, headers, names, and images.

"Bloody hell. And I thought that film *Ring* was bloody ghoulish." Mullens broke the silence.

"Do we know who the victim is?" Baxter asked.

"We don't have a definitive ID as yet, but it is most certainly Donald Fagan," Bone said.

"I assume the man in black and his team are on the scene now?" Harper said.

"Yes, they were barely back at base when they all had to repack the vans and return. We'll hopefully have an initial report from him shortly. But we have more."

"More than that?" Mullens asked.

"Rhona and I found a way into the Sneedons' house via the basement, and it was clear someone was living or squatting there. Following a quick search, we discovered a man, possibly homeless, in the property. He attempted to flee, but we caught him."

"I caught him," Walker added with a smile.

"He's now in custody, waiting for an interview."

"Any idea who he is?" Baxter asked.

"He was very uncooperative."

"And nothing on him?"

"Aside from fleas and some dried-in cereal in his beard, no," Bone replied. "As I said, he may be homeless and using the empty property for shelter."

"But it's like Northlands High-Security Prison, isn't it?" Harper asked. "You think he may be responsible for the death of Mr Fagan?"

"Maybe Fagan disturbed him attempting to break in."

"But, sir, the food, bedding, and dirty plates suggest he'd been there for quite some time," Walker said.

"Could he have somehow evaded Fagan's eye until last night?" Bone suggested.

"Fagan was obsessive about security, and it seems unlikely he'd miss a bumbling old down-and-out breaching his line of electronic and steel defences. And what about the elaborate setup at the well—the radio, the rope?"

"True. We can hold him for now on breaking and entering until we find out who he is."

236

"The destruction of Fagan's cameras and removal of recordings also suggests that someone doesn't want us to see them," Walker said. "Perhaps he captured our killer on the night of the hit-and-run who then needed to get rid of the evidence and the witness."

"If the killings are linked. We have no concrete evidence to assume they are at this point."

"Oh, come on, sir," Mullens interrupted.

"I repeat, as we have absolutely zero evidence linking this apparent squatter to the crimes, then for now, we have to assume the killer is still at large."

"And increasingly desperate by the looks of things," Baxter said.

Bone turned back to the incident board. "What's this?" He pointed to an arrow linking the pub landlord and Burns.

"I was just about to tell you, sir," Baxter said. "I did a bit more digging into the residents of Cullenbrae, like you asked, and came up with something interesting. The Clachan Arms landlord, Gronin, has quite the shady past with a record as a fence. Five years ago, he was convicted for handling stolen goods and served eighteen months for repeat offending, which included two counts of GBH."

"Well now."

"Not only that but I also discovered that he had an accomplice who was also charged and sentenced alongside him. None other than Mr Martin Burns."

"So they were partners in crime?"

"Apparently, Burns helped Gronin source the knock-off gear. The procurator fiscal couldn't prove

Burns was the actual thief, but he was caught with stolen goods in his car so was done, Gronin went down and Burns received a nine-month suspended sentence for a first offence."

"Why would Gronin fail to mention this? He surely knows we'll unearth his records?" Bone asked.

"Especially when he'd employed him to work in his pub," Walker said.

"Okay, we need to speak to Gronin again. Mark and Will?"

"On it," Mullens said.

"Then there's Burns' car," Walker said. "I found it in a lock-up this morning with damage to the rear that looked consistent with a severe collision."

"Burns' car?" Harper asked.

"Yes, the plates match the ones you gave me yesterday, sir."

"That doesn't make any sense. Did he run himself over?" Mullens said.

"There was a box of tools in the back, full of instruments similar to the murder weapon."

"Tapered reamer," Baxter said.

"Yes, that." Walker nodded. "The car has been impounded. Forensics is examining it now."

"I also ran checks on the second set of plates you got from the innkeeper, and the car was a rental from a company called Happycars, based in Milngavie," Baxter said. "I rang their office and spoke to a very officious employee."

"I bet that didn't last long," Mullens said.

"Yes, once we'd overcome our initial misunderstanding, she was very cooperative and found the details. The car was rented on the second and tenth of October to a woman from St Andrews, called Kathleen Fisher."

"St Andrews? Burns' net stretched far and wide," Bone muttered.

"I wonder if it was one of his clients," Walker suggested. "Maybe he was fitting a new kitchen for her?"

"That old euphemism," Mullens said.

"Do you have an address, Sheila?" Bone asked.

"Of course. And I rang a landline number, but there was no reply. I also checked the land registry and council records on the property, and Kathleen Fisher inherited the property from her parents when they passed away."

"We might need to ask the St Andrews nick to pop round to Ms Fisher's home," Bone said.

"I can sort that." Baxter nodded.

"Excellent work." Bone smiled. "What about Burns' next of kin and anything more from forensics?"

"Burns' mother died when he was three. He was brought up by his father, now also deceased. No prints, identification marks, or DNA from forensics, including the tapered reamer."

"Tyre marks and paint?"

"Traffic has indicated acceleration burns. The tyres are most likely cheap Goodyear rip-offs, but samples still to confirm. Let me double-check the paint." She went back to her desk and tapped her keyboard. "Checks ongoing. Sorry."

"Frustrating all round."

"And even more frustrating news," Harper interrupted. "The results from the sample taken from the bumper of Gary Speed's Saxo came back."

"And?"

"Dried-in deer blood. So it looks like he's off the hook."

"Aside from his skunk farm in the loft, of course," Mullens said. "We got him to admit to cultivation, but he insisted he never sold it. He said it was for personal and friends' use only."

"He's trying to reduce his sentence," Bone said.

"Aye, but the two thousand in fives and tens recovered from his house will be enough for the procurator fiscal, I'm sure," Mullens said.

"But Will is right, he is off the hook when it comes to Burns' murder."

"He did say some of these so-called friends lived in Cullenbrae, but refused to elaborate."

"Okay, so we'll need to re-interview residents."

"A second murder in Cullenbrae is going to go down really well," Walker said.

"Aye, the press muppets will piss themselves with glee over this," Mullens said.

"They already have." Walker went back to her desk and returned with the *Chronicle* newspaper. The headline read *Horror Hamlet* with the tagline underneath: The Evil Curse of Cullenbrae Returns.

"… sake," Bone muttered.

"More fucking ham than old Jake Whyte's pig farm," Mullens said.

"Okay, let's start with Gronin, and see where it goes," Bone said. "And try not to wreck another pool car, Mark."

"Have supplies been moaning to you again?"

"Never a good idea to upset them down there."

"True. I'll be good." Mullens followed Harper out.

"That'll be a first," Bone replied.

"Okay, Rhona, let's go and see what Brody's done with our homeless suspect." Bone turned to Baxter. "Once Sergeant Brody has processed him, can you send his mugshot to shelters, charities, and support agencies to see if we can identify our mystery guest? I suspect he won't be forthcoming, but I did notice he has a fairly posh Glasgow accent, so may originate from West End or leafier neighbourhoods on the south side."

"Okay. I'll chase forensics as well," Baxter said. "A busy morning. May I refuel first?" She removed a pack of cigarettes from her handbag.

"Go on then."

"What about the Super?" Walker asked Bone.

"I'll call him soon. Let's just see where all this goes first."

"Are you sure? I mean, he's usually on your case if you don't keep him updated."

"I will, but not yet," Bone said. "Come on."

Walker followed him out.

They went out the back door to avoid the press and passed Baxter, lighting up.

241

"You go on a sec, Rhona," Bone said.

She carried on.

"Can I ask a favour, Sheila?" Bone asked.

Baxter turned her head and blew a plume of smoke away from him.

"Can you go back through Robert Meiklejohn's files and check if there are any photos of him as a child, maybe aged nine or ten?"

"You want me to check the Peek-a-boo Killer's records?"

"Yes."

"I don't mean to pry, but is everything okay, sir?"

"Yes, I'm just following up on something, trying to tie up a loose end. All part of my healing process."

"Ah, yes, of course."

"I'd have a look, but you're way quicker than I am at this sort of thing."

"Absolutely, no problem at all."

"But keep this to yourself, okay? I wouldn't want the Super finding out and worrying unnecessarily."

"It's between us." She waited until he was of sufficient distance before she took another long, deep drag of her cigarette.

TWENTY-FOUR

A squad car pulled up at the edge of the village square. Two officers climbed out and joined Mullens and Harper.

"Right, you go round the side of the pub with DC Harper and cover the back," Mullens said. "We'll take the front door."

Harper chuckled.

"What?" Mullens frowned at him.

"*Die Hard* five. The village boozer." Harper giggled.

"The guy has form, Will. Just watch yourselves, okay?"

They carried on across the square. Harper and the PC disappeared around the side, and Mullens continued to the entrance. The door was closed, and the sign advertising lunch that usually sat on the pavement was gone. He glanced at his watch.

"A bit late to still be shut, isn't it?" he said to the PC.

He tried the door, and it swung open.

"Hello? Mr Gronin?" he called into the gloom.

The counter and drinks dispenser lights were all out.

"DS Mullens from Kilwinnoch station, are you there, Mr Gronin?" he called again.

A loud crash followed by a high-pitched scream came from the other side of the rear wall. Mullens and the PC raced through the connecting door to the lounge, but the tiny room was empty.

A second and third thump sounded from the rear of the pub. They ran back to the public bar, around the counter, and out the back. Harper and Gronin scrambled around on the kitchen floor, by an upturned table. Harper's legs were locked around Gronin's waist, but he was rapidly losing his grip.

Mullens rushed forward to help, but Gronin broke free, thumped Harper in the face with his elbow, and jumped up.

He turned and roared at Mullens, his fists raised. Mullens approached calmly. Gronin swung his arm, but Mullens landed a single punch on the landlord's double chin that sent him airborne for a second. He careened backwards over the upturned table and landed with an almighty clatter on top of a cookware tower, sending pots, pans, and utensils flying in all directions.

Harper got to his feet, clutching his cheek. He ran over to Gronin, who was on the floor in a heap, out cold. He cuffed him.

"That'll teach you to underestimate us." Mullens shook his head. "Where's the officer you were with, Will?"

"Here, sir," the second officer said, kneeling by his colleague at the back of the room.

"He came charging straight at me from the yard," the disorientated PC said from the floor, rubbing his head. "Clocked me with that." He pointed to a steel frying pan lying at his feet.

"Was there a woman here with him?" Mullens asked.

"No, I don't think so," Harper said. He pushed his palm against his jaw.

"I heard a woman scream." Mullens frowned.

"Ah, er… I think that might have been me. He grabbed my hair. Right at the roots, you know, the worst bit."

"*Die Hard*, my arse," Mullens moaned.

Gronin shifted sideways. The soup ladle teetering on top of his chest slid off and clanged onto the stone floor.

"Right, tumshie face. David Thomas Gronin, I'm arresting you for, well, let's start with assaulting two police officers and resisting arrest and see where that goes."

While Mullens continued to read out the caution, Harper stumbled out the back door.

245

Gronin's minivan was parked up outside the yard's gate. The boot was open. It was loaded up with antique furniture. There was a box pushed under a Georgian chest. Harper pulled it out. Inside, there were bubble-wrapped silver and gold ornaments and bagged-up jewellery. A crimson-red square box in the middle caught his eye. The top was embossed with the Omega watch company logo.

He returned to the kitchen. Gronin was now sitting up and protesting loudly.

"Assaulting officers? Try the other way round, you wankers." He rubbed at his chin. "And that was a lucky punch. You won't be so fucking lucky the next time."

"Oh, I do hope there is a next time," Mullens said. "Give me a chance to use my actual punching fist." He turned to the two officers. "Are you okay?" he asked the first, who was back on his feet.

"I'll live," the PC groaned.

"No thanks to Hans Gruber here," Mullens snarled at his captive. "Take him back to the station."

"Here we go." The PC cautiously approached and grabbed Gronin's handcuffed arms.

"Boo!" Gronin yelled in his face, and the PC jumped. "This little piggy went to market, this little piggy…"

"Button it or I will do it for you, permanently," Mullens said.

The two PCs led him away.

"Looks like the landlord was having a clear out." Harper nodded to the van in the yard.

"Knock-offs, I would assume, hence the siege of Nakatomi Tower."

"All right, can we drop my *Die Hard* clanger?"

"Ah, you've watched it then?"

"Catriona made me. She loves it."

"Oh, she's gone right up in my estimations. I might steal her from you. If I suggest anything like that to Sandra, she threatens to cut off my gonads in the night. I thought you two were vegan-munching *Star Wars* geek nutcases?"

"I'm way more of a geek than her."

"You set the bar very high, Will. You okay?" Mullens turned to examine his colleague's face. "You're going to have a bit of a shiner there. Your fiancée will think it's sexy."

"She'll worry even more about me."

"If you scream like that every time you paper-cut your finger, I'd be worried as well."

"Please don't tell anyone about that."

"How long have you known me?"

Harper groaned.

"Any damage on the vehicle?"

"Nothing."

They followed the PCs back through the pub and out into the square.

Mullens stopped at the pool car. "I won't say a word, but in return, there might be something I need you to do for me."

"Oh God, I don't like the sound of that."

"Right, let's see what bollocks-for-brains has to say for himself."

247

"What is it?"

Mullens started the engine. "That would spoil the surprise."

Harper's stomach sank a little further.

TWENTY-FIVE

Up in reception, Bone rang the desk buzzer, and Brody came through from the back.

"What room is the homeless guy in?" Bone asked.

"That was the incident team on the blower, the guy collapsed in the wagon on the way in. They've taken him up to Falkirk General."

"A&E?"

"Yes. Apparently, he had some kind of seizure, and they called paramedics to assist."

"Good God. This investigation. I've just been up there. Someone's definitely pulling my chain today."

"Sorry, sir."

"Yes, I'm blaming you entirely, Sergeant. You and that lucky unicorn of yours."

"He's not so lucky now. On his way to the nearest landfill."

"Exactly, it's karma."

Bone headed for the doors. Walker followed.

"No, I'll go on my own. You'd better hold the fort here."

Sir," Walker said and returned to the incident room.

Bone took a deep breath and carried on out. The gaggle of journalists gathered outside had multiplied since he'd come in.

"I hope they haven't got wind already."

He turned around and left via the rear exit.

***

In A&E, a registrar doctor marched across the busy waiting room.

"Are you the police officer who wants to speak to the man who was fitting?" he asked.

"Yes, DCI Bone from Kilwinnoch station."

"Follow me," the doctor said.

They went down a corridor with cubicles on either side.

"Is he okay?" Bone asked.

"He's a little groggy, but stable and his seizures have subsided."

"Is he an epileptic?"

"No, he suffered a severe panic attack, and the sudden drop in oxygen levels brought on a seizure."

"Has he told you his name?"

"He told one of the nurses he was called Ronald, but no surname as yet." He stopped at an examination room at the end and drew the curtain back. "Hi, Ronald, there's a police officer here to see you."

Ronald was propped up on a high bed, his skeletal body barely visible under a white linen sheet that matched the colour of his drawn, furrowed expression. A nurse hovered by his side.

"You," the old man croaked.

"You suffered a panic attack, Ronald, and that caused a seizure. But we've checked you over and you're fine now," the doctor said.

"I don't wish to speak to that man." Ronald raised his arm and pointed a gnarled finger at Bone.

"I'm afraid I have to speak to you, Ronald. Is that your real name?"

The old man continued to frown.

"Why did you have a panic attack in the police vehicle, Ronald?"

"I just want to be left alone," the man grumbled.

"How did you get into Brae Hill House?"

The nurse dropped a clipboard and it clattered on the floor.

"Sorry," she said and attached it to the bottom of the bed.

"Did you use a set of bolt cutters on the lock?" Bone continued.

The man breathed hard.

"Inspector, perhaps you should give Ronald a little longer to recover," the doctor said.

"It would really help if you could tell us your full name," Bone persisted.

The old man shook his head.

"Excuse me," the nurse interrupted. "Could I speak to you for a moment, Inspector?"

He followed her out, and she briskly pulled the curtain shut.

"I think that's Craig Sneedon."

"What?"

"You know, the brother of that guy who killed his parents, neighbour, and some townsfolk. It was when you mentioned Brae Hill House, that's when I knew I was right. I recognise him and his voice from a documentary I watched a few months ago. He was on there being interviewed after it all happened. That programme really stuck in my mind."

"But he says his name's Ronald."

"Well, I'm pretty sure that's Craig Sneedon in there. He was a lot younger, of course, but it's that voice. That whole story gives me the heebie-jeebies. I remember I spoke to an older colleague who was on A&E that night. He said the gunshot injuries were horrific. And you know the father survived a few hours? Just awful."

Bone went back in. "So why are you back at your old family home, Craig?"

The old man looked up in surprise. "The name's Ronald."

"Come on, Mr Sneedon, we know who you are. This is pointless. Why did you break into your own home?"

The old man sighed. "I didn't break in. I live there."

"What?"

"Just let me go home."

"You are the brother of Henry Sneedon?"

He nodded.

"So why change your name, Craig?"

"Wouldn't you change your name after what happened?"

"And you say you live in the house?"

"Yes." He wriggled around under the sheet. "There is an ongoing dispute between my sister and me over our parents' will and our inheritance.

"Which included the house?"

"That's right. My damned sister refuses to accept that my parents left the house to me even though she received the rest of their estate. Things just went from bad to worse, and then in 2018, around Christmas time, I found out she'd hired a demolition company to come in and flatten Brae Hill House. That was the last straw, so reluctantly I returned from abroad to try and sort out the mess she had created, and rid my sister from my life for once and for all."

"So you're saying that you've been living in the house for over four years?"

"Correct."

"But how is that possible? No one in Cullenbrae has mentioned this to us, and the property is like Fort Knox."

"When I moved in, I just never came back out."

"Never?"

"I had what you might describe as a breakdown, and my pre-existing agoraphobia spiralled."

"So you've not left the house?"

"I use a small corner of the back garden that's not overlooked."

"But if you never left, how did you eat? Surely in all that time you must have needed a doctor or dentist, or someone like that?"

"I'm blessed with good genes. And Mr Fagan looks after me well. I pay him to buy my essentials and keep the house secure."

"Mr Fagan told us you were abroad."

"He's very loyal. He's kept me safe all this time, and I'm very grateful to him."

"So your relationship with Mr Fagan is good?"

"I would say he's like a brother to me, but that would be ill-judged. Now, if that's all, I would like to go home." He glanced over at the doctor. "I feel well enough."

"I'm afraid the body you saw in your garden was that of Mr Fagan," Bone said.

"What?" Craig exclaimed. "No!" His body shook.

"It won't be possible for you to go home at this stage, as your house and garden are now a major crime scene."

"No… No," he repeated. "How? I just saw him. That can't be."

"When was that?"

"He came round with some food and warned me. Three days… That…" The old man's mouth fell open.

"Warn you about what?"

254

"That the police were attending an accident down the lane, so not to worry if I heard sirens. He was very considerate like that, always."

"Did you hear anyone breaking into your property last night?"

"I heard some noises from the garden, but assumed it was the foxes that have been setting off Donald's alarms." His head dropped. He took two or three deep breaths. "Why does this keep happening? When is all this pain going to end?" he muttered.

"And you didn't see him the next day or later that evening?"

"No. He usually calls in every couple of days, so I wasn't expecting him."

"I'm sorry, but I have to ask you this, Mr Sneedon. Did you kill Donald Fagan?"

"My God, no! Why would I do that? Why would anyone do that? He was so kind. He was my lifeline to the world. I rely on him every single day. Why would I?" His breathing intensified.

The doctor came forward and checked the old man's pulse.

"Slow breaths, Craig, as I showed you before," he said to the man, whose frame heaved up and down under the sheet. "Gently does it." He pressed his palm on Sneedon's forehead.

The old man's breathing slowly calmed.

The doctor stood back. "Inspector, a quick word?"

Bone followed him out into the corridor.

"He's on the brink of another panic attack. I think he needs more time. If you carry on, he could fit again."

"Okay, I'll leave it for now, but I'm going to have to send a PC over to keep an eye on him."

They returned to the room.

"We'll need to ask you some more questions when you're feeling better, Mr Sneedon," Bone said.

"I just want to go home," the old man whimpered.

Bone nodded to the doctor and left.

On his way back to the car, his phone rang.

"Rhona?"

"Forensics have pulled prints from Burns' car's steering wheel and have matched them to Stuart Mason."

"The hippie electrician?"

"Yup."

"Bring him in," Bone said.

"Uniforms are already on their way to collect him," Walker replied.

Bone sighed. "We'll be running out of interview rooms at this rate."

TWENTY-SIX

Gronin leaned back in his chair and scanned the interview room. "Harassment, plain and simple. I'm on your books, so you think I'm easy pickings. Same old stuck record."

Mullens stared at him in silence for a few moments longer. "Okay, let me make it as clear as I possibly can, Mr Gronin. Were you involved with Mr Burns in the acquisition and sale of stolen goods?"

"And why would you think that, Detective?"

"Oh, maybe because of the way you assaulted two of our colleagues. You just fancied another spell in Northlands High Security then, is that it?"

"The copper came at me. I was defending myself."

"DC Harper?" Mullens said.

Harper flicked open his notepad. "On searching your property and van, we recovered four items of antique furniture, a Georgian-era dresser, two Regency chairs, and an oak cabinet. Also, two miniature silver vases, jewellery pieces, including a lady's gold necklace, bracelet, and a collection of diamond, ruby, and emerald set rings, and a boxed antique Omega gold watch."

"The jewellery was my mother's. I inherited it when she passed away. Or I should say when my dad passed away. Then in probate they were passed down to me. I have proof."

"And the furniture?"

"They are all restored reclamation."

"And who restored them for you?"

"Okay, I know where this is going."

"And where would that be?" Mullens asked.

"I paid Martin to help me."

"Ah yes, partners in crime."

Gronin looked up.

"Why didn't you tell us about your criminal history with Mr Burns? Is that the real reason you panicked and thumped two police officers? Trying to do a runner, were we?"

"I told you, your uniform had a go at me first." Gronin sighed and laid his hands on the table. "Okay, look. Once in a while, I find something interesting at a car boot or clearance sale and I ask Martin to help me repair and restore it. I sell it on, and he gets a cut. It's all mostly junk, though. Sometimes we'd strike lucky and land something actually worth a bob or two, but it's only ever happened once, I think."

"Amazing." Mullens scoffed.

"What?"

"A fence and supplier dealing in legit goods."

"Former fence. I'm telling you, that is all behind me now. I have receipts for all those goods."

"So you employed your former criminal associate as a barman out of the kindness of your heart?"

"I gave him a leg up. I felt sorry for him. To be honest I probably felt guilty for landing him in it."

"Very noble, and a great cover, too. Clever."

"It wasn't a cover. It was my fault he got nicked and banged up. I was a stupid arse and I shouldn't have involved him. He's a very talented carpenter. I just wanted to help him out, make amends, you know?"

"Must have rankled a bit though, what with him escaping prison while you were still inside."

"As I said, I was a prize prick back then and I got what I deserved. He should have been cautioned, and that's it. It was completely over the top."

"And so you welcomed him back with open arms. Back to your firm."

"Give it a rest. No."

"And in those long, dark nights, when the punters had all gone, and you counted out your pittance barely lining the till, the two of you were never tempted to go back into that lucrative easy money-making business together, perhaps expand into an even more lucrative enterprise?" Mullens persisted.

"Utter bollocks. Why is that so hard to believe? We both have years of experience, so why not put it to use legally?"

"I'd describe it as form rather than experience."

"That's the truth. I know it might surprise you, but there is a thing called rehabilitated."

"I noticed you haven't mentioned where you got the antique watch," Harper interrupted.

Gronin shifted in his chair.

"Well?" Mullens pressed.

"I know this looks bad, but Martin asked me to have the watch valued."

Mullens laughed.

"It's the truth. Jesus."

"And when was this?"

"About a fortnight ago. He told me someone had given it to him as a gift and he wanted shot of it."

"Why?"

"Why do you think? For the money. He was skint."

"And you believed him that it wasn't a knock-off?"

"He reassured me that someone had bought him it as a joke, since he was always late for everything. To be honest, initially, I thought it was a bit cock-and-bull, as it seemed like a very expensive gift to give someone as a joke. I even went as far as asking him to provide me with a receipt."

"And did he?"

"He promised to, but I was still waiting."

"This tale is taller than the Nakatomi Tower, Mr Gronin."

"It's bloody true. I have drawers full of pictures of my mum wearing some of that jewellery."

"What was your relationship with Donald Fagan like?"

"CCTV man up the hill? I saw the police wagons up there. Has something happened to him?"

"Answer the question."

"He's a strange wee man. He comes into the pub and winds folk up with his strange wee theories about aliens. A harmless headbanger."

"Do you have cause to harm him?"

"Oh aye, and if I did, I'd tell you, wouldn't I? Of course not. He's just that loony who's appointed himself as Head of Security for Brae Hill House."

"What do you know about that?"

"Nothing. I never go near the place. So, are you accusing me of doing something to him now, as well?"

Mullens sat back.

"I said it before and I'll say it again. Harassment. I've told you the truth, and you have absolutely nothing. Admit it." Gronin folded his arms.

Mullens leaned over to the recorder. "Interview paused at one thirty-eight." He hit the button.

"Is this charade over? Am I free to go?"

"Wait here, please," Mullens said and stood.

"Oh, come on."

Harper followed Mullens out.

"He's a slippery bastard. I don't trust his eyebrows," Mullens said.

261

"His eyebrows? I'm more wary of those bloody bulldozer fists of his. I know I'll regret asking this, but what is it you don't trust about his eyebrows?"

"He says one thing and his eyebrows say another."

"I'm now convinced more than ever that when you died for a few minutes out at that hotel, you never actually recovered and are now some kind of walking, joking zombie. What the hell do you mean?"

"He was professing his innocence, but his eyebrows were twitching and all over the place."

"They were grassing him up. Is that what you're saying?"

"Exactly."

"Oh God. I've heard it all now. So what do we do?"

"We run checks on these goods, and if receipts turn up, we start again, but in the meantime, his fists alone have earned him an overnight stay."

"Yes, that was not how an innocent man would welcome police officers into his home."

"Let's just clear it with the boss. Is he still interviewing?"

"No clue," Harper said.

They went along the corridor and Mullens knocked on the next door, but the room was empty.

"Wait here," Mullens said with a shrug and returned to the reception.

"Where's the boss?" he asked Desk Sergeant Brody. "I thought he was interviewing the homeless guy in room four?"

"He's gone to the hospital. The guy collapsed in the wagon on the way over."

"Collapsed?"

"Some kind of seizure, according to the PCs."

Mullens found his phone and called Bone, but there was no reply.

"Shit." He went back downstairs. "The boss is at the hospital. The homeless guy took a funny turn on the way over. I tried calling him, but he didn't answer."

"What do we do?" Harper asked.

"Send him back to the cells until Bone gets back," Mullens said.

Harper pushed his glasses up his nose.

"Something bothering you?" Mullens asked.

"If what Gronin said is true, who do you think bought Burns such an expensive watch?"

"Sounds nicked to me, to be honest."

"His thing about Burns always being late for work chimes with what that HR lady from the Love Candy factory said about Martin, though. If he's lying, that's a weird detail to throw in."

"But then there are those demented eyebrows."

"He knows he's looking at probable jail term again, so his eyebrows are worried. God, you've got me doing it now."

"Mmm. You're definitely getting a bit too good at this for my liking, young Obi."

"I might just duck down to the goods room and have another look at that watch."

"Fancy it yourself, do you?"

"I'd just like to check it over again. Satisfy my curiosity."

"Okay, I'll check in with the boss, or try to anyway."

They parted, and Harper headed out across the courtyard to the storeroom.

TWENTY-SEVEN

The evidence store manager glared at Harper. "You have authorisation?"

"I just want a quick look."

"Sorry, but no sign-off, no lookie," the store manager replied. "I mean, you could be a master criminal attempting to tamper with vital evidence."

"You're taking the mick, aren't you?"

The manager chuckled and disappeared into the storeroom. She emerged moments later with an evidence bag and handed it over. "I'm keeping my beady eye on you, Raffles."

Harper reached to pick it up.

"Hold your horses." The manager stopped him. "These first." She reached under the counter and produced a pair of examination gloves.

Harper slid his hands in, removed the watch box, and placed it on the counter. He carefully unclipped the latch and flipped the lid.

"Nice kit," the manager said, leering over the desk. "My grandfather had one of those."

Harper turned the box around to examine all sides of the watch.

"His was eighteen or twenty-four carat. The distillery where he worked gave it to him when he retired. Just what you need, a precision-engineered timepiece to remind you that your time's running out. Sure enough, he pegged it six months later."

Harper glanced up.

"Sorry, am I distracting you?" she asked.

"A bit, yes," Harper replied.

He removed the watch from the box. It felt heavy in his palm. He turned it over and checked the back.

"It's self-winding. I reckon issued sixty-eight or nine. Worth a fortune now, I would think."

"Hold it a sec." He held it out.

"Are you deliberately trying to contaminate this?" She found a second pair of gloves and snapped them on with an officious twang.

"Feel the quality in that," she said and placed it by her wrist. "I think I quite suit it. If I was a master thief like you, I wouldn't mind snaffling this one."

Harper gently eased out the velvet-covered mount insert.

"What are you doing? Don't wreck the bloody thing."

Underneath, there was a tiny card tag tucked into the bottom corner of the box. He prised it out and held it up.

"Grassmarket Antiques."

"Edinburgh," the manager said. "Posh. Makes sense."

He found his phone and took a snap of the tag and the box. Then he put it back and replaced the mount. "Watch?" he said.

"Aww, I was hoping you'd forget I still had it."

He slipped it into the holder and snapped the box shut.

"Thanks," he said.

"No problem, Raffles." She was about to drop the box back in the bag when she stopped. "Hold on. You still have the watch, don't you? I bet you performed some kind of sleight-of-hand trick there. Maybe I should check inside again?"

"Give it a rest." Harper sighed and left.

He ran back across the car park and took the stairs three at a time to the incident room.

"I think I might have a lead. I found a company tag in the watch box." He sat at his desk. "Grassmarket Antiques." He tapped at his keyboard. "Bingo. Twenty-three Victoria Street, Edinburgh. They will have a record of the purchase and the buyer, maybe."

"But if Burns pinched it, then the rightful owner might be just some unfortunate random," Mullens said.

"Go check it out, Will," Walker cut in. "Good work."

"Shall I accompany young Poirot?" Mullens asked.

"No, you're needed here. Carry on, Will."

"Free at last." Harper sneered at Mullens. He grabbed his jacket and dashed out.

TWENTY-EIGHT

When Bone returned from the hospital, Walker intercepted him, and they went straight down to room two.

"I'm sure the gods are determined to keep me from the coffee machine today," Bone said.

They went in. Stu Mason sat on the edge of his chair, elbows on the table, chewing at his nails.

"Thanks for coming in, Mr Mason," Bone said.

"I didn't have much choice, did I?" He wiped his hands on his torn Led Zeppelin T-shirt and flicked his greasy hair out of his eyes.

"Oh yes, that's right." Bone smiled.

The two detectives sat opposite.

Mason sat back, his gaze dropping to the floor.

"DCI Bone. We've met before, and this is my colleague, Detective Inspector Walker."

Mason glanced up.

"I've heard so much about you. It's good to finally meet, eh?" Walker said.

Bone leaned over, turned on the recorder, and went through the preamble. When he'd finished, he sat back and stared at Mason for a moment. Mason returned to gnawing off his fingernails.

"Do you know why we've asked you to come in today, Mr Mason?" Bone asked finally.

"No." Mason shrugged.

"Not an inkling?"

"I have no idea, and to be honest, I'm quite upset."

"Yes, I can see that. Why are you upset?"

"Why do you think? I've never been in trouble with the police, and you're intimidating me."

"Well, we both know that's not quite true, don't we?"

"Ach, that was years ago. I got caught with a tiny amount of hash, and some jobsworth copper nicked me. I got off with a caution."

"Which escalated to a suspended sentence when you were caught again, by another jobsworth copper."

"Okay, I like the odd smoke, big deal. It's legal in California, you know."

"The road incident victim has been identified as Martin Burns." Walker paused to allow the bombshell to land.

"What? No way. That can't be…This is insane." He sat back shaking his head in apparent disbelief.

"Earlier, we recovered Martin Burns' car from a lock-up in Cullenbrae."

"Right." He swallowed, and his eyes widened.

"The rear bumper of the car was quite severely damaged and fragments of dried-in blood taken from the paintwork and side-mirror have been identified as belonging to Mr Burns. In other words, his car was used in the hit and run."

"None of this makes sense. Why are you telling me all this? It's so distressing."

"Following further detailed forensic inspection, we found your fingerprints on the steering wheel. Why would that be?"

"Oh, Christ." He rubbed at his head.

"Well?"

"Hold on, I can explain that."

"We are all ears, Mr Mason," Walker said.

"A few months ago, I rewired Martin's house in exchange for the use of his car. Our van was off the road, and we needed to take Cait's ceramics to craft fairs and the like. We couldn't afford to miss any. It's our only income, and the gas bill alone on that kiln is through the roof. So that's what we did."

"Do you have anything written down, emails, texts, receipts to prove this arrangement?"

"I don't know. I used to meet him in the pub, and we'd arrange it like that."

"That's quite convenient, isn't it?"

"Well, it was. It saved our bacon, and I thought the arrangement was fair," Mason said, his apparent shock rapidly turning to anger.

"Having no proof…"

"Oh, come on. You can't possibly think…I mean, look at me. He raised his arms. "Do I look like the kind of guy who'd want to kill anyone?"

"You'd be very surprised, Mr Mason."

"This is madness. I didn't kill Martin. Why would I? He saved us from destitution."

"They were the only prints found on the vehicle."

"Well, I don't wear driving gloves. What can I say?"

"I put it to you that, for some reason you had a falling-out with Mr Burns, perhaps over money. Did he refuse to pay for materials you'd purchased?"

"No. I told him how much stuff cost, and he gave me the amount in cash to go and buy it from the cash and carry. I have those receipts somewhere."

"You said yourself that you struggle with bills and keeping your head above the water. You are on the edge, close to destitution, as you called it."

"We are poor, Inspector, not psychotic."

"And him taking advantage of you in this way would be enough to push you over."

"Fantasy land."

"And then, enraged, did you march over to the lock-ups and take Burns' car out? Maybe you were just going to destroy his property or torch it as payback, or maybe you knew he was on his way home from his late shift, on his bike, on a dark lane, an accident black spot. It would be anyone's chance for real payback. The only kind that would compensate for his betrayal of your arrangement."

"Where do you get this garbage from? No offence, Inspector, but do you lot live in some kind of parallel universe where everyone is presumed guilty of brutal murders? I had nothing to do with Martin's awful death. I might not have been best buddies with him, but we respected each other. I thought his cabinets were fabulous. Cait does, too. It's heartbreaking that he's been killed. But my prints are on the steering wheel of his Volvo because I borrowed his car three days before the accident. I have receipts to prove I bought materials for his house rewire and I can also dig out the invoice for the rent of the stall at the craft fair."

"When I interviewed you at your property, I saw some lights in a frame at the back of your studio," Bone continued. "You said you used it for taking promotional shots of your wife's ceramics."

"Where are we now? Okay, yes." Mason folded his arms.

"A little earlier we arrested a Mr Gary Speed, who admitted he supplies residents with skunk and other forms of recreational drugs. When we searched his property, we found a skunk lab in the loft with a UV lighting rig that looked remarkably like the one I saw in your studio."

Mason exhaled. "Look, I'll admit, I like the odd puff. Gary Speed asked if I could build him a frame. And in exchange, he'd give me some weed, for my use only. But that has absolutely nothing to do with Martin. We're not part of some big drug cartel, if that's where you're going with this. Next thing you'll be accusing me of is being Pablo Escobar."

"You seem to be doing quite a bit of exchanging, Mr Mason," Walker said.

"It's called old-fashioned bartering, Detective. It's what us poor unfortunates do. I'm sorry, but I have told you the truth. Now if you're going to charge me with possession of skunk, go ahead, but you don't have any evidence other than my admission. But I'm telling you now, if you carry on with this offensive farce about me murdering Martin, I'll be going straight to the Police Complaints Authority for wrongful accusations, not to mention the press. It's an absolute joke and another example of coppers trying to fit a square peg in a round hole to make up the numbers and keep your fucking powder dry."

"You seem a little angry for someone who is claiming innocence, Mr Mason," Bone said.

"Oh, so I'm supposed to feel happy about all of this, is that it?

"This?" Bone asked.

"Wrongful convictions. You just can't help yourself. You have no right to hold me here."

"Did you have a beef with Donald Fagan?"

"The tin-hat nutjob? I don't bother with him. As long as he keeps his cameras away from my house and his insane conspiracy theories to himself, then I have no issues with the sad old man."

"So never a cross word?"

"In the past, we've had heated discussions in the pub, but I don't waste my energy on him anymore. Life's too short, too precious. And I'm wasting it right now in here."

"Interview paused at four-eighteen p.m.," Bone said.

He stopped the recorder.

"What?" Mason threw up his hands.

"Please wait here." Bone stood.

"Are you charging me? Can I go? What's it to be, Inspector?"

Bone left, and Walker followed him out and shut the door.

"I think he's telling the truth," Walker said.

"Which parts?"

"All of it. He's claiming he has evidence to support his story, which is easily checked. To be honest, it's all very plausible."

"But he's so angry."

"Understandable, considering what we've just accused him of. And I think he has a thing about authority. I just don't think there's a motive there, or at least one that's strong enough to explain multiple, brutal murders. And his story about Gronin's contempt for Fagan ties in with what Gronin said to me the first day I met him. He called him 'mad as a brush.'"

"But is that enough to slit someone's throat and hang them in a well? These murders are premeditated with consistent patterns. Gronin's an animal, but Mason may be a little more sly."

"I just don't think we have sufficient evidence to keep him. We could ask for an extension, based on the fingerprints alone, but I don't think we'd get it."

Bone sighed.

"I suggest we hold him for a little longer, see what we can find. Then take it from there," Walker said.

"Thank you, sir," Bone said with a smile.

"Sorry, am I leading again?"

"No, you're spot-on as usual." Bone pressed his finger into his scar to try and alleviate his oncoming migraine.

They returned to the interview room to break the good news to Mason.

TWENTY-NINE

Grassmarket Antiques was located about halfway down Victoria Street in central Edinburgh. Gleaming gold and silver ornaments, jewellery, and timepieces filled the Georgian bay window. Harper tried the door, but it was locked. He peered through the pane and spotted a hand-drawn arrow pointing to a bell with a sign underneath that shouted, RING! He pressed the button, and a faint tinkle sounded inside. A shadowy figure emerged from the gloom, and with a clunk and a click, the door swung open.

"Sorry about that. I was having my lunch," an elderly man in a beige misbuttoned cardigan said. He dabbed his mouth with a napkin and glanced down at a long dribble of drying egg yolk on his front. "What a slitter." He wiped at the mess and ushered Harper in.

The shop was a gleaming clutter of antiques of many shapes and sizes. A mass of ornate chandeliers and ancient light fittings hung low from the ceiling, making the space feel even more crowded.

"Are you looking for anything in particular?" The man sidled around a glass-case countertop.

"I'm Detective Constable Harper from Kilwinnoch Police Station. I want to ask you about a watch you may have sold."

"Detective Constable, my oh my. You don't look old enough, son. I thought you must be in looking for something for your mother's birthday perhaps."

"Don't worry, I get that all the time. I blame my Nordic genes."

"Well, Detective, a watch, you say?"

"Yes, an Omega Constellation, possibly circa nineteen sixty-nine. I believe it was purchased from your shop. I'll show you."

He found his phone and opened the gallery.

The shopkeeper searched the counter and then behind.

"Are you looking for your specs?" Harper pointed to the pair swinging from a chain around his neck.

"Oh God. Don't get old, son. That's all I can say." He put them on and studied the photo. "Ah yes, I remember that watch. Very handsome, and these ones with the diamond inset are quite rare, a very limited edition, which hikes up the price. Eighteen-carat gold, boxed, and aside from a few scratches on the glass frontage, all-in-all, a beautiful timepiece."

"Do you know who bought it and when it was sold?"

The storekeeper reached up to scratch his head, but his hand caught on the chain, and he knocked his glasses off. He sighed. "Let me check the ledger."

He opened a door behind the counter and shuffled into a workshop room with ancient iron machines, work lamps, and a messy bench crammed into the space. He rummaged around under the bench and returned.

"Do you restore antiques as well, then?" Harper asked.

"Jewellery mainly, and the odd minor tinkering with watches, but something like the Omega, I'd recommend clients send to official repairers, or the manufacturer for restoration work, otherwise it can reduce its value."

He placed a tatty, thick leather-bound ledger on the glass top and opened it up. "I have a feeling it was three months ago."

He flicked forward and ran his finger down the rows of hand-scribbled entries. He continued on, page by page, until finally his finger stopped halfway down a page.

"There." He tapped the book. "I remember now. A lovely young lady. Very pretty."

"Did she give you her name?"

"I wouldn't think…" He stopped. "She paid by cheque." He nodded.

"A cheque? I haven't seen one of those for a while."

"Yes, believe it or not, I hadn't either. But it worked fine. She said something about using an old account so that her husband wouldn't find out. It was an anniversary present, I believe."

"May I ask how much she paid for it?"

"She drove a very hard bargain. I think she got me down to two in the end." He checked the entry in the book.

"Two hundred?"

"No, no. Two thousand. Ah, I'm wrong, nineteen hundred, an even tougher negotiator than I remembered. To be honest, it's probably worth double that, but I have overheads and, well… It was a quick sale."

"Do you have bank records of the sale? That might have her name?"

"Give me a minute and I'll see if I can dig out the statement." He disappeared into the back again.

Harper wandered around the shop and stopped by a cabinet full of brooches. He leaned in to examine a penny-sized silver rose with a tiny ruby in its centre.

The storekeeper returned. "Here we are. I can't believe I found that so easily. My wife must have organised them behind my back. She does that, and I'm very grateful, otherwise, I'd be opening the shop in my pyjamas." He coughed out a laugh.

Harper went back over to the counter.

"Here's the payment, nineteen hundred, paid by a Ms Kathleen Fisher."

"Can I take a picture of this?"

"Of course, aye. Is there a problem with the watch, or has it been stolen or something?"

"No, no, nothing like that."

"I have the purchase record on the watch, in case you might think I deal in stolen goods."

"Oh no, not at all. But purchase history would be very useful. Perhaps if you could send copies of those to me." Harper checked his pockets and found a card. "My telephone and email are on there."

The storekeeper studied the card. "I still can't quite get over that you're not at school." He looked up and smiled.

"Sometimes I wish I was," Harper replied. "By the way, I noticed a brooch in your cabinet over there. How much is it?"

"Let's see." The storekeeper followed Harper.

"That one there."

"Yes, very pretty. I assume that might not be for your mother?"

"My fiancée. She loves roses."

"Don't all ladies? How romantic." He opened the case and unpinned the brooch from its mount. "Sterling silver with ruby inset. I believe it's late Victorian. It's marked as forty pounds, but seeing as it's for your fiancée, I'll drop it to thirty."

"Twenty-five?"

"Oh, another Del Boy. Twenty-eight, and that's my final offer.

"Deal."

"As long as you invite me to the wedding."

"We haven't found a date yet, and they cost so much."

"Ach, well, don't leave it too late or she'll go off you, and the wedding is about the two of you. What does it matter if you marry in a shoebox under a bridge, as long as you love each other?"

"Tell that to Catriona's relatives and friends."

The storekeeper carefully boxed up the brooch, skilfully gift-wrapped it with a champagne silver bow, and handed it to Harper. "There you are. And you can thank me after she thanks you." He winked.

Harper paid, took a shot of the bank statement, and the shopkeeper showed him out.

THIRTY

In the stairwell, Bone was about to descend to the cells when Baxter called from above.

"Where's the fire, Sheila?" He ran up to meet her.

"Will just rang from Edinburgh."

"What the hell is he doing over there?"

"Long story, but he followed up Gronin's claim that Burns asked him to have the Omega watch valued, and that the watch was gifted to Burns by a female admirer."

"To put it politely, can you cut to the chase?"

"The person who bought the watch was a Ms Kathleen Fisher."

"This mystery woman from St Andrews?"

"I did more digging."

"Yes, and?"

"Remember I said that the property was inherited by Ms Fisher from her parents? Well, when I called the local police station, they said the house was used for holiday lets. I checked a few rental companies online and finally found it. The contact name for the property is listed as Kathleen Anne Hepworth."

"What?"

"The letting agents' records were changed four years ago, when Kathleen Fisher got married."

"Good God. But Rhona said she insisted she told him to do one," Bone said.

"Apparently not. The room at the Methuen Inn, the car hire, and the expensive watch were all purchased by her using her maiden name and a bank account registered to the property in St Andrews."

"Presumably so that her husband wouldn't get wind. What a murky wee place Cullenbrae is. Right then. More interview rooms are required. We now have more persons of interest than an Agatha Christie dinner party. And I think we're going to need a support unit to follow us up to Mrs Hepworth's house."

"Also, Cash was in earlier looking for you."

"Is he back from the crime scene?"

"Temporarily. He said he'd be in his office for an hour or so."

"When was that?"

She checked her watch. "About two hours ago."

"Missed him. Did he say what he wanted?"

"No, sorry."

"And no feedback yet from the crime scene?"

"No, not yet."

"Okay, I'll call him."

"Oh, sir." She stopped him. "You asked me to find that info on Peek-a-boo? I found something. I don't know if it's of any use." She handed him a sealed A4 envelope.

"Thanks."

She disappeared back up the stairs. Bone stared at the envelope for a second. He folded it in three, tucked it into his suit pocket, and called Cash, but it rang out. He checked his watch and went to find Walker.

At the Hepworths' property, Bone and Walker jumped out of the Saab, and a squad car pulled in behind them.

Bone went over. "We have a person of interest in the property, Mrs Annie Hepworth, mid-thirties. There is a possibility she could attempt to run, so I need you to cover all escape routes front and back."

"Sir." The female constable nodded.

Bone approached the house and knocked on the door. There was no reply.

"Police, open up!" Bone called out. He rattled the door again. "Mrs Hepworth, are you in there?"

Walker peered through the bifolds. Mr Hepworth's head popped up from the kitchen island. Moments later, the front door opened.

"Sorry, I didn't hear you there, Inspector Bone. Have you got some news about the hit-and-run?"

"We need to speak to your wife, is she in?"

"No, she's gone out."

"Do you know where?" Bone asked.

"She normally goes fell running at this time of day." He checked his watch. "Yes, she'll be out for another couple of hours."

"Can we come in?"

"Of course, yes, but I do have a Zoom meeting in ten minutes with clients in Saudi."

"You might want to cancel that. I'm afraid we have a warrant for the arrest of your wife, Mr Hepworth."

"What?" Hepworth said, alarmed.

"In connection with the murder of Mr Martin Burns."

Hepworth laughed. "Are you serious?"

"Is it okay if my colleague has a quick look around?"

"How, I mean... How could you possibly think that?"

"It's imperative that we find your wife, sir."

Hepworth's face fell. Walker disappeared deeper into the house.

"Where does your wife go running?" Bone continued.

"You think Annie killed him?" Hepworth asked, his voice shaking. "This has to be some kind of joke, right?" He stuttered over his words.

"We have reason to believe your wife is directly involved in the death of Mr Burns."

"That's bloody ridiculous. She's not capable of something like that. For God's sake. There has to be some mistake, an error somewhere. You lot make them all the time."

"We have reason to believe your wife had an affair with Mr Burns."

Hepworth stared at him for a moment. "Him? And her? This is utter madness. He's…"

"Our evidence indicates this. I'm sorry."

He stared at Bone for a moment and then slumped down at the kitchen table. "He's a charmless, ugly toad. Why would she? How could she?" He shook his head. "This is all wrong."

"You had no idea?"

"What a bitch," Hepworth mumbled.

"Where does your wife go running?" Bone asked again.

"Up Brae Hill, somewhere along the top of the Campsies. I've no idea, just like I have no idea what the hell I've married." He looked up at Bone. "But hold on, what about her car? It's absolutely fine. There's no damage. How could she possibly have run him over? Surely there would be dents or blood or something all over."

Walker reappeared and shook her head at Bone. "No sign, sir."

"I told you, she's out running. You think I'd harbour that slut now?"

"Sorry, sir. We'd appreciate your help here by remaining calm," Bone said.

"Calm? You've got to be joking. You come in here and tell me my wife's been fucking some troll and then murdered him. Not exactly a transcendental meditation class, is it?"

"I understand that this is very distressing, but we do need to find your wife before she does something stupid."

"Like what? Sleep with someone else, or run them over with a fucking tractor?" He fished his phone out of his pocket and angrily stabbed at the buttons.

"What are you doing?" Bone asked.

"I'm calling her."

"Please don't do that. It's important that we don't alert her to…"

A phone rang on the other side of the kitchen.

"Great. She's left her phone now as well."

Walker went over to a large sofa in the far corner and found the phone buried beneath a cushion. She brought it over.

"There are two messages on the screen here. One was sent at two forty-three and the other at two forty-four p.m., from a CM. The first says 'Where?' and the second reads, 'I'll be there.' Do you know who CM is, Mr Hepworth?" Walker asked.

"Another of her fuck buddies? I don't know."

"Can I see that?" Bone asked. He studied the screen. "Do you know her password, sir?"

"Oh yeah. If I'd known that, I might have found out what a cheating whore she is."

"Sir, please," Walker said.

Bone clicked the on button, and the screen illuminated again.

"Two officers will remain here with you, Mr Hepworth," Bone said.

"What, in case I top myself? That's probably what she'd want. I wouldn't give her the satisfaction."

"Please remain in the house, and if your wife contacts you, let us know."

"Oh aye, I'll do that all right."

Bone marched out of the house. Walker raced after him.

"Sir?" Walker said, catching up with him.

"I know exactly who CM is. It's sewer rat McKinnon. I recognise the moron's mobile number."

"The idiot! He's gone to meet her."

"We're going to need Will and Mark. Can you tell them to wait by their phones?"

"Where are we going?"

"*Chronicle's* offices. Shake the bastards down."

THIRTY-ONE

"I'm sorry, the editor is in a meeting. You can't just barge in," the flustered *Chronicle* receptionist said, chasing after the two detectives as they marched through the building.

"Where's the meeting?" Bone asked.

"Er, his office on the fourth floor, but I really think you should wait here while I..."

But Bone and Walker were already in the lift.

At the end of the glass-lined corridor, Bone shoved the editor's door without knocking. A small team of hacks sat around the editor's expansive desk. They all spun around in unison.

"Mr Lampard?" Bone asked, eyeballing the balding, scruffy man behind the desk.

"DCI Bone," the editor, said and stood.

"We need to speak to you now."

"If you give me five minutes, I'll wrap this up."

"Now!" Bone roared.

The editor gestured for the attendees to leave, and once the room was cleared, he approached Bone. "This is out of order, Inspector. We're in the middle of a meeting here."

"Where's McKinnon?" Bone cut him off.

"What?"

"Where is your social affairs editor?"

"He's out on a story, I think."

"Where?"

"He hasn't shared that with me, I'm afraid. All he said to me yesterday was he was on a major scoop, but wouldn't tell me what until he had more."

"Oh, come on. You gave him the nod to proceed, surely. Did he arrange to meet Annie Hepworth?"

"The witness in the hit-and-run case?"

"Stop bullshitting me. If McKinnon has arranged to meet Mrs Hepworth, then his life might be in danger. So tell me where he is."

The editor returned to his chair. "So, is she responsible for the death of Martin Burns?"

"Are you serious? You're digging for a story now? Tell me where he is," Bone snapped back.

"I honestly don't know." He thought for a moment. "But there is someone who might." He picked up the desk phone.

"Carol." He paused. "Yes, don't worry. It's okay." He glanced at Bone. "Can you get Charlie Parrie to come to my office as a matter of urgency?"

"Who's he?" Bone asked when he hung up.

"Colin's photographer. He usually goes out with him on stories, but I saw him in the canteen about twenty minutes ago."

A couple of minutes later, there was a knock at the door, and a young, long-haired man in a waistcoat and flared jeans came in.

"You wanted to see me?" He looked over at the two detectives, frowning at him. "Oh, police."

"Charlie. Do you know where Colin is meeting Annie Hepworth this morning?"

"Who's that?"

"Come on, we haven't got time." Bone sighed.

The editor nodded.

"He didn't say, but he told me to be on standby and he'd call."

"So no address or location?" Walker asked.

"No, he said she'd insisted he come alone, so he told me to wait for him to ring."

"Colin might be putting himself in grave danger, Charlie," Walker said.

"I honestly…" He fumbled for his phone. "Hold on." He flicked at the screen.

"What are you doing?" Bone asked.

"A while back, we were on a job together at some busy event, can't remember where now."

"And?" Bone pressed impatiently.

"I missed an important photo opportunity, which was annoying, so I persuaded him to add Find My Phone to his work mobile." He tapped the screen again. "He appears to be..." He widened the map. "Up at Craigmallon Reservoir."

He turned the phone.

"That's him there, see, close to that building just off the forest track."

The icon disappeared.

"Weird." He fiddled with the image.

"Where's it gone?" Bone asked.

"Don't know."

"Has he turned off his phone?"

"That shouldn't affect anything."

"Right. If he gets in touch with you, inform us immediately." Bone turned to the photographer. "And don't even think about it."

"What?" The photographer shrugged.

"I'm serious. Even as much as a ball hair gets within ten miles of Craigmallon and I'll have an armed officer blow your fucking head off. That goes for any or all of you. Are you listening, Mr Lampard?"

"Threats?" the editor said.

"Who said anything about threats?"

Bone stormed out.

THIRTY-TWO

McKinnon stopped at a crossroads and checked Annie Hepworth's message again.

He'd been driving for nearly an hour, deeper and deeper into Campsies. He stopped at the turning she'd told him to take. The waterlogged track looked almost impassable in his Corsa. He shrugged, inched the car through a narrow gate, and continued on. The car bobbed violently as it hit pothole after pothole. About a quarter of mile in, the front suddenly lurched forward, and the car stalled. He restarted it, revved the engine, but nothing happened. He tried again, and the tyres skittered in the mud.

"Bollocks."

He opened the door and climbed out. His shoes disappeared into the quagmire.

"Dear God!"

The track wound along the edge of a stream with the fells looming on either side. He checked ahead. An indistinct building stood in the distance, its roof peeking above low-lying mist. He plodded and splodged up the track, stumbling a couple of times. As he neared the building, the mist cleared. It was a dilapidated, tumbledown bothy with part of its roof missing.

"Why the fuck here?" he muttered, and attempted to negotiate another muddy puddle, but landed right in it.

When he reached the bothy's side wall, he used it to lever himself through the mud to a wet-rot-consumed front door. He squatted, and squinted through a low window, the panes cracked and filthy. He rapped on the door.

"Annie, it's me."

No answer.

He pulled at the rusting metal knob, and the door almost fell off its rotting hinges. He manoeuvred it out of the way and stepped inside.

"Hello? Are you there? It's Colin McKinnon, Kilwinnoch *Chronicle*."

The interior was a filthy, squalid mess of mud and old rotting furniture.

"You asked me to meet you. I'm here." He moved further in, almost toppling over a broken cabinet lying in pieces at his feet.

"Ms Hepworth, Annie?"

He spotted a second door. He crept over and pushed it open. A gust of wind blew through, and the door slammed against the side wall.

He jumped back. "Jesus!"

He moved forward into a room even worse for wear than the previous. The walls were blackened, a gaping hole in the roof with burnt-out sodden rafters lying in a tangled mess on the floor. The wind whistled and whipped around him, pelting his face with icy rain.

"You said on the phone you wanted to set the record straight about Martin Burns. I'm here to help you do that," he called out. "I would have preferred a nice comfortable hotel bar, but hey, it's your call."

He wiped his eyes. The sound of music blew about him. He pressed his finger in an ear and listened again. It was coming from the furthest corner, a wall unit still clinging bravely to an exposed wall. He shuffled through the sludge and pulled open the door. It fell off and landed on his toes.

"Bastards!" he yelled. He glanced over his shoulder. "Is this some kind of wind-up?"

A small portable radio inside played an indistinct melody. He plucked it out and turned up the volume.

"Taylor Swift, really?" He returned it to the cabinet, removed his phone from his coat, and took a couple of snaps.

"I told you no phones!" a voice shouted behind him.

He spun around, but he was struck with force on the side of the head with the end of a shovel. He toppled, unconscious, onto the muddy floor, his cheekbone cracking as it smashed against the hard flagstone.

THIRTY-THREE

"This one?" Bone asked.

"Yes, Craigmallon Reservoir is through the gate on the left and at the end of the track."

Bone stopped the car. "Where are they?" he said, checking for Mullens and Harper, who were supposed to meet them there.

"Here they come, with the cavalry." Walker pointed to the line of vehicles appearing over the top of the hill.

They got out. The wind blew Bone sideways against the car.

"Jesus, it's wild up here." He scanned the storm clouds racing across the top of Graigend Cap, towering over them. He buttoned up his coat.

"Sir, look at this." Walker knelt by the open gate. "This has been rammed open." She picked up a broken chain link.

The vehicles arrived, and two officers jumped from one of the armed response vans and set up a roadblock. Mullens and Harper approached, with a third ARU officer following behind.

"Why do our suspects always pick these bloody godforsaken places?" Mullens asked, wrestling to control his coat-tails that flapped wildly about his waist.

"Compliments of ARU," the officer said, and handed the team body vests.

"Afternoon, Sergeant Dalgleish," Bone said.

"What are we looking at?"

The team huddled around to try and block the worst of the wind, horizontal rain and hail.

"A possible hostage situation. Female, mid-thirties, could be armed and dangerous, holding a male *Chronicle* journalist, mid-thirties."

"It's not Colin McKinnon, is it?"

"Who else?"

"Shall we leave them to it, then?" the sergeant said.

"Tempting."

"You said it might be a hostage situation?"

"Yes, that's why we need to tread carefully here. It's unlikely, but there could be a perfectly innocent explanation for all of this."

"Aye, right," Mullens said.

"McKinnon's GPS location indicated that they could be holed up in a building less than a quarter of a mile away, just short of the reservoir. There are two tracks. I suggest you split your team, Bill, but stay back and remain on hold until I give you the word."

"Speaking of which." Dalgleish reached into the box and produced field radios.

"Okay, let's go. Mark and Will, you take the high road and we'll take the low."

"And I'll be in pishing-down Scotland before yo..." Mullen tried to sing it but coughed the last word.

They put on their vests and split at the gate. Bone and Walker carried on up the main track. Bone turned and gestured for the ARU officers to slow their pace. They carried on, and at the bend, he stopped again.

"Any sign, Mark?" He clicked the button on the radio. "Mark?"

The radio crackled.

"Nothing, sir," Mullens' voice hissed.

They trudged on, the track growing increasingly waterlogged.

"Good job I put my waterproof boots on today." Walker glanced down at her mud-splattered Docs and shook her head.

At a bend in the track, the edge of the reservoir appeared in the distance, shrouded in mist and lined with conifers.

"There's a car on the verge up ahead," Walker said.

"That's McKinnon's bloody Corsa. It's always parked up on the road outside the station."

They approached cautiously. Bone gestured again to the ARU officers to keep back.

301

"Looks like he got stuck in the mud." Walker kicked the half-submerged rear tyre.

Bone opened the driver's door and searched the glove compartment and side pocket.

"Nothing." He called Mullens again.

"We've just reached the top side of the reservoir, but there's no sign of life," Mullens' voice crackled through the tiny speaker.

"There are fresh boot prints on the track here, heading on towards the water," Walker said.

They carried on. A tumbledown bothy appeared on the far side of the trees.

"This could be it," Bone said. "You go round the back. Be careful."

They crept up to the door that swung back and forth in the wind. Bone gestured for Walker to go around the back. He edged through the doorway. The room was empty. He continued past the debris and a deep pool of water in the centre to a crumbling hole in the internal wall. He scrambled through into a deluge of rain. By the far wall, he spotted a portable radio lying on its side inside a wall unit. He climbed over the burnt-out A-frame and picked it up, but accidentally tapped the on button. A screaming pop song blared out.

A hand gripped his arm. He dropped the radio and spun around.

"It's me," Walker said, jumping back before his swinging fist connected with her nose.

"For God's sake, Rhona." He retrieved the radio and switched it off.

"I thought you heard me. There's no one here," Walker said.

"But looks like our suspect has been. There are muddy scrape marks on the ground over there, and some of the rotting wood has been shifted."

They followed the trail as it disappeared and re-emerged from puddles and debris to a door with three of the four panels missing. Walker pushed it, and with a crack, it came away from the frame and toppled to the ground, spraying muddy water up Bone's already-soaked trousers.

"Sorry, sir," Walker said.

"I'm beyond caring now."

The deep heel scores in the wet soil continued along the side of the bothy and down onto the track, where they disappeared.

"A car's been here," Bone said. "It's driven off in that direction towards the reservoir."

They walked on. Beyond a line of Scots pine trees, the view of the reservoir opened out.

A BMW had been parked at the end of the track a few yards from a low, narrow jetty that extended some distance over the reservoir.

Bone squinted through the murk. "Are there two people in that car?"

"Yes," Walker said.

"Shit, she's got him in there with her."

THIRTY-FOUR

McKinnon roused and opened his eyes. A searing pain rushed across the top of his skull. He reached up, but his hands were tied together. He tried to make sense of the shapes in the fog swirling around his semi-conscious state. He leaned back and focused on the shifting object directly in front of him. Annie Hepworth's features slowly formed. She sat beside him. He screwed up his eyes and refocused. He was in a car, the open expanse of the reservoir directly ahead.

"Wha…" McKinnon tried to speak, but his throat was locked dry. "Water…"

She leaned over and held up a bottle to his lips. He took an awkward sip and choked again.

"We don't have much time," she said quietly.

"Why did you...?" He winced as another shock of pain raced across his face. He lifted his hands and felt blood pouring from a deep wound in his cheek.

"I told you not to bring your phone."

"You didn't need to clock me."

"I couldn't risk you running away when I tell you."

"Tell me what?" he moaned.

"I want you to do something for me."

"If it involves getting whacked by a shovel again, count me out." He winced when he spoke.

"I want to give you a statement I've prepared, and I want your word that you will publish it."

"Did you kill Martin Burns?"

"You have to promise that you will publish my statement in full, and then I will let you go."

"I can't just promise to publish anything anyone wants. How do I...?"

She opened the glove compartment, removed a vegetable knife, and placed it on the dashboard.

"Okay, okay. I promise. Word for word."

From her coat, she produced a bundle of folded papers. About to hand it to him, she stopped. She exhaled.

"I have spent my whole life having to survive the relentlessness of male abuse. Being talked down to, leered at, cat-called, groped, fondled against my will, body shamed, and humiliated in every way conceivable. I'm too good-looking, not good-looking enough. I'm a sexless robot, I'm a whore. I'm too ambitious. I'm asking for it. I'm a ruthless cow."

"Did you kill Martin Burns?"

306

"Don't interrupt me. I don't deserve the job because my skirt's too short or my hair is blonde. I'm stupid. I'm too clever by half. I've been treated mean to keep me keen. I'm a gold digger, a devious man-eater. I'm asking for it. I'm a slut. I must be a dyke. My whole life, on and on it goes until it becomes normalised. Just shut up, lie back, and take it."

She took another deep breath.

"And then there was Burns. I just wanted a moment where I was in charge of my own desires, my own body. I thought Burns was my way out. A way to regain some control and escape the abusive, misogynist I'd married."

"Your husband abuses you?"

"Not with fists. But barely a day goes by without him debasing me in some way or another. I thought Burns was different, but how wrong and stupid was I? I should have known he would be just the same as all the rest, but it turned out worse."

"What did he do?"

"It was all romantic claptrap for a few weeks. He suckered me right in. He had a way of making you feel, well... Then I found out he couldn't keep his dick in his trousers. I told him it was over and to get the fuck away from me, but..."

"What?"

"He threatened to tell my husband. Deliberately break up our marriage. And the only way he'd keep quiet was for me to continue to sleep with him."

"And did you?"

"I felt so ashamed, so broken. But his threats escalated, and in desperation, I relented."

"But why, if your marriage was so awful?"

"That's the twisted irony of it all. I still love my husband. I just couldn't do that to him."

"Or was it his fat bank account that you were worried about losing access to?"

"Here we go. I wondered how long it would take for you to revert. I have my own money. I sold my business two years ago and I have more in the bank than him. Another misogynistic hammer for him to hit me with. Apparently, me having more money than him is an affront to his manhood. Nothing more dick-shrinking than a successful woman."

"So, how long did this go on?"

"A few weeks. But then I just... snapped."

"And you ran Martin down?"

"I never meant to kill him. Not at first, anyway. I just wanted him to suffer the pain I was going through. The day it happened, I went round to his house. I made some excuse to avoid sleeping with him and stole his car keys."

"But why his car?"

"I don't know. Maybe I thought it would be the last place the police would look. That night, I waited for him to come home from his shift. I only intended to injure him. Make him feel what it's like to be abused the way he was hurting me. But when I saw him crawling around on the road like the filthy maggot he is, I just saw red. All those years of shit came piling in, and I ended it, once and for all." She took a

308

shuddering breath. "You know when I begged him to stop, to leave me alone, all he said was, '*Hey, what can I say? I have an eye for the ladies.*' Well, I fucking fixed that."

"But what about the second murder victim?"

"I wanted it all to stop, but it went on. That lunatic, Fagan, had filmed me on one of his fucking security cameras and he tried to extort money out of me. By then, I'd had enough. I was done."

"So you slit his throat. Did he deserve that?"

"That was an accident. He cut it when I pushed him over."

"Oh, come on. This is all calculated. I mean the radios. That's just psychotic."

"Don't say that!" Hepworth exclaimed.

"So, is that your plan? To slowly work your way through the entire male species? Am I next?" He wriggled in his ropes.

She glanced in the rearview mirror. She spotted Bone on the bank. She quickly folded her statement, and pushed it into his jacket pocket.

"Okay, I have it now, so let me go and I'll get on with it," McKinnon said, the panic rising again in his chest.

She picked up the knife.

"No, wait. Please don't," McKinnon pleaded.

"Give me your hands." She checked the mirror again.

"I promise I will. Please don't do this."

"Do it!"

He held out his shaking arms. She sliced through the rope.

"Now get out," she said.

"What?"

"Get the fuck out."

THIRTY-FIVE

An ARU officer ran up. "Shall we take it from here now, sir?"

"No, hold your line. Let me talk to them. We don't want this to kick off. Do you have a megaphone or a means of communicating with them?"

The officer went back to his group and returned moments later with a pocket megaphone the size of his fist.

"Is that the best you can do?"

"They're more powerful than they look."

"I bloody hope so."

Bone took the device and searched for the on button. The officer leaned over and flicked the switch on the bottom. The speaker let out an ear-piercing, high-pitched squeal. The officer snatched it back and turned down the volume.

"I see what you mean," Bone said, rubbing his ear.

"The volume control is on the side here."

"Yes, I can see that one, Officer," Bone said. "I need to get closer."

"I'm really not sure that's a good idea, sir," the officer said.

"What he says," Walker added.

"Just wait for my order, okay? We need to try and talk her down from this."

Bone took a few steps forward and then a few more. When he was within thirty or so feet, he turned on the megaphone.

"Annie, it's DCI Duncan Bone." The speaker screamed again, and he turned it down. "Listen, Annie. If you let Colin McKinnon go, you can talk to me face-to-face, one-on-one. Tell me what happened. I can help you. Just let him walk away, and I'll sit with you. I'm a very good listener."

The car's engine started up.

"We can work it out together. Colin is not part of any of this." He stopped himself from adding: *Oh yes, he bloody well is.* "Come on, Annie. Me and you. We can take all the time you need. I'll send all the others away."

The passenger door opened, and seconds later, McKinnon stumbled out.

Bone spun around. "It's the hostage! Stand down!" he hollered.

The door slammed shut, the engine roared, and the car accelerated away, but the corner of McKinnon's coat was trapped. He ran alongside, frantically tugging and then attempting to remove his arms from the sleeves, but the speed increased and he fell over his feet, his arms and legs flailing and battering against the side of the car.

Bone dropped the megaphone and gave chase. The car raced along the jetty, and with a loud thump, it jettisoned off the end and careered into the reservoir, sending a huge spray of water high into the air. Bone sprinted down the track and pounded along the jetty. The car floated forward, the waves settling around it. McKinnon was nowhere to be seen. Then, slowly, the front end started to go down. Within seconds, the chassis upended, and the car sank like the Titanic on speed.

As Bone ran, he shed his coat, suit jacket, kicked off his shoes, and leapt into the freezing water just as the rear of the car disappeared beneath the surface.

Bone frantically swam to the hissing circle that remained. He took three deep breaths and dived under. The car rested vertically on the bottom, directly below him. He reached down and grabbed hold of the rear bumper. McKinnon was below him, thrashing around, tugging at the belt to try and free himself from the passenger door.

Bone swam around the chassis and, using the rear door handle, he levered himself towards McKinnon. The journalist stared back, his eyes full of terror and panic. McKinnon snatched at Bone's shirt, but Bone pushed him away and yanked at the passenger handle. But the door wouldn't budge. McKinnon threw his arm around Bone's neck. Bone thumped him this time, and he let go.

Bone tried the door again, and it swung open, releasing McKinnon's trapped coattail. Free at last, McKinnon kicked wildly for the surface. Bone swam into the car. Annie Hepworth was unconscious, slumped forward over her seat belt. Bone's oxygen-starved lungs burned, and he fought the urge to return to the surface. He fumbled with the lock until finally it released the seat belt.

Mrs Hepworth tumbled sideways towards him. He yanked her by the shoulders and hauled her over the gear stick, but her feet were stuck on the pedals. He ran his hand down the seat and hit the recliner lever. Mrs Hepworth's limp body sank backwards, and Bone manoeuvred her legs free.

He hauled her towards the open door, but his cognition started to fail. He couldn't remember which way was up or down. He was losing consciousness, his lungs now a furnace of pain. His grip slackened, and Mrs Hepworth floated free. Two ARU officers appeared by his side. One caught Mrs Hepworth, the second grabbed Bone, and together they swam up to the surface.

The officer turned Bone onto his back in the water and swam to shore. Bone gasped for air but swallowed mouthfuls of water. More officers hauled Bone up onto the jetty. He flopped down onto his side, choking and coughing. Officers nearby worked on

Mrs Hepworth, who lay flat out on her back. And on the other side, McKinnon was on his knees, coughing his lungs up.

Walker rushed over.

"Is… she… okay?" Bone wheezed.

Mrs Hepworth's body convulsed. The officers turned her on her side, and she threw up half of the reservoir.

Bone looked over at McKinnon. "You… fuck… idi…" he spluttered again.

"I think what my boss is trying to say is, what a total fucking idiotic thing to do."

McKinnon raised his hand to try and speak, but another coughing fit got the better of him.

"Paramedics are on their way, sir. Looks like you've just saved two today," one of the ARU officers called over.

Bone's phone rang from his jacket halfway up the jetty. Walker went to retrieve it.

"It's Cash," she said.

Bone gestured to take it.

"Duncan, I've been trying to get a hold of you all afternoon. We found a hair on the well victim's clothing. We've identified it as belonging to a female, blonde, approximate age thirty-five. Hello, are you there?"

"For once, we're way ahead… of you, Andrew," Bone said and hung up.

Mullens and Harper came running along the jetty.

"Just in time, lads. Not," Walker said.

"What the hell's happened?" Mullens asked.

"I fancied a wee bit of… wild swimming." Bone wheezed. "Arrest her and kick his arse." He turned and scowled at the half-drowned journalist. "You owe me now. You're mine."

McKinnon gagged again and retched over the side.

After paramedics checked Bone over and provided him with some warm clothes, Walker insisted on driving him home.

She drove his Saab into Alice's yard and turned off the engine.

"Okay, I'm going to admit something, and I don't want you to hold it against me," she said, handing him the keys.

"What?" Bone asked.

"Bertha is actually quite a pleasant old car to drive when you're not in a hurry."

"Ha, I told you. She's very special."

"I wouldn't go that far. I'd say more like an endearing batty old relative that the family just about tolerate." She looked over at him. "Would you like me to help you in?"

"Don't start that again. I'm a wild swimmer. I feel fine."

"It's just that you look a little peaky in that pink fleece the paramedics gave you."

"I think it's quite fetching," Bone said. "I'm more than happy to run you home. There was no need to drive me."

"No, no. I can walk from here, don't worry. I could do with clearing my head."

"Be it on your own legs." He shrugged.

"You did good, sir." Walker nodded.

"I'm not sure Mrs Hepworth will thank me when she starts her life sentence at Northlands. See you tomorrow, Rhona."

Walker got out. Bone sighed. She tapped the window.

"Sorry, sir. I almost completely forgot. This fell out of your suit pocket when you stripped it off on the jetty."

She handed him Baxter's envelope.

"Ah, the blackmail payment. I thought I'd lost that." Bone said.

Walker waved and headed off out of the yard.

Bone stared at the sealed envelope for a moment, wondering if his weary frayed brain could cope with the contents. He glanced up. Alice was running over from the house. He quickly pushed the envelope into the glove compartment, snapped it shut and climbed out to meet her.

EPILOGUE

"**O**kay, where are we going?" Harper asked. He gripped his seat belt as Mullens careered around another bend. "And why so bloody fast?"

"Shush, we're already late." Mullens grinned.

"For what?" Harper exclaimed in frustration.

But Mullens carried on driving like a maniac. Finally, and much to Harper's relief, he slowed at a junction and pulled into a residential road.

"Isn't this where your dad's care home is?" Harper asked, then he spotted stalls, bunting, and a small marquee on the playing field opposite. "What's going on here?" he asked again.

"Jesus, you ask a lot of questions. You're nipping my heid."

"I'm a bloody detective. It's my job." Harper groaned.

Mullens turned into the car park and pulled up by a minibus that was close to a concrete changing block by the perimeter fence. A group of scruffy teenagers, some in school uniforms, shirts hanging out, slouched around by an open side door.

"Wait here a sec." He jumped out.

"What the hell is happening?" Harper stared in confusion.

A man in a tracksuit appeared from the side of the vehicle and spoke to Mullens for a moment. Mullens went inside the van and moments later re-emerged clutching a box. He returned to the car and thumped Harper's window with the box. Harper got out.

"This is Malc Skene, Will. He co-coaches the Raphorse Youth Football team with me. Malc meet Will."

"What he means is, I coach and big mouth here eats the team's packed lunches while they're out training.

"That's libellous, that is," Mullens replied.

"Okay, in what way am I helping you out?" Harper replied, fearing his response.

Mullens thrust the box into Harper's arms.

"What's this?"

"We're a player down for the five-a-side."

Harper opened it up. "You've got to be kidding."

"Oh, come on, I promised my da's care home I'd set up a special match for the old codgers and help raise money for their garden fund."

"But I'm hopeless at the best of times, but in this?" Harper squinted into the box again.

"I'm sure you are, but this kit might just give you that killer edge."

"Aye, suicide."

"But you do owe me." Mullens winked.

"I haven't played football since school and even then I usually refused as a conscientious objector. Are you deliberately trying to humiliate me?"

"Of course I am, numbnut. Let's give the residents a bit of a laugh. All the others are up for it, aren't you folks?" He glanced over at the sea of sullen faces.

"Mark, you really are a nightmare. Don't worry, the lads are harmless, mostly."

"Hey!" the girl at the front yelled.

"That's Rachel, our top goal scorer," Mullens said. "How's it going, Rach?"

"Oh aye, fine now I'm a lad apparently. I'd be the useless girl if I didn't win all your games for you." She scowled.

"Sorry, Rach. Slip of the tongue."

"It'll be a slip of my boot right into your fucking nuts if you say that to me again."

The team sniggered.

Mullens turned to Harper. "I'd stay away from her if I were you," he whispered.

"Fuck's sake. Just make a decision, ya dick." Rach said. "You think your strip's bad." She exhaled.

"You've put me in an impossible situation, you bastard," Harper said, finally.

"Oh, yes. Come on, Will," Mullens nudged his disgruntled colleague. "It's all for a good cause."

"Not my good cause." Harper squinted into the box again and winced.

"Are we in?" Malc asked tentatively.

Harper sighed. "This is a nightmare. Go on then. Where can I change?"

"That's the spirit. Give Will a big cheer team," Malc said.

"The players collectively stared at the coach in silence." The bean-pole at the back furtively drew his finger across his throat.

"Ignore them, Will. They're just pulling your chain," Malc said. "There are cubicles in there. Don't be long. We're about to kick off."

"It might not even fit me."

"I hope not." Mullens smiled. "You'd better get on with it before the rest of the team grabs all the lockers."

Harper disappeared.

Mullens winked at Malc and smiled.

Malc checked his watch. "Shall we say kick off in ten minutes?"

Mullens glanced across the playing field to the lines of stalls and bunting flapping gently in the sunshine. Some of the residents were already out by the edge of the pitch. He scanned the faces but couldn't see his dad. The care home manager approached.

"So glad you could make it, Mark. Sorry again about the date change, but look at this amazing weather."

"No bother. The team were all happy to get out of school early, so win-win. In the end, we were only one down, but I found an emergency replacement. See if you can spot him." Mullens sniggered. "Are those pies I spy over there?"

"Homemade steak and mince, and we've had so many donated cakes we've had to bring out a couple more tables."

Mullens gawped at the towers and racks of Victoria sponges and custard slices. His stomach rumbled loudly.

"Don't even think about it," Bone said, creeping up behind him.

He thumped Mullens' arm and roused him from his ecstatic stupor.

"You made it. Thanks for coming." Mullens grinned.

"Are you kidding? This, we definitely had to see."

"We?"

"Oh, aye." He nodded to the care home.

The rest of the RCU appeared in the entrance, along with Harper's girlfriend, Catriona.

"When's the Boy Wonder on?" Walker asked, hopping down the bank onto the field.

"Aww, that's bloody fantastic. I wasn't expecting you all to show up. And Catriona, thanks for your help," Mullens said.

"Pleasure."

"Though after what you are about to witness today, you might be tempted to call off those wedding plans," Mullens added.

"What wedding plans?" Catriona smiled.

"You two," Walker interrupted.

They hugged.

"It's lovely to see you all," Catriona said.

"Aye, long time no see," Bone said.

"This is Fiona, the long-suffering manager of the care home." Mullens waved her closer.

"Don't listen to him. I love my job. It's nice to meet you, and thank you for coming and supporting the event."

"And check out all that nosh over there," Mullens said.

"That's an awful lot of cake!" Baxter said. She unbuttoned her tweed jacket.

"A wee bit hot in your flock of sheep, Sheila?" Mullens asked.

"A tad."

"Yes, the community has rallied round to support us. It's been quite humbling," the manager said.

"What's all this then?" Mullens' dad appeared in his wheelchair, pushed by a carer who looked like they needed counselling.

"Awright, Da?" Mullens asked.

"It's a wee fundraiser for our gardens, George," the carer said.

"I hope it's no' another of your mother's girlie nights, Mark. We'll have to barricade ourselves in the living room again, keep all they feral women away from us, especially what's-her-face?"

"Jean Churnside?"

"Aye, Voddy Churngut. We let her in, and she'll suck you dry in seconds."

Bone winced.

"No, you're safe, don't worry," Mullens said. "Da, these are my colleagues at work. You know my boss, DCI Bone?"

"It's Duncan, George. We've met a few times," Bone said.

"Are you one of that big dunderheid's interlopers who hibernates in his room day and night, playing that horrendous shite you pass off for music?"

"Yup, that's him," Walker interrupted.

"Ah, your new click, Mark?" George asked, and pulled a face as though he approved.

Walker laughed. "I'd rather have a colonoscopy through my eyeballs than go out with your son, Mr Mullens. No offence."

George bellowed with laughter. His chair rattled around, and the carer grabbed the handles. "I like her," he spluttered.

"Check out the stalls and all the food, Da," Mullens tried to distract him.

George frowned. "Where's the ice cream van? I fancy a double nugget."

"There's going to be a picnic in a wee while, George, with loads to eat," the manager tried.

"Or a ninety-nine. And get yer mother a Mivi."

"I'll take you over to your mates, eh, George?" the carer said.

She pushed him over to the growing line of residents, and the detectives followed behind.

A whistle sounded from the other side of the park.

"Aye, aye, here we go," Mullens said.

The players emerged from the changing block kitted out from head to toe in fancy dress costumes.

"It was Geek Features' idea." Mullens waved an accusatory finger at Catriona.

"It's a *Star Wars/Star Trek* face-off," Catriona said. "Well, it was supposed to be, but the fancy-dress shop near our flat in Stirling could only afford to lend us two or three costumes, so we had to improvise."

"I can see that." Bone chuckled. "But they all look brilliant. How did you manage to persuade them to do it?"

"They were all up for it right away, well, except for our number one striker, Rachel McAdams. She told me to shove the Princess Leia outfit, so she's Chewbacca, and big Lanky Lennie drew the short straw. He's the one in the tight miniskirt with the Dawsons' donated doughnuts attached to either side of his scone."

"I love the guy in the bedsheet and rubber bald wig that looks like it's ready to swallow his entire head. Who's he supposed to be?" Bone asked.

"Talosian Observer, from Talos Four, original series. They appeared in a two-parter called *The Menagerie* where—" Catriona started.

326

"Thank you!" Mullens interrupted. "You see what I mean? I've had to deal with this demented lunatic all week."

"So where's our star player?" Baxter asked, now jacketless and a lot less flushed.

"Here he comes now."

Harper sidled out from behind the minibus in an oversized Darth Vader outfit, complete with a shiny black helmet, a cloak that trailed perilously along the ground, and an illuminated kid's plastic light sabre. He ran to catch up with his teammates but stumbled over his cloak, and his sabre skittered across the field.

The team erupted with laughter.

"Poor Will." Walker choked back tears.

"But he looks so sweet," Catriona cut in.

Harper looked over sheepishly at his fiancée and colleagues, in fits, holding camera phones aloft. He shook his head, did a little dance and bow, but almost lost his balance again.

"What the fuck is this?" George interrupted. "Is the Kilwinnoch Rangers squad all on the crack cocaine again?"

Bone heard a familiar voice behind him.

"Skiving again, I see." Gallacher came marching down the path. "I was just passing and thought I'd drop in. Hope I haven't missed the show."

"Just in time, sir," Mullens said. "How's Carol?"

"You know?" Bone asked in surprise.

"Yes, sorry about that, Duncan," Gallacher said. "I had a change of heart and rang everyone up individually to tell them what was going on, on the

327

proviso no one said a word to each other. Just to keep it under the radar."

"Well, your plan worked. So how is she?" Bone asked again.

"She's out of surgery, and the consultant was very positive. More so than they were before the operation. They still have more tests to run, but they think they've caught it and it hasn't spread."

Bone exhaled. "That's such a relief."

"She's not out of the woods yet and more rounds of chemo are likely, but it might be a little more optimistic than it was a few days ago."

"We all have everything crossed, sir," Baxter said.

"Anyhow. Well done with the case. Maybe I should stay out of the office more often. You seem to solve investigations at a rate of knots."

"Aye, possibly the fastest resolution in Police Scotland's crime history. I do like it when things come together."

"Ignoring the fact you nearly drowned," Walker said.

"Ah yes, I heard you're officially a hero now, Duncan."

"Yeah, right." Bone scoffed.

"Have you spotted our young DC yet, sir?" Mullens asked.

"Oh, dear God. The lad's drowning in that."

"Exactly." Mullens laughed.

Malc blew the whistle, and the game commenced. The carers on the sidelines, cheered and encouraged residents to wave flags, but only one or two obliged.

The first kick of the ball landed at Harper's feet. He staggered back as though the ball was an unexploded bomb, but he fell over his cloak again and tumbled onto the top scorer, Chewbacca. The two of them rolled around, tangled up in each other's costumes.

"Get up, Darth!" Bone shouted.

"Whit's that yeti doing to that nun?" George said.

"It's not a nun, Da. It's Darth Vader."

"Garth? Does Mother Superior know? I bet Garth's having a bloody field day in that nunnery."

"Da!"

The game continued in haphazard, ridiculous chaos. When Malc blew the final whistle, Harper had managed to fall over or avoid the ball more times than the eighteen-goal scoreline. He collapsed onto the pitch, exhausted. The team, carers, and a few less startled residents clapped and cheered.

Catriona ran over and helped Harper out of his helmet. Mullens joined them.

"Are we quits now?" Harper huffed.

"Oh, I think so." Mullens laughed. "I've signed you up for training next week."

"On the Death Star," Catriona said.

"Don't you start. I know exactly who's cooked this up." Harper wiped the sweat streaming down his beetroot-coloured face.

"You did brilliantly. I think you'd make a great Darth Vader." Catriona leaned over and kissed his cheek. "Ugh, you're soaking."

"If the main job requirement is remaining horizontal as long as possible," Mullens said.

"I'll never look at Chewbacca the same way again," Harper said.

"Picnic in five minutes," the manager called out.

Malc came over. "Well done, new recruit. You done great. Well, not really, but it's the thought that counts. You'd better get changed before the locusts descend on all that food."

The carers moved residents over to a long table, overflowing with food and soft drinks. Mullens returned to his dad.

"I'm going to love you and leave you. I need to get back to the hospital," Gallacher said.

"Thanks for taking time out, sir," Mullens said.

"Worth every penny. I'm assuming all those photos on your phones will mysteriously make their way to the staff canteen noticeboard Monday morning?"

"Of course, sir," Mullens said.

Gallacher gave them a nod and left.

A couple of minutes later, the young players, now in their civvies, sat down, poised to gorge.

"Okay, everyone. Tuck in," the manager shouted from the top of the table, and the feeding frenzy commenced.

"Da, this is Will. He's my colleague at work. He was Darth," Mullens said.

"Nice one, you dirty dog, you."

"What?" Harper asked.

Mullens raised his hands. "Don't even ask, Will. No, I mean it. Don't."

George turned to his fellow resident, Frankie, who was busy ramming a whole triangle of ham sandwich into his mouth. "The lad's a nun. Would you believe it?" He elbowed his pal.

"A wee squirt of WD-40," Frankie mumbled through a mouthful of bread. He sprayed wet crumbs all over George's arm.

"Fuck's sake, Frankie." George flicked at the debris.

Bone placed a single triangle of bread on his paper plate.

"Is that it?" Walker said. "Goodness sake, sir."

"Okay, okay." Bone picked out the smallest cake on a four-tier stand and pushed it next to the sandwich.

"I reckon the last time I saw you eat was four months ago."

"Three, don't exaggerate."

"Such good news about the Super's wife, isn't it?" Walker said.

"Aye, it was looking pretty bleak before, but he seemed in better spirits."

"Always difficult to tell with him. His mood face is generally stern to smacked arse, but yes, you're right. I think I even caught him smiling once or twice."

"Good God," Bone said. He took a nibble of the sandwich.

"You know you probably will get a commendation," Walker continued.

"For saving a killer and a dung beetle? Self-congratulatory crap. I don't think so." Bone sighed. "Did you read McKinnon's article?"

"I did, yes. And to be fair to the leech and his rag, they did publish Annie Hepworth's statement in full. It was quite something. If I'd been treated the way she had, I'm not sure if I'd been able to contain my rage."

"An absolute indictment of men's horrific behaviour towards women."

"But in the end, she did murder two of them, so perhaps she's undermined her argument somewhat." Walker took a bite of a massive slice of Victoria sponge. "Oh my God, this is incredible."

"A sad, sorry affair," Bone said.

"As always."

A commotion at the far end interrupted their conversation.

"What are you laughing at?" George roared at one of the young players sitting opposite him.

"Nothin'," Lanky Lennie said, but his grin widened.

George reached over and picked up an angel cake from one of the stands and launched it at the boy. It hit him square in the face and slid down his chin into his lap.

"No, Da!" Mullens grabbed his dad's arm.

A Mexican wave of laughter rippled along the table. The boy retrieved the cake and flicked some of the cream back at George.

"Christ, don't do that," Mullens said.

His colleagues turned to see what was going on. George broke free from his son's grip and, snatching up handfuls of sandwiches and cakes, he fired them across the table. His friend, Frankie, followed suit and tossed his half-eaten sandwich over his shoulder. It landed in George's hair. The carers rushed forward, but it was too late to stop George's retaliation. He thrust a custard slice into Frankie's face.

"How dae ye like they bananas, eh?"

"A wee squirt of WD-40," Frankie said, and licked at the creamy mess.

The team on the other side were now fully armed, and fired a battery of food at the residents opposite.

"That's enough!" Malc bellowed, but the teenagers ignored him and continued their assault.

The carers snatched food away, but the food fight was now past the point of no return, and there was too much tempting ammunition on the table. Mullens shook his head, retrieved a giant triangle of Victoria sponge from a cake stand, sat back, and tucked in. Carers pulled residents one by one from the front line. George turned to his son and, seeing him tuck into a second cake, he leaned over and slammed the end of it into his face. The cream spurted out the sides of the sponge.

"Enjoying your picnic, son?" George chuckled.

The carer wheeled him away.

"Aww, where are we going?"

"Time to go home, troublemaker," the cake-splattered carer said.

The manager came over, her hair full of jam, dripping down her cheek.

"Well, that went well," Mullens said.

"What a stupid thing to do," she said angrily.

"That's my da for you," Mullens said. "I did warn you."

"No, not him. Those idiots over there." She pointed accusingly at the food-drenched teenagers who still fired food missiles at each other.

"Well, they all had a laugh, didn't they?" Mullens smiled.

"It's not funny." The manager tried to stifle a grin. "Look at all that wasted food."

"Oh, I don't know. I'd be happy to clear all that up for you. I'll see you tomorrow, Da!" Mullens called back to his father, who still protested loudly and explicitly.

George gave him the Vs again and licked the ends of his fingers.

"Just another uneventful day in the life of George Mullens." Mullens chuckled.

"And his liability of a son," Bone said, peeling a flattened chocolate éclair from the lapel of his jacket.

After instructing the Raphorse youth football team to individually apologise to the manager and care workers, Malc and Mullens corralled the cream and jelly-smeared teens back onto the minibus.

Bone said his goodbyes and went back to his car. From the glove compartment, he removed the envelope and picked out a six-by-four faded colour photo print. He immediately recognised the Peek-a-boo Killer's father's tumbledown, dysfunctional wreck of a farm. Stern-faced Meiklejohn senior was standing by a battered, paint-blistered front door. A red-haired boy was by his side. They were hand in hand. The boy was smiling, his beady-eyed, intense stare drilling deep into Bone's skull.

"What are you up to now, Peek-a-boo?" He studied the boy's now-familiar features a moment longer, searching for clues in the expression that might provide some answers to this new unwanted manifestation of his PTSD. With a weary sigh, he slid the image into his pocket, started the Saab, and headed home.

The End

TG REID

DCI BONE RETURNS IN...

Burn it All Down
A DCI Bone Scottish Crime Thriller
(Book 7)

IF YOU PLAY WITH FIRE...

TG REID

JOIN MY DCI BONE VIP CLUB

AND RECEIVE YOUR *FREE* DCI BONE NOVEL

WHAT HIDES BENEATH

Secrets Always Surface

Scotland's hottest summer on record is already too
much for DCI Duncan Bone. As if the water shortage
wasn't enough, a body turning up at the bottom of
Kilwinnoch's dried up reservoir sends Bone to boiling
point.
With three suspects on the loose and time running out,
the Rural Crime Unit needs to find the smoking gun and
nail the killer before another victim is slain.

Visit tgreid.com to sign up and download for *FREE*.

**Your monthly newsletter also includes updates,
exclusives, sneak peeks, giveaways and more...**

TG REID

THE DCI BONE SCOTTISH CRIME SERIES

Dark is the Grave

Blood Water Falls

Dead Man's Stone

The Killing Parade

Isle of the Dead

Night Comes Falling

Burn it all Down

More thrillers by TG Reid

Agency 'O'

TG REID

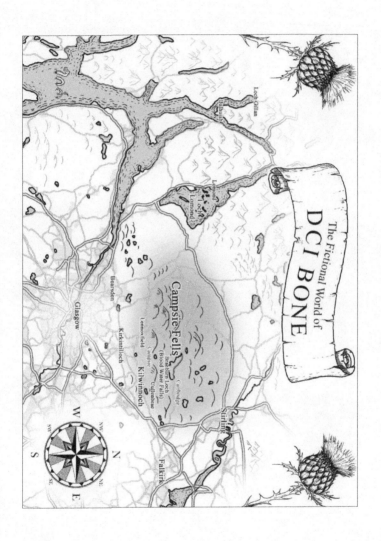

The Fictional World of
DCI BONE

343

ABOUT THE AUTHOR

TG Reid is a bestselling British crime novelist. His DCI Bone Scottish detective series has topped the Amazon charts in the UK, USA, Canada and Australia. Since publication of Book 1 in the series, Dark is the Grave, in 2021, he has sold over 300,000 books and surpassed 50 million page reads on Kindle Unlimited.

This bestselling series continues to grow from strength to strength, with many more books still to come, and plans to adapt DCI Bone for TV. Sign up to the author's mailing list to keep informed about future release dates, giveaways, and exclusives.

TG Reid grew up in his native Scotland and the DCI Bone series is set in and around his hometown, among the brooding hills and glens of Scotland's Campsie Fells. After working as a musician and English lecturer, TG turned to full-time writing and has never looked back. He now lives in Bath with his wife, daughter and hyper-neurotic cat.

TG Reid's books will appeal to readers who enjoy dark, atmospheric, edge-of-you-seat mysteries with added touches of Scottish humour.

Readers can reach him via his website at www.tgreid.com or find him on Facebook, Instagram and Twitter.

ACKNOWLEDGEMENTS

This book would be nothing more than a doorstop
if it weren't for the expertise, wise words and
kindness of the following people:
Andrew Dobell, Emmy Ellis, Hanna Elizabeth,
Diana Hopkins, Meg Jolly, Dylan Jones, Wes Markin,
Kath Middleton, Gordon Robertson, Shakey
Shakespeare, Lisa Wright
My majestic ARC Team – The Mighty and
magnificent Boners!
My dear friends, bloggers, reviewers and crime
champions: Lynda Checkley,
Deb Day and Donna Morfett,
Steve Worsley, the voice, heart and soul of DCI
Bone for his outstanding narration of the series and
support for the Bone!
Also a huge debt of gratitude to the admin team
and readers at UK Crime Book Club and Crime
Fiction Addict Facebook groups.
BBCC for our lunchtime meets!
The British Crime Authors Group
The Cassia Collective for desks, inspirations and
the best scrambled egg in Somerset.
The residents of Kilsyth and surrounding
Campsie Fells … So sorry I keep murdering you!

And, of course…
Jeni and Erin x

Made in the USA
Las Vegas, NV
02 December 2023

81995718R00204